# In the shadow of a hero

Jenny Herbert has a PhD in creative writing from Deakin University. She is the author of the best-selling *The Intelligent Traveller*. *In the Shadow of a Hero* is her first work of fiction. She lives in Metung, Victoria with her husband Fred.

Jenny Herbert

# In the shadow of a hero

ARCADIA

The project was assisted by the Faculty of Arts and Education at Deakin University, for which I am deeply grateful.



First published 2014 by Arcadia the general books' imprint of
Australian Scholarly Publishing Pty Ltd
7 Lt Lothian St Nth, North Melbourne, Vic 3051 TEL: 03 9329 6963 FAX: 03 9329 5452
EMAIL: aspic@ozemail.com.au WEB: scholarly.info

ISBN 978-1-925003-76-5



Cover design: Amelia Walker
Printing and binding: Tenderprint Pty Ltd

This book is typeset in Stempel Garamond 10.5/14.5

*For mum*

# Acknowledgements

First and foremost, thank you Fred, for your constant encouragement, faith, and endless hours reading and commenting on my work.

I owe much to Maria Takolander, David McCooey and Michael Meehan for their unstinting advice, direction and support. They made the journey expansive, positive and rewarding.

# Chapter 1

They gathered up the body, at least what they could find, and laid it on the Union Jack. One hand and the feet were gone, taken by dingoes most likely. Howitt had brought four men with him: Edwin Welch, Alexander Aitkin, Dr Wheeler and Weston Phillips. They each took an edge of the flag and folded it inwards—the bones shifted unnervingly—and secured it with rope. They wiped their hands down their trousers, and stood bare-headed in the blazing sun, trying to keep the thirsty black flies from their eyes and sweaty faces without too much disrespectful waving. Howitt read from his Bible: 'Though he were dead, yet shall he live'. When he'd finished the reading, he nodded to Aitkin and the men picked up the rope tails and lowered their bundle into the hole they had dug at the foot of a box tree. They reached for spades and scooped up the red earth, and it fell like dry rain into the grave.

Howitt looked past the burial scene to the land beyond. While they had been travelling, spring had crept up behind them, leaving a swathe of wildflowers in its wake, and now the gravelly landscape was patched with violet and yellow, bright blue and crisp white. He closed the Bible and thanked his men. Burke's was their second burial in a week: they'd found Wills a few days earlier at Breerily Waterhole, half buried by sand. Aitkin had retched at the sight of the headless torso, and his own stomach had heaved when his spade struck bone.

Phillips stamped the earth firm over the grave with his heavy-booted feet, making Aitkin wince. In silence, they tied their spades to their saddles, mounted their horses and turned back towards camp. The sun was heading towards the western horizon, casting long black centaur shadows behind them.

Their camp was set under a stand of box trees, on the banks of Coopers Creek where it widened into the Bullah Bullah waterhole. The tents formed a ragged semicircle around a campfire, and shirts and trousers had been washed and hung out to dry, giving the scene its one domestic note. Red desert pea flowers ran across the bare earth like wildfire and green budgerigars foraged for crumbs of damper. Approaching the camp, the men could see William Brahé pacing to and fro amongst the trees, one moment his blonde hair brightly lit by sunlight, the next, dulled by shade. He looked up anxiously at the sound of horses, his gnome-like face crumpled. Howitt nodded to him as he came alongside and slid out of his saddle.

'You found him?' Brahé asked in his cumbersome English.

'We did,' Howitt responded, squeezing Brahé's shoulder. He placed his reins in Phillips' outstretched hand, grimly smiled his thanks, and strode off to his tent without a further word.

'Come on, William lad, you can give me a hand with the horses.' Phillips spoke cheerfully to Brahé as he gestured to Welch, Aitkin and Dr Wheeler that he would see to their horses, too.

'You found him, then?' Brahé's German accent had become thicker.

Phillips nodded. He would spare Brahé what they'd found. 'And buried him like a hero. Mr Howitt read the service.' Phillips was a tall, loose-limbed man, disheveled and gangly as a wolfhound, with just enough Welsh blood to put a lilting edge to his speech. Feeling too tall beside Brahé, he slouched his shoulders as they walked the horses towards a patch of green shade. Without speaking, they removed the saddles, rubbed the horses down, hobbled them, and slung chaff bags around their muzzles.

Brahé looked despondently in the direction of the camels that were a little further away, quietly chewing their cuds. The beasts were molting to a new level of ugliness.

'Dost will see to the camels later,' Phillips reassured him.

Dost Mahomet had been imported from Afghanistan into Australia along with Burke's camels but he and beasts had only got as far as Menindee, left stranded with most of the gear by the impatient explorer. He was still there when Howitt's relief party arrived. The cameleer had begged to join the mission, trying to convince Howitt of the valuable role the camels could serve. Howitt had reluctantly agreed to take the cameleer on, along with the mangy-looking camels.

'What do you say to a swim, Will? I could do with washing this sand away.' And the smell of death, Phillips thought.

They stripped off and winced their way across the stony ground and into the water, which folded like cool silk around their skin. Phillips swam out to the deep centre and dived below the surface, rising streaming and spouting water from his mouth. Brahé stood waist deep looking down at his white wavering legs, then up at shadows dancing like smoke on the trunks of trees that lined the opposite bank.

Phillips dived again, his eyes open to watch the fish as they swam towards him in packed schools, then parted and flowed around his body. He pushed back up to the surface.

'You should see the fish,' he called to Brahé, but the man frowned into the afternoon sun.

A pink flush of sunset coloured the water as Phillips swam back to the shore. 'How could they have died of starvation?' he asked the still distracted Brahé. 'There were fish hooks in King's pockets.' He hit the surface of the water with the palm of his hand.

Brahé shrugged and shook his head, not taking his eyes off the opposite bank. Phillips followed his gaze but all he could see were the trees and a flock of galahs pecking around the trunks, breasts the same colour as the sunset.

Dr Wheeler appeared from one of the tents and led John King towards the water, nodding to Phillips and Brahé as he approached them, and easing King down to sit in the shallows. They'd found King first, the only survivor of Burke's small party that had pushed north. He was no more than a skeleton, covered by shedding skin that the natives had coated with foul-smelling fish oil. The man was so very weak; it had taken all his strength to point his finger in the direction of the bodies.

Since finding King three days ago, the doctor had brought him to the water to wash away, layer by layer, the tenacious fish oil, gently so as not to break the man's ravaged skin. Phillips positioned himself behind King, holding his bony shoulders so that he would not topple backwards. Brahé watched the pecking galahs, not offering to help.

'There, there,' the doctor spoke softly as he rinsed the cloth and soaped it, then wrung it out so the soapy water flowed over King's head and body. Gradually the smell of tar soap was replacing rancid oil.

As they led King back into the camp, Howitt emerged from his tent, pencil and journal in hand. He had lit a candle in his tent, and the canvas shone golden in the fading light.

'Not yet, Mr Howitt,' Dr Wheeler instructed. 'He needs a couple more days before you start asking your questions.' He could be dead by then, Howitt thought, but he nodded his agreement.

ᔓ

The great comet that had lit their nights for the past two weeks was once more appearing in the night sky, its tail streaming like ocean spume. Up there, it would be a viciously molten fireball, but from the ground it looked like a fleet-footed angel. Howitt nodded his greeting to the comet as he approached Brahé, sitting alone by the campfire, crumbling a heel of damper in his hand. Most of the men sat yarning quietly on the other side of the flames.

'I'll tell them how invaluable your help has been. In my dispatch.' He spoke to Brahé in German, but still the man only nodded without lifting his eyes.

'We'll all speak up for you. They can't blame you.' Howitt poured water from the boiling quart pot into two mugs. Brahé tossed the last of the damper into the fire.

'They will, you know. Blame me. They'll need someone.' The mug of tea Howitt passed to him shook in his hands until he carefully placed it on the ground, as if the tin mug might break.

Howitt sat down beside Brahé and pointed to the comet. 'It's been like the star guiding us to Bethlehem, don't you think?' But Brahé didn't stir. Howitt looked at him: the light from the flames was casting dancing shadows across his face, but it was the only animation.

It was becoming increasingly hard to be in Brahé's company: the way the man's eyes grew duller each day; the way his shoulders hunched lower; the way he chewed at the skin around his fingernails; the way he obsessed at mealtimes that the portions of food not touch each other, as if they bore mutual contaminations. Howitt would have liked to tell him to pull himself together.

He heard footsteps behind him and turned to see Phillips returning to the circle of campfire light from between the trees, buttoning his flies.

'Just the man.' Howitt called to Phillips. 'He's the one to cheer you up,' he told Brahé. Phillips and Brahé exchanged looks, Phillips raised his eyebrows but Brahé looked down into his empty hands. 'Remember that time in Gippsland?' Howitt asked Phillips brightly. 'You kept our spirits up even though we were starving.'

'Looking for gold, we were. For the government,' Phillips explained to Brahé as he sat down beside him. 'In country so unlike this you'd think it was on the other side of the moon. Hard to believe in that freezing, dripping bush when you're out here.'

Brahé lifted his head and looked surprised to find himself in the desert. 'God, I hate this place.'

Howitt rose to his feet. 'I'll go and check the horses.'

The horses stood together in a grassy spot beneath some trees, close enough to the camp that their jangling hobbles could be heard. The light from the moon cast shadows as sharp as ice and Howitt found himself walking through a tracery of branch shadows that reminded him of cats' cradles. His own horse, a grey stallion he'd named Dubbo, raised its head from the long grass and whinnied softly. Howitt ran his hand down the horse's nose.

'We'd expected more adventure than this, hadn't we?' he asked the horse. He had dreamed of weeks, months, of searching; riding north until the hot odourless air took on a briny edge to be tasted before it was smelt. He'd dreamed of mapping and naming and learning, of hardship that pitted him against the land. Not this quick, almost effortless success.

Welch, his surveyor, was pleased. He didn't say as much, but he carried a smugness about him. His father had served with Lord Nelson which, Howitt assumed, accounted for his priggishness.

Speak of the devil, he thought.

'A rum business, these dismembered bodies.' Welch addressed Howitt as he appeared from the direction of the river, his hair wet. When he bent down to inspect the hobbles, Howitt tensed, having just checked them himself.

Welch was, as always, as immaculate as desert travel allowed. While the others in the party had become comfortably ragged and bushy, Welch kept his military beard trimmed and his clothes neat as a uniform. He was a well-built, handsome man, towering over Howitt by a good five inches. Howitt put his hand up to stroke his own shaggy beard and ran it across his knotted black hair.

'They had hooks.' Welch spoke with naval-trained disapproval as he put his hands on his knees and pushed himself upright.

Howitt was tired of hearing about the fishhooks. 'Perhaps it wasn't starvation.'

In the silence that followed, he could hear the camels, hobbled a little further off, making their drawn-out nuurr noises and occasional bleats that sounded eerily like the hubbub of a distant crowd.

The horse blankets and saddles were slung over the lower limbs of trees. Welch watched as Howitt took each blanket, one after another, shook it out, folded it neatly and rehung it.

'Well, it couldn't have been defeat,' Welch finally spoke as he slapped a mosquito on his arm and rolled down his shirtsleeves. Success was clearly recorded in the journal they'd found near Wills' body. The explorers had waded through tidal mangroves, smelt salt, and seen hundreds of wild geese, plovers and pelicans. So they'd reached the Gulf; they'd crossed the continent.

Howitt ran his hand over his horse's warm flank, its muscle trembling beneath his fingers. He could imagine how the spring desert would have seemed benign when the explorers first pushed north, only to have summer hunt them down as they trudged the final desert miles to the Gulf. The autumn had brought torrential rain and floods, with rivers rising out of nowhere and blocking their return passage. What did this country care for a small troupe of miserable white men with glory in their sights, hungry to scratch their name into the land's memory? It had mocked their efforts and paid them back for their arrogance. They must have wondered, towards the end, what demon had driven them to attempt the feat in the first place.

'Perhaps the heat sent them mad,' Welch said. 'Or the space.' He was fastidiously buttoning his shirt cuffs.

It was tedious, Howitt thought, the way the man dug around for explanations: the way he felt he had a special right to answers. 'A space that needs filling, wouldn't you agree?' he muttered.

Welch looked down at him, genuinely bemused. 'I'm not one to forget my duty.' Howitt watched the man turn and walk with his quarter-deck strides back to his tent, to his maps and sextant.

The hooks *were* a mystery. Howitt had brought dozens with him and they'd been put to good use. He, too, had trouble reconciling the starved explorers with the creek full of fish.

Burke had included hooks in his inventory, and so much besides. By comparison Howitt had insisted his party travel light. He recalled the suggestions he had received regarding vital equipment to pack. It seemed every second man in Melbourne was an expert in desert exploration; they would have seen him even more encumbered than Burke. He remembered the man who had instructed him to take an air balloon from which he could spy across the endless flat desert. This would be easily accomplished, the inventor had instructed: hang the balloon between tall poles and inflate by burning a pile of straw underneath. Anchor a long cord to, say, a tree, to allow for a smooth descent. Even more absurd was the idea that they erect a large water tank on the banks of the Darling River, at great elevation and with a steam engine to pump water. They would then carry vast coils of India-rubber piping, uncoiling it as they travelled into the desert. When they struck camp they need only turn a tap for instant water.

The world was full of experts, Howitt thought with a shake of his head as he relieved himself onto the trunk of a tree. He buttoned up his trousers, patted Dubbo one last time and returned to the campfire.

❦

Two days later, Dr Wheeler gave his permission for King to be interviewed, although the man was still a wreck. Howitt propped King against the trunk of a tree, hemming him in with swags to keep him upright, and sat on a stool facing him, pencil poised above the blank page of his journal. King would say a few rusty words then sink his head into his hands. 'Two camels and three scarecrows. . . one and a half pounds of dried meat . . . Charley Gray dead . . . still smoking campfire . . . Mr Burke's insistence . . .'

Come on, man, Howitt silently urged him. 'No hurry,' he reassured him aloud as he leaned forward and brushed away the flies that crawled across King's face. He could not bear the way the man did not seem to notice them on his lips and in his eyes.

Brahé crept by and Howitt called to him, enlisting him to help with the account of what had happened. Gradually the story unfolded, between long silences when Brahé stared off into the distance, chewing his lips, and King dozed. Howitt tapped his pencil on the page of his journal and cleared his throat loudly.

Burke had left Brahé and most of the exploration party at the Coopers Creek depot, saying he'd be back within three months and taking rations only for that length of time. Brahé waited out the three months, then a further five weeks, watching his men become weak and sick. His own gums started to bleed and his legs were weakening. When he could wait no longer, he left rations—all he could spare but there wasn't much of anything left. He buried the cache, marked a tree, left a spade and rode away. That very evening, just as the moon was rising, Burke appeared on the horizon, an emaciated figure in rags, using the last of his strength to coo-ee across the empty space. There was no answer. Wills and King joined him at a still-smoldering campfire. Burke howled like a dingo; the other two sank to their knees.

❧

The following morning, Howitt sought Welch out to discuss which route they should take back to civilisation. They squatted down side by side outside Welch's tent and the surveyor opened out the map that he was gradually filling in with contours and English words. Howitt put his hand into his jacket pocket to retrieve his compass so that he might check Welch's bearings. He rubbed the lacquered brass case up and down his trouser leg to give it a sheen before flipping off the cover to reveal the compass face: a bold dial of black and white vectors and a filigree-tipped black pointer.

It had been a gift. Years ago, the poet Wordsworth and his wife had come to stay with Howitt's parents. Alfred had been reading *The Swiss Family Robinson*, lost in a tropical-island fantasy of shipwreck, tree houses and ingenious acts of survival. When asked what he was reading, he had told Wordsworth about the island and its animals, which he could describe vividly: a monkey called Knipps, a pet flamingo, a kangaroo and two large, bounding hounds—Turk and Juno—who were so much smarter than his family's bull terrier. He confessed to the poet, shyly, that he'd like to be an adventurer when he grew up. 'Only, I don't want to shoot all the beasts I find.'

When it was time for the Wordsworths to leave, the poet handed Alfred a blue velvet bag. The boy first looked to his father, for permission, then slipped the contents onto his hand: the gleaming brass compass. 'For the young adventurer,' Wordsworth spoke down to him from his great height. 'To find your way through life.'

His father had put it away 'for safe keeping', although Alfred had begged to keep it by him; he could recall how angry and frustrated he had been. His father had finally handed it over when he was sixteen, after eight years of yearning and asking. It had been the first item he packed to travel to Australia, and he'd used it on the goldfields, in the Dandenongs, through Gippsland, and now this inland trip. He was forever putting his hand in his pocket to feel the heft of the instrument.

'Can I see that for a moment?' Welch asked with interest. Howitt hesitated, then passed the compass to him.

Turning it over, Welch looked for the maker's mark. He found the small engraving directly under the North point. 'James Parkes. Made to last a lifetime.'

Howitt held out his hand and Welch handed the compass back to him.

'You probably feel about that compass like I feel about my camera. I wish I had brought it with me, there's so much to photograph out here.' Welch spoke with longing for the craft he had become so passionate about. 'It's just that you have to carry so much clobber for developing the daguerreotypes.' Howitt made no reply and Welch merely shrugged.

They turned to the map laid out on the flat ground. 'I've given this some thought,' the surveyor began confidently, using his pencil to show the route he was proposing. 'This route here seems to make the most sense.'

Howitt followed Welch's pencil. He could feel the pulsing in the vein that snaked down his left temple. It was immediately clear that Welch's plans were faultless.

The sun had risen, molten, into the morning sky, and in the perfectly still air, the surface of the creek was as smooth as a satin ribbon. A dozen spoonbills waded in the shallows, their beaks swinging back and forth like pendulums. Howitt could feel the sweat beading on his face. He swatted away the flies and scratched at an angry crop of mosquito bites on his neck.

'And what about here?' he asked, pointing to a wide tract of unmarked land. 'Have you thought about what might happen if there's no water?'

'We will never be more than fifty miles from a known waterhole, and we can carry enough for that. There's been good rain so it will simply be a matter of ensuring that we always fill up at every possible chance.'

Was it the training, Howitt wondered, that put that confidence into the voices of naval officers? His leg was cramping and he stood up and looked towards the creek. Something disturbed the spoonbills and, as one, they took flight. 'I'm sure you're right. The plan seems adequate.'

'Adequate?' Welch frowned at the map and then looked at Howitt. 'I've been up half the night doing this, making sure the route is achievable and that the party will be safe. I understood that was what I was employed for.' His voice was even and full of certainty.

It was, Howitt realised, like listening to his father speaking. A whisper of breeze lifted the corner of the map and both men immediately went to put their foot on it, Welch's foot getting there first. Howitt stepped back. 'As I said, it seems quite adequate.' He picked up the map, causing Welch to shift his foot, and folded it neatly.

'More than,' he offered in a more conciliatory tone, handing the map to the surveyor. 'We should prepare to be underway in one hour. Now that King is fit to travel,' he added as an afterthought, before walking away.

He returned to his tent feeling tense and angry with himself. Enmity was frowned on in the Quaker household in which he had been raised, although plenty of times he'd heard his father fume and rant about matters best forgotten. It had been a home built on strict morals. His mother knew the days of the weeks by numbers, unable to utter their pagan names. He had never wanted that degree of goodness, if that's what it was, but there were times he wished for a little of her humility.

Dear Father, I think you will be pleased to learn . . .

The racket of hundreds of frogs clonking and croaking in the muddy creek bank intruded on his thinking. Mosquitoes buzzed around his head. He rolled over and pulled his swag up around his ears.

Dear Father, I trust you will feel some pride for your once prodigal son . . .

No matter how he shuffled the words around, they reduced his achievement to trivial bragging. At least, that's how his father would read it.

The ground was giving up the last of its warmth into his body. Stones dug into the arm he was lying on and he rolled onto his back. He'd given up sleeping in his stuffy tent, where he felt cut off from the wonders of the night. In the cloudless night sky above him, millions of stars hung close, an indigo infinity stretching away beyond them. The comet had gone, and the moon had lost its shoulder, making the shadows of the trees soft and smudge-edged.

Better, he thought, to wait and send cuttings from *The Argus*. It was even possible that his father would read of his success in the British newspapers before a letter could reach Nottingham.

He rolled onto his side again, ignoring the stones, and stared at the glowing embers of the campfire. The other men, too, had relinquished their tents for cold nights under the stars. He could hear King, close by, snuffling and muttering in his sleep, and Phillips' gagging snores.

'You're a fool to want to stay in this uncouth land,' his father had told him. They had travelled to Australia, his father and he and his brother Charlton, and Prince the family dog, along with thousands of other hopefuls with gold in their sights. His father called it a country without culture or faith, although he really meant a land that hadn't given up its easy wealth into his hands. 'Return with us to England, lad, where you can make a good life in journalism.' It was all mapped out for him. But while his father thought Australia all muddy gold diggings and carousing drunks, he had felt the stirring of adventure. Here was an unmapped place awaiting discovery.

He remembered a book by Lord Byron that he had found in his father's bookcase—he must have been about thirteen—and how he'd pictured himself as a real-life Childe Harold. Not the unchivalrous, debauching Harold—he could hardly be that after all of his mother's teaching—but the young knight-errant who travelled to escape his past, who journeyed through unknown lands in search of independence and freedom. He wanted to copy the knight's aloofness, to adopt his detached observation of even the most surprising sights.

Would the press, Howitt wondered, report that he'd been the one to find King? Most likely: he was the expedition leader, so the honour was his due. Still, it rankled that it was actually Welch who discovered the wretched man. It wasn't that he wanted to be a hero—he had no stomach for the hoopla that would probably greet him on his return to Melbourne—but he would still need to make sure that those who needed to know saw the triumph as his.

King called out sharply in his sleep, and Howitt could hear him thrashing about before settling back into a murmuring slumber.

If he were honest, Howitt conceded, it galled him that Burke would be accorded the status of hero, despite all of his errors of judgement. The rash explorer had divided his party and rushed north to the Gulf with Wills, Gray and King: it was a case of the siren of glory drowning out the voice of prudence. Howitt didn't doubt that the Royal Society had encouraged Burke's impetuosity, determined as it was that the Victorian expedition be the first to cross the continent. Now the members were anxious that their lavishness not be seen as folly.

There was a deeper nagging that took longer to surface: he didn't want to be forever known as the explorer who discovered the fate of Burke and Wills, to be a mere label attached to another, more celebrated man's name. He looked down the years to a future shackled to the heavy lead ball of Burke's lunacy. Yet he was coming to understand, through the quickening of his own ambition, what drove men like Burke for a place in posterity. There was plenty of scope in this country to carve out individual fame. His father would call it arrogance: he liked to believe that everything he did was for the good of mankind, although Howitt had witnessed often enough how the Quaker spirit was easily swamped by personal crusades.

A dingo howled in the distance, its cry like a round hole opening up in the darkness. It sent a thrill through Howitt's body: the primordial cry of a predator; the ageless sound of death and the desert. A camel coughed and the horses jingled their hobbles. This should be enough, he told himself sleepily, recalling his mother's gentle admonishments when he complained of wanting more from life. 'Don't try to remake the world,' she would advise him. 'Be content; be grateful.'

☙

'One hundred and thirty degrees in the shade, can you believe that?' Phillips tapped the small thermometer in his hand as if he might bring down the soaring heat.

Howitt ran his tongue over his dried and cracked lips, tasting blood. He put on his hat, stepped out of the trees that had offered lunchtime shade, and looked off into the shimmering distance. Voluminous, rainless clouds were being pushed along by a scorching wind. Everything was grey: the sky, the earth, the saltbush, the hazy distance, even the dust-covered men and horses. He wondered how much further they might ride before the heat overcame them.

The relief mission had ended in Melbourne to all of the anticipated fanfare, subdued only slightly by the tidings of the explorers' deaths. Even before Howitt's return, the Royal Society had agreed to a further mission to recover and return Burke's and Wills' remains. Within a fortnight of returning home, Howitt was instructed to return to the desert. This time, the exploring party set off in high summer.

'Beware the bones,' Phillips cautioned humourously, making attempts at ghostly noises. Howitt tightened the straps one last time on the boxes strung on either side of a packhorse that contained Burke's and Wills' remains. He patted the boxes, as if for luck, and he and Phillips mounted their horses. The other men, led by Welch, were riding ahead, and behind them, Dost Mahomet was kicking his reluctant camels to their feet.

'Melbourne's conscience,' Howitt called the bones. It hadn't been good enough for Melbournians to know that their neglected heroes had been laid to rest in the desert; they wanted them home, even if incomplete. They wanted the third body, too—Burke's man Charlie Gray who had not survived the trudge back from the Gulf. But those in charge of the purse considered Gray's lowly status not worth the expense of the search.

Howitt wasn't complaining. He was in good humour, provided he didn't think too much about those rattling remains. He was back in the desert, with most of the men who had accompanied him on the first expedition. Now with the bodies disinterred, he could turn his attention to planning the second part of his mission: to explore and map the inland country and open a route from Coopers Creek south to Mount Hopeless and down to Adelaide.

'The desert's a temptress.' Phillips removed his hat, wiped his brow with the back of his hand, and pointed with his hat across the sepia-coloured emptiness into the distance. A hazy mirage hung the few stunted trees upside-down and offered a string of teasingly cool waterholes.

It was like travelling into a deepening sunset: the earth gradually changing from lemon-pink to blood red. Howitt now knew that the barrenness and monotony of the landscape concealed a deeper beauty, one that set his pulse racing. It was the way the desert swept away the past, its uncompromising demands leaving no room for vanity or regret. He'd learnt to submit to its implacability; he could think his way into that emptiness and find a purpose beyond anything his previous life could have predicted.

'It's wonderful, for all that,' he answered Phillips. 'Perhaps this is what it means to be Australian.' He felt the weight of the vast, empty land, the triviality of their small party upon it.

'To be your own man,' Phillips agreed with him as he ran his hand gently over his horse's damp neck.

ఌ

In Melbourne, a letter from his father had awaited Howitt's return, sent before news of the relief mission's success could have reached England. His father wrote of Alfred's sister's wedding and hinted none too subtly that Alfred's absence was the only dark cloud that hung over the day. He praised the success of Alfred's old friends in their range of suitable professions.

Howitt knew how close he had come to being ensnared in the web, and not for the first time he marveled at his father's uncharacteristic decision to travel to Australia. The Antipodes of all places, despite the fact that his cultured father had declaimed it as being full of inebriated convicts, desperate bushrangers and foul-mouthed miners. Seeking gold, for goodness sake, when he was the one who preached that avarice was the work of the devil. He liked to call Australia God's vault, envisioning God as the banker and himself as the honest withdrawer of funds that he had previously deposited in the form of good works. It turned out to be more of a raffle than a savings account, but Howitt could forgive his father's rush of blood to the head. He was even more grateful for the return of sobriety that sent his father back, two years later, to the sanctuary of England. And now this second expedition was a further reason for gratitude.

They were following the course of Coopers Creek, riding through red country towards Cullyamurra Waterhole where Howitt planned to establish a depot and from there, travel out to map the land. Galbraith, one of the youngest of the party, rode up to join Howitt and Phillips. He pointed to a mob of kangaroos, erect and motionless as tree stumps, ears pricked and ready for flight.

'Makes you wonder what God was thinking to create a beast like that,' Galbraith exclaimed. He was enthusiastic about everything he saw. He had a broad open face and a compact body in which he seemed entirely comfortable, and sat erect in the saddle with the reins held loosely in one hand.

Phillips turned his horse in the mob's direction and with a holler and a wave of his hat, went racing towards them. The kangaroos turned as one and bounded away.

'How do you think Noah confined those hopping creatures within his ark?' Galbraith added, laughing at Phillips' antics.

'It must have been a mightily crowded ark when you add all the animals of this land to what we'd already thought was onboard,' Howitt answered with amusement in his voice. They fell silent for a while, the gentle rocking motion of the walking horse lulling Howitt into a reflective mood. 'Charles Lyell, the geologist, might be right: that the Deluge didn't cover all the earth.' He had lost faith in the literal truth of the Bible, and this country often gave him the feeling that he was travelling back in time rather than across space—all the way back to Genesis and then much further. He spent wakeful nights trying to reconcile 6000 years with the ageless spirit of the desert, counting backwards and forwards until the jumbled figures brought on a restless sleep of sorts.

Galbraith kept his eyes on Phillips who had finished with the kangaroos and was joining the other men up ahead, but Howitt could sense in the young man a willingness to consider this challenge to his Bible. The horses' hooves scattered small stones, the sound tinny in the vast space. The land ran flat and colourless to the west, to a line of hills that rose out of the plain like a long blue wall.

'Perhaps it was a kookaburra rather than a dove, with a sprig of wattle, that carried the message that the flood was over,' Galbraith ventured diffidently, but Howitt hooted to imagine such a ludicrous sight.

'My pa's a minister. You wouldn't credit it, would you?' Galbraith shook his head. 'He always thought I'd follow in his footsteps, but that's not possible now. I could no more return to England than I could stand in a pulpit.'

Howitt nodded, enjoying the companionship of shared thinking. 'What will you do, Henry, when we've finished out here?'

'Farm. Some land, a family. It's not very ambitious, is it?' Galbraith pushed his hat to the back of his head and squinted into the fierce light and wind.

'That depends on how you do it.'

They rode on, the sun pressing them down into their saddles, and in time came to a broad sheet of water that mirrored the blue sky and drifting clouds: Oontoo Waterhole was not one of Phillips' mirages. Howitt and Galbraith dismounted and led their horses through the sparse clumps of trees to the water's edge. The other men were already strung out around the shoreline. Water bags and bottles were being refilled, heads doused, shirts removed and rinsed. The horses had waded into the water up to their hocks and were drinking noisily. Howitt searched the ground and collected a handful of stones. He inspected them closely, then sent one skipping across the water's surface. It skipped six times, leaving a series of rippling circles in the cloud reflections.

'Ducks and drakes, we used to call it.' He passed a stone to Galbraith. The young man tossed it, but it sank as soon as it hit the water.

'Like this.' Howitt bent his knees and skipped another stone. 'You need a flat, round stone for bounce, and spin and speed to stop the stone from sinking immediately. But it's the angle that makes the difference. Twenty degrees between the stone and the water is perfect.' He sent another stone hopping across the surface.

'You should be a scientist, Mr Howitt, with all the things you know. Australia's very own Sir Isaac Newton.'

Howitt slapped him on the back and laughed. 'Perhaps I will be, who knows?'

ɕ∽ɔ

It was like holding the world in your hand. Howitt didn't want to be impressed, but it made the hairs stand up on his arms. There was the copse of coolabahs, their shadows dark against the pale pebbly ground, and a dusky smudge to the right from which he could just make out a mob of kangaroos, perhaps on the move. He'd only known portraits before this, nothing more unusual than looking in a mirror, but this picture captured the world. It would make it possible to carry back to civilisation an unrivaled record of the desert landscape.

Welch stood beside him; Howitt could feel the man's eyes on his face, judging his response. The smooth glass surface of the plate in Howitt's hand caught the sun's rays and a reflection of light fell on the trunk of a nearby tree. Overhead, white cockatoos screeched and filled the sky with a mad flickering of white and grey, and small clouds had formed along the horizon like smoke signals. The two men were standing close to the grassy bank of the Oontoo Waterhole. Howitt's eyes kept drifting to the water; he felt a rising longing to shed his clothes and dive into the green coolness.

While the others were intrigued by the craft, Howitt had tried to avoid being present when Welch set up his camera, until now, when the photographer had specifically called Howitt's attention to the daguerreotypes. Welch had learnt the craft from the renowned photographer, Perez Batchelder, and if anyone asked, he loved nothing better than to talk about potassium iodide and silver nitrate, of lenses and exposures.

There'd been an argument at the outset of the second expedition. Welch had arrived laden with his camera and tripod, boxes of glass plates, distilling apparatus, troughs and chemicals. He even had an extra tent that he'd made lightproof, which he would not leave behind. It was like Burke and Wills all over again, Howitt had silently complained, looking at the unnecessary baggage.

It wasn't that Welch neglected his surveying duties, but at every opportunity he could be seen framing the desert between his fingers and thumbs. Howitt suspected that the man had been emboldened to exceed his assigned tasks by his success in being the one to find King. Not that the surveyor had said anything during their short spell in Melbourne. Howitt had been annoyed when he applied to join the second mission but he had no grounds to refuse Welch's appointment.

It was science, Welch insisted, as he threw crystals of silver nitrate into a dish of water. When they had dissolved, he submerged a collodion-plated glass sheet into the solution. He then inserted the glass into its carrier and the carrier into the camera. Outside, he took the photograph he had set up, directing his subjects as if he were the producer of a Covent Garden show. Out loud he counted off the seconds of exposure: one, two three. Then he dashed back into his darkened tent. He had three minutes to develop the image before it was lost. Woebetide any man who stood in his way and caused the hoar frost of crystals to blossom on the glass, undoing his work.

Howitt glared whenever he saw the 'development in progress' sign that Welch hung outside his tent. And when there was precious little water for men and beasts, Welch expected special dispensation to use gallons for his processing, insisting that his role of obtaining accurate pictorial records was a vital aspect of the mission.

And so it had become. The pictures were laid out along the grey blanket of Welch's swag: brolgas poised for dancing on their long stick legs, and tree martins perched in a row along a branch looking for all the world like a chorus line. Plants of all description, and the straight, thin black bodies of natives holding spears, standing in canoes, wrapped in animal skins. There was a picture of a lizard puffed up into a sentinel pose, and one of Galbraith and Phillips holding a string of perch between them, laughing like clowns. These pictures made Howitt's own scribbling accounts seem inadequate and his sketches amateurish. Howitt's fingers itched to close around the daguerreotype in his hand, to crush and shatter it. He handed the plate back to Welch with his best attempt at a compliment, but the voice was not his own.

'How's your eye?' Howitt asked, to change the subject. Welch had burnt his right eye the previous day while taking observations of the sun, and Howitt had been careful to record the injury in his day journal. A broad bandage wound around the surveyor's head, covering the eye. He shrugged noncommittedly.

'Any problems taking bearings?'

Welch touched his finger to the bandaged eye. His fingernail, Howitt noted, was clean and trimmed. For a moment Welch studied the daguerreotype in his hand, then crouched down and carefully placed it in the box at his feet.

'I have another eye,' he finally answered without looking up at Howitt. 'The work will still be done.'

❧

The party woke in the calm antelucan dimness to the sounds of calling and singing floating across the desert. The waterhole was shrouded in a soft mist that seeped into the spaces between the trees along the banks.

'That will be the blacks coming for their reward,' Howitt announced as the men rolled out of their swags. 'You'd better go and calm the horses,' he instructed Phillips as he set about rolling up his swag. He looked up at the big man. 'And ask the Doc for something for your face.'

The previous evening Phillips had shaved off his beard—Howitt could not convince him it would be no cooler—and angry red welts covered his cheeks and chin. Phillips poured water from the bottle he was carrying into the palm of his hand and held the coolness against his skin.

It was half an hour before about twenty natives ambled into the camp, accompanied by haloes of black flies. By that time, the men were sitting around the campfire eating their breakfast of beef jerky, damper and tea. A white-hot sun pushing up into the firmament had burned off the mist, and dozens of waterbirds had flown in to feed around the waterhole: sooty black cormorants, sleek egrets and sickle-beaked ibis.

'More flies,' Phillips grumbled. 'Just what we need.' He irritably swatted at the flies gathering on his face and plate.

The natives inspected the white men's breakfast, pushing their faces towards the plates the men held on their knees, and crinkling their noses in disgust.

They looked like a big, happy family, Howitt observed; men, women, children, ancient and newborn, all of them filthy and embarrassingly naked. These were, he supposed, the same natives who had cared for King. He told his men to leave their breakfast and stand in a group, and asked Galbraith to collect a sack from his tent. The natives chattered excitedly and Howitt held up his hand for silence, which had little effect. Feeling slightly ridiculous, he made a short speech about the gratitude of the Royal Society. His own men clapped, somewhat sardonically. He took the sack that Galbraith handed to him and distributed the Society's largesse of tomahawks, knives, necklaces, ribbons, old clothes and looking-glasses, and small quantities of flour and sugar parceled up in Union Jack handkerchiefs.

Squatting on his haunches, Howitt watched the women, trying to keep his senses in some sort of equilibrium. He was used to the sight of his men bathing naked, but he had never before seen a woman without clothes. Did it make a difference that they were natives? He focused his attention away from their breasts to the fingers that they licked and dipped wet into the sugar, laughing at the explosion of sweetness on their tongues. He watched as they sorted the items using their own unfathomable criteria of value. A young woman smoothed the ground between her legs—Howitt hardly dared to look— and used a tortoise-shell comb to rake swirling patterns in the sand.

Phillips inspected his own raw skin in a looking glass, fingering the welts, and then held the mirror before one of the natives. The old man, thin as a whippet, with a bonnet of grey corkscrew hair, touched his reflected forehead, and Phillips laughed at his astonishment and distrust. 'Didn't know yourself, did you old man?' he asked the native. The native pushed aside Phillips' hand.

'You leader?' Howitt pointed at the old man's chest. 'You boss here?' The native merely raised his eyes to look past Howitt towards the women.

From the bottom of the sack, Howitt extracted another item and presented the old man with a brass breastplate embossed with the words: *Presented by the Exploration Committee of Victoria for the Humanity Shewn for the Explorers Burke Wills & King 1861*. He helped the native tie it around his neck, using the leather thongs that were threaded through holes in the tips.

'That's thank you from the Royal Society,' he commented wryly. He'd thought blankets would have been more to the point.

The sun had climbed towards noon and the shadows on the sand had grown darkly stunted. Heat like molten lead drove both white men and natives into the shade of trees where the horses waited patiently, surrounded by another cloud of flies and smelling of sweat and leather. If the natives were wary of the big animals, they seemed terrified of the camels that stood in the blazing heat, their jaws working in a contemplative, circular motion. Dost Mahomet was walking amongst the camels, checking their shins and straps; carrying the large slab of timber he used to subdue bad behaviour.

Galbraith and Aitkin were also still out in the sun, surrounded by a group of piccaninnies all jumping and laughing for the twists of sugar the two men had prepared and now held above their heads. Galbraith especially was completely at ease with the blacks, as if, Howitt thought, there were no difference between the races. A small girl, pushed to the ground by a bigger boy, began to cry. Galbraith bent and swept her up into his arms, tossing her grease-plastered body into the air and catching her as if she were no more than a bag of flour. The toddler screamed with glee.

A woman broke away from the group in the shade. Half crouching, she ran towards the circle of children and stopped a few feet away from Galbraith. A young black man close to Howitt slowly rose to his feet. He put his hand on the boomerang tucked into the girdle of string around his waist.

Galbraith noticed the mother and passed the child into her arms. 'She's a mite pet, that one,' he remarked to the woman, who smiled shyly and withdrew.

The young black man had now moved towards Galbraith. Howitt stood tensely and nodded to Phillips, who had put his hand on his pistol. The black man handed Galbraith the boomerang, then pushed his empty hands in small movements towards him, indicating the gift.

Howitt relaxed and walked over to the group.

'Well done, man,' he congratulated Galbraith. The young man took the compliment easily and turned back to his game with the children. They were now playing a game that looked uncannily like Ring around the Rosie. It transported Howitt back to a childhood in Nottingham, playing on a frosty street with his sister Mary and neighbourhood children. Their home had been one of a terrace of tall red brick houses facing the market square that even on the coldest days smelt of offal and rotting cabbage leaves. *Atishoo atishoo we all fall down*: it was the black death the rhyme told of—a contagion he could not imagine in this place of dry, clean heat and open space. He watched the black children as they laughingly crumpled to the ground and wondered what the origins of their game might be.

❧

The exploration party moved on from Oontoo Waterhole, following the course of the Cooper, and made camp the following day at a drier, less agreeable spot where the creek had narrowed to little more than a gutter. It was only midday, but they had set out before dawn and now the heat was scorching. They were sunburnt and weary, and the horses, too, were tired. The men erected tents along the miserly watercourse in the only patch of shade available. A little way off, Howitt could hear that the camels were fractious. They could smell the water but he had insisted they go without for another day: the creek water was for the men and horses only. Howitt was nursing a pain that seared through his jaw and into his ear that made him short-tempered and deaf to Dost's pleas.

Despite the loads the camels could carry, Howitt thought their oddness turned the mission into a circus: why not an elephant or two, a performing lion? He wanted to travel lean and spare, modeling himself on the South Australian explorer Stuart who survived his desert treks with no more than a few horses and a water bag. By comparison, Burke had not only imported the camels to take on his mission, but had also amassed twenty-three tons of paraphernalia: everything from Chinese gongs to enema kits and dandruff brushes. Enough to sink a ship of the desert.

Howitt sat on his horse blanket on the stony ground to write up his journal as the other men set up the tents and watered the horses. He ran his hand through his hair, which had become coarse with dust. Camel hair, he snorted with disgust as he wiped his hand on his trousers. He had acquired the camels during the relief mission, against his better judgment, but he included them on this second journey because they had proved more useful than he had expected. He'd put Alex Aitkin in charge of them, hoping the man's stolid nature might help to calm the foul-tempered beasts.

Dost Mahomet, who had also rejoined the party for the second trip, offered Aitkin constant advice: how to water the camels, standing them apart to allow room for their swelling girths, and the necessity of being always on guard, for these crazy camels could switch from docile to dervish in the blink of an eye. Watch for their legs, he instructed, lifting the legs of his pantaloons to reveal scars and bruises. He never hesitated to strike an unruly camel on the nose with his length of timber. The struck camels looked down at Dost, unharmed and indifferent. Nero, the Black Devil, was especially untrustworthy.

He knew camels, Dost regularly boasted; cameleering ran through his blood. It had been his father's trade, and his father's before him: a lineage as long as a trade route. Watching him, Howitt could imagine the cameleer's mind's eye following the earth's arc, over the rim of horizon to a desert many moons away where his ancestors were buried, lying on their right side facing Mecca.

Aitkin accepted most of what the cameleer said with a casual nod. The others of the party laughed at Mahomet: at his pantaloons and turbaned head; his black hedge-like beard and twirling moustaches; his invocation to Allah to preserve him from snakes and British food. He badgered Howitt for his compass to calculate the Qibla before laying his carpet and forehead on the foreign sand. Around evening campfires, he recited poems and folktales as old as the world itself that made the white men nostalgic and subdued. Howitt had grown used to him, as one grows used to a loyal dog, and was happy to have him along on this second mission.

As the afternoon wore on, the mosquitoes became as

relentless as the ache in his jaw. Howitt retired to his tent to finish writing up the day's entry.

'Get him!' The yell was as sharp as a gunshot on the hot, dry air. 'Go for his legs!' A brief pause, and then, 'Get a rifle!' The voice was hoarse and edged with fear. Hearing the fracas Howitt dropped his pen and ran out. Welch was already ahead of him, running towards the commotion with his rifle. Howitt held a handkerchief over his mouth, trying to contain the pain.

He could just make out the shapes of Aitkin, Phillips, Burrell and Galbraith racing about in the dust with lengths of rope. Burrell was an older man, lean and tough-skinned from a lifetime outdoors, and was the only native-born of the party. He was the one yelling instructions.

Dost Mahomet was being chased by the mercurial Nero and they were trying to trip up the beast's long scissoring legs. The camel pulled its lips back and brayed wildly, swerved and dodged, kicking up great plumes of red sand but always keeping its unblinking eyes on the Afghan. Mahomet looked over his shoulder as he ran, shouting Afghani insults and beseeching Allah. Galbraith yelled a warning but it was too late: Mahomet tripped over a fallen branch and fell heavily to the ground. The camel was on him in a moment, sinking its yellow teeth into his upper arm, lifting him off the ground and shaking him as if he were no more than a mouse in the jaws of a cat. The cameleer screamed with terror and pain.

Welch, approaching the scene, raised the rifle to his shoulder. He automatically went to sight through his right eye before remembering the bandage that wound around his head. Howitt was immediately at his side.

'Hold your fire.' The handkerchief at his mouth muffled his voice. Welch looked at him with disbelief. Mahomet was screaming for help.

'The camel's *magnoon*,' Welch snapped, using the cameleer's term for crazy. He shot a quick look at Howitt, expecting him to see reason. Howitt looked away and yelled at the men.

'Now. Quickly.' Pain tore through his jaw.

The four men raced in front of the camel with their ropes

strung between them. They caught the front legs and quickly crossed over behind the beast, pulling the ropes tight so that its four legs were lashed together. The camel thundered to the ground and Dost rolled from its jaws.

Howitt felt a surge of victory; there were better ways to bring down a camel than a bullet. In his outback trips he had lost neither man nor beast. The press had been full of praise after his relief mission, about horses returning fresher than when they'd set out; of Burke's camels made useful again, great weeping sores cured with creosote. It was a reputation he did not wish to have blemished. He could feel Welch's eyes on him. The camel was writhing in the dust, the men trying to keep it down. Mahomet was groaning, holding his bloody, oddly bent arm to his side.

Howitt held up a delaying hand, palm flat towards Welch. 'Wait. It will quieten.' Talking was the worst. The air, even though it was hot, speared the hole in his tooth.

'The camel's rabid.' Welch answered furiously, raising his rifle to his left shoulder, putting his left eye awkwardly to the gun-sight.

'Put it down. You'll kill one of the men,' Howitt snapped. The camel still thrashed about on the ground, growling and bleating like a demented sheep, its lips pulled back, teeth snapping wildly. Burrell caught a kick on the shin and let go his hold for a moment, allowing the camel to strain its neck and nip Galbraith on the shoulder. Both men screamed curses.

Welch pushed his rifle into Howitt's hands and strode away.

Howitt glared at the man's straight back. With the rifle heavy and ominous in his hands, he turned back to the struggling men. Phillips, sitting on the camel's legs, yelled at him to do something. Phillips, too? Howitt felt a moment of shock.

He looked to see if Welch was returning, but his long strides had already taken him back to his tent. So it's left to me, he thought bitterly, although an uncomfortable awareness of his own inconsistencies didn't escape him. He approached the camel, aimed the rifle at its head and pulled the trigger. The sound cut through the heat like a whiplash and ricocheted between the sparse trees. The camel went limp and the men fell about, crawling exhausted to their hands and knees, coughing and spitting. Red dust filmed their sweaty faces, making their eyes stand out, white and accusing. Phillips rose to his feet, shook his head at Howitt and stepped over the dead camel's legs to see to Mahomet who was still moaning in the dust, his turban unraveled around him.

Dr Murray, bulky and short of breath, came running from the camp, his big leather bag thumping against his leg. He had been alerted by Welch, no doubt. Howitt tossed the rifle to Aitkin who caught it without looking at him. The surgeon made straight for Dost, fell to his knees and started to inspect the wound.

There were only two men on the team Howitt couldn't abide. One was Edwin Welch. The other was Dr James Murray, who was in no way like Welch. Murray was undisciplined, in attitude, appearance and duty. It should have been Dr Wheeler who had made this trek with them, instead of remaining in Menindee; Murray, fleshy and pale skinned, was next to useless. The odd little man cared more about plants than patients but he had friends in the Royal Society. Up until now, without Wheeler, he'd only been called upon to dress a couple of minor burns, lance Galbraith's boils, remove a small beetle that had burrowed into Burrell's ear and see to Welch's eye. At day's end, when everyone was occupied with horses and tents and firewood, Murray wandered off in search of rare flora, or sat amidst the bustle with his eyeglass trained on a bird, a love-struck look on his face.

Howitt felt in his pocket for a clove, placed it gingerly on the diseased tooth and bit down on it. His mouth filled with the cruel sharp taste and his eyes watered. The men avoided him as they moved about, coiling ropes and helping the doctor.

He walked back into the camp, his heart pounding, the vein in his temple throbbing. Take deep breaths, his mother always said when he was anxious or irritated. 'What does your anger accomplish?' she would ask him, genuinely perplexed, laying her cool fingers on his cheek. She could even placate his father's rage—a fury as wild as the Valkyries—with a hand on his arm or a bowed head. It never diminished her.

Small black flies, made languid by the heat, crawled across his face and he swatted at them angrily, then mopped his brow with his handkerchief and shoved it in his pocket. At Welch's tent he pushed aside the front flap and stood in the entrance. He tried to ignore the pain as he watched Welch fold his clothes into his saddlebags and roll his swag neat and tight.

Say something; it shouldn't be that hard. Turn the other cheek. His mother's voice counseling forgiveness could not drown out his rage. He and Welch had argued in the past, and Welch had always finally given way to his leader, as he should. As Howitt drew in a breath to speak, Welch brushed past with his saddle and went to find his horse. Howitt was left marooned and vexed.

Mahomet was carried into the camp. Dr Murray had dosed him with laudanum and was holding the mangled arm against the Afghan's body. Blood soaked their clothing and left a dripping black trail across the sand. The splintered end of a bluish bone was visible through the muddy, bleeding wound. Howitt signaled for Mahomet to be carried to his tent. He instructed the men to boil water, tear cloths for bandages, prepare splints. He took another clove from his pocket. He could have almost wept with the pain.

When he entered his tent it was filled with a thick heat and the stench of excrement. Murray beckoned him over to the camp bed and told him to hold Mahomet down with one hand and, with the other, grip his arm firmly between the shoulder and the wound. The surgeon, eyes bulging with the effort, slowly rotated the lower arm until the dislocated elbow joint clicked back into place. Mahomet's face was slick with sweat, his eyes squeezed shut against the pain. He turned his head and vomited over Howitt's hand.

Dr Murray placed crystals of morphine on the point of his lancet and carefully deposited them into the laceration. He cut away the ragged edges of skin and used forceps to pick out minute fragments of bone, cloth and gravel. Mahomet's face had turned the colour of bile and he cried feebly as the surgeon manipulated the fractured humerus back into place as best he could, then pulled together the torn muscle and skin. Howitt wrung out cloths in a basin of clear water and bathed Mahomet's forehead and, as the surgeon stitched the wound, swabbed away the blood. From time to time, Dr Murray beckoned for his own forehead to be mopped. Mahomet's body arched as the astringent to prevent gangrene bit into his raw flesh. Howitt held two splints in place so that the surgeon could set the limb, binding the roughly cut timbers tightly. The tent had become unbearably hot and stank like an abattoir. Howitt tipped laudanum into a mug of water and held it to the cameleer's lips; he would have given him rum, but Mahomet was more of a teetotaler than himself.

Murray picked up a clean cloth and wiped his face and hands. He looked as done-in as the Afghan. He passed the cloth to Howitt.

'You've done a fine job.' Howitt had thought he would never have cause to praise the doctor. He wiped blood and vomit from his hands. 'A very fine job indeed.'

'It's a nasty wound. He'll need to be taken back to Menindee.'

'I'll take him.' Welch was standing at the tent entrance, a black silhouette with the late afternoon sun behind him. Howitt could just make out the white bandage.

'We can't afford to be without you, Welch.' It was meant to be conciliatory, but even to himself his voice sounded harsh.

Welch stood his ground. While he'd been saddling his horse, he'd mulled over past injustices—one in particular. It didn't take much to bring up the memory: it was like a scab he couldn't leave alone. He'd been the one to find King, looking like a scarecrow, the excited blacks moving away but gesticulating and laughing. He hadn't known who the man was, even that he was white, until King spoke to him—a rasping voice out of a scabby mouth. 'Thank God, I'm saved.' Welch had ridden wildly to the top of a ridge and fired his pistol to alert his leader, and was holding the broken, sobbing man in his arms when Howitt rode up.

When the party had returned to Menindee, a copy of the *Colonial Post* awaited them, in which Howitt's dispatch appeared, setting out the details of the relief mission. Welch had read the dispatch but made no comment. There was no doubt, when they returned to Melbourne, who was the hero. No one so much as shook Welch's hand.

'You'll be able to have that eye of yours seen to in Menindee,' Dr Murray said. Welch put his hand to his right eye.

'I thought your eye was improving.' Howitt again spoke more bluntly than he meant.

'When will it be safe to move him?' Welch nodded towards Mahomet, his face in shadow, inscrutable.

Dr Murray looked enquiringly to Howitt who made no move to respond.

'He'll need to rest overnight. Tomorrow morning, if that suits Mr Howitt.'

Howitt touched his fingers to the outline of his compass in his pocket. 'I trust you can wait until morning, Mr Welch?' But Welch was gone.

Phillips' lean face, with the stubble beginnings of another beard, appeared at the entrance of the tent. 'How's he doing?' He had Mahomet's turban and made an attempt to wind it back onto the cameleer's head. Mahomet gave him a look of gratitude, even though the turban looked like a tent collapsed in a storm.

'He'll leave tomorrow for Menindee. Welch will take him.' It was the surgeon who answered.

Howitt felt a prick of relief. He was tired of the strapping figure that infested his dreams, striding ramrod through his nights, making him feel small and pathetic. There were times when Welch merged into his father, so Howitt couldn't make out who was standing over him. But he felt angry, too. The man was not only burdening him with the extra duties of surveyor, he was taking away any chance for Howitt to rid himself of the nightmares. He might have found a way to make peace, given time.

Phillips interrupted his thoughts. 'You should get the Doc to see to that tooth, while you have him.' Howitt had asked Phillips for the cloves, thinking he'd keep the matter to himself. He waved him away crossly. Phillips shrugged. 'I'll round up the lads and we'll carry Dost to another tent. Leave you in peace.'

Howitt listened to Phillips walking away, whistling. Further off, a bird gave a harsh 'graank' call, as if in reply.

'White-faced heron?'

The surgeon was wiping his instruments. 'Hardly a thrush.' The two men looked at each other and laughed. Howitt's hand shot to his jaw.

'Might as well see to that tooth before I pack away my weapons.' The doctor gestured to a stool for Howitt to take a seat.

There had been a time, that very morning, when Howitt would no more have let Dr Murray near his mouth than kiss a camel. Now the surgeon was humming and hawing as he poked around the rotted tooth, releasing arrows of pain that Howitt could feel down to his feet.

ꝏ

He slept badly, nursing his painful jaw, his tongue constantly finding the soft, raw hole in his gum. The pulling and twisting to extract the tooth had, at times, almost lifted him from his stool. It wasn't just the pain that kept him awake: there was the anguish that came from his self-questioning. Am I becoming a monster? Is it the empty, endless desert? The diet of stringy meat and dry damper? Does that feed a meanness of spirit? Phillips and the others managed an easy companionship, but then they didn't make the decisions. It was hard to recall, in the cool hours before dawn, what Welch had done that was so grievously wrong. But his body tensed, under the rough grey blanket, to think of the death of the camel at his own hand.

It was still dark when he rose, lit a candle, and wrote the letter he'd thought about during the night. He would need the signatures of every man involved in the shooting; he couldn't see why the responsibility for the loss of the asset should fall on his shoulders alone.

When the dawn was no more than a thin orange line on the horizon, he went out to find Welch. The air was soft and fresh on his face, and the moon hung translucent in the dawn sky. Welch had already saddled his horse; Burrell and Aitkin were carefully strapping Mahomet to another horse, just as they had done with King. Burrell had his head buried in the cameleer's side to hold him upright while he used both hands on the straps.

'One last duty, Mr Welch.' Howitt passed the letter to him. Welch scanned it quickly then looked at Howitt with such contempt that Howitt stepped backwards. Welch held out his hand and Howitt passed him the pen, the nib loaded with ink in preparation, and his journal on which to rest the page. Welch balanced the journal on his saddle, signed with a flourish and handed letter, pen and journal back to Howitt. Without a word, he then turned and mounted his horse.

'So you won't be convinced to stay, Welch?' Howitt asked. Welch's boots gleamed in the stirrups. Howitt could picture him spitting and polishing for his departure.

'Hasn't been any convincing. At least, not that I'm aware of.'

Howitt took a deep breath. The air found the hole where his tooth had been and his hand shot to his jaw. 'I would be grateful if you would stay. Galbraith could go in your place. Your skills are vital to the mission.'

Welch harrumphed and leaned down to check his saddle's girth straps.

'I'll remind you, Mr Welch, that you have an obligation to this party. You signed a contract to remain as surveyor for the duration of the expedition.' Howitt could have bitten his tongue. That wasn't at all what he had planned to say.

Welch looked at him with hard, cold eyes until Howitt was forced to turn away. 'Ready?' Welch asked Mahomet. The dazed Afghan nodded. His splinted arm was strapped diagonally to his body; his good hand clutched the saddle pommel. He looked like death. Welch came alongside and picked up the reins by which he would lead Mahomet's horse. A packhorse followed behind on a long tether.

'I've left the maps and equipment with Bill O'Donnell.' Howitt bristled at the insinuation that Welch had selected his successor; and O'Donnell, as the most junior member of their party, was obviously chosen as another slight. 'You'll find everything in order.' Welch addressed his words to Howitt over his shoulder as he nudged his horse forward with his heels. As the packhorse followed, Howitt saw the black box amongst the other gear. It was the box in which Welch packed his daguerreotypes. He was taking away with him what he possessively called his light writing. It would be Welch, arriving back in civilisation much sooner than Howitt, who would amaze the world with his miraculous images of the desert.

Howitt held his aching jaw as he watched Welch and Mahomet become black shapes with the sunrise before them. He wanted to call Welch back—command him—but how would he appear before the other men if Welch ignored his command? He looked at Welch's ostentatious signature on the letter in his hand: the man was all show. He was better off without him.

ᔕ

He chose Aitkin, Phillips and Burrell to head south with him to survey new country. The other men he left at Cullyamurra Waterhole, along with the camels and Burke and Wills' boxed-up bones, with instructions to establish a depot. Burrell was an odd-looking cove, with close-set eyes, a large hooked nose and stooped shoulders. He wouldn't have been chosen, if Howitt hadn't seen the way the man had dealt with the camel. It seemed an act worthy of this reward.

They turned westward towards Lake Warrakalanna. In the afternoon, the sun bored into their eyes, making the spindly scrub dance like hordes of blackfellows. The countryside was parched and colourless, and they saw little wildlife. They filled their water bags at Lake Warrakalanna and turned south towards Mount Hopeless.

Howitt reached into his pocket for his compass to check their bearing, then held it out in the palm of his hand to show Burrell. 'James Parkes' best,' he told Burrell, who was riding alongside.

'Yes, Mr Welch was quite envious of it.'

Howitt bridled at the mention of the man's name and pushed the compass into his pocket. His journal was on the saddle between his thighs—he'd become adept at reading and writing on horseback. Now he lowered his head over the page, jotting down figures in his spidery hand.

'Some lose all sense of direction when they first come to Australia,' Burrell said to ease the tension. 'The night sky so different and the sun in the wrong quarter. Whereas for me, it's all I've known. And you've certainly mastered it.'

'You need to be practical, willing to change. Some never do, Welch included.'

Burrell gave him an odd look. 'Mr Welch was alright. A bit of a stickler, but good company for all that.'

Howitt raised his eyebrows, but they were hidden under the brim of his hat.

Burrell coughed into his hand. 'He was a good surveyor, and clever with his daguerreotypes.'

Howitt scowled. 'Well, we'll manage just fine without him,' he said to close the conversation.

ꟹ

They rode into ever-increasing barrenness, along a length of watercourse that had gone dry. For days on end they found no water, and sucked on bullets, trying to draw out a drop of spit, till the taste of metal was like blood filling their mouths.

Two day's ride from Mount Hopeless, the sky turned the colour of lead, the sun became a fierce, brassy disc. Then a strong sand-laden wind wiped out the light: a dry-dirt blizzard that flayed exposed skin and eyes, and bit into already cracked and bleeding lips. The men tied handkerchiefs across their noses and mouths, pulled the brims of their hats down low and worked to calm their skittering horses.

Visibility was reduced to mere inches. Phillips leaned over on his horse and yelled into Howitt's ear: 'We need to string the horses together, so we don't lose anyone.' Howitt nodded and Phillips passed a length of rope down the line, linking men and horses.

Howitt struggled to retrieve his compass from his pocket and held it up to his eyes for some idea of direction, but the needle swung wildly. 'Where on God's earth are we?' he asked himself in rising panic. Sand had choked his senses; the wind spun his mind into turmoil.

He reined in his horse and to Burrell, riding behind him, he instructed word to be passed down the line that they would have to stop. They drew into a tight circle and covered the horses as best they could, lashing blankets around their heads, and then covered themselves with canvas, fighting with the sheets against the wind. We could be buried alive, Howitt thought, as they hunkered down, sand drifts piling up around their bodies. A strong gust caught the corner of his canvas so that it flew up like a sail and dragged him a few feet across the ground. The other men helped him to reef it back in around his body.

They looked like a circle of bulky mummies; part of an ancient rite of sacrifice to Seth, the Greek god of the desert, of sand storms and chaos. Inside their canvas wrappings, each man sweated in fear and prayed to their one true god. Howitt, too, tried to pray, but the words wouldn't come. He might pray that he wished he could still pray, for the relief it might bring him. But what a hollow shell that would be, now that the last shreds of belief were gone. Instead, he thought about his death and how little he would leave behind: no wife or children, no significant contribution to science or society. If he were remembered at all it would be as the man who led his team to their death. In his pitch-dark, fetid tomb he was becoming lightheaded and nauseous with thirst and heat, and nightmare images danced before his eyes.

Towards sunset, the wind suddenly dropped and with it, most of the sand. Howitt unwound himself from his canvas and stood up unsteadily. The others emerged from their coverings, exhausted and sickly. Howitt asked each man, individually, if he was alright. There were no physical injuries, but each man's eyes were stark with the horror of the dark places they had seen. Howitt told them to rest while he removed the blankets from the horses and checked each one. There had been no loss of life: he felt a flood of relief that made him sink to his knees.

The following two days provided easier riding and the watercourse once again offered up water: a sludgy trickle at first that gradually cleared and broadened. Ahead, the plain was flat and barren; Mount Hopeless rose like a great carbuncle on the horizon. They reached the base of the mountain almost to the day that Howitt had predicted, their spirits high. Not so hopeless after all, he congratulated himself.

It was the Welch episode that was hopeless. He imagined that Welch now felt sorry for his rashness, wished he were here at Mt Hopeless, with compass and watch in hand, taking bearings, and making notes. Surveying wasn't all that difficult. The pages of Howitt's journal were smudged with sweat and dirty fingerprints, but the reckonings were readable and, he believed, as accurate as Welch could have made them.

Up close, Mount Hopeless was not so much a mountain as a mass of rounded, tussock-covered hillocks from which emerged sharp black pinnacles. Howitt sat in a niche out of a wind that had sprung up from the north, soughing through the saltbush. A more gentle, sighing wind, he thought, as his pencil scratched across the pages of his journal. But from time to time he closed his eyes against what might have happened. The others were setting up camp beside the small waterhole they had found, and he could hear, without looking up, the horses snuffling as they drank. The air filled with the sound of tent pegs being hammered into the red, flinty ground, the noise bouncing back and forth amongst the hillocks. They were laughing now, his men, but they could have ended up as a pile of bones, no different from Burke and Wills. He swallowed hard and returned to recording his account of the dust storm. Unwittingly, his mind rolled back to the memory of other bones, scattered amongst the rocks of a river gorge in Gippsland. The bones he should have recorded, but never did.

After the work had been done, Phillips sat on the bank of the waterhole with his rifle between his knees, waiting for the ducks he was sure would appear with the sunset. Burrell was with him, and the two men yarned quietly.

Howitt finished his journal entry and went to find Aitkin who was sitting on the ground, his back against a boab tree, plaiting thongs of greenhide into a whip. From the quarter pot on the campfire, Howitt poured two mugs of tea, put them on ground beside Aitkin and sat down with his knees drawn up and his arms around his shins.

'Do you ever think of those bones we found in Gippsland?' Howitt asked softly.

Aitkin kept his eyes on the plaiting, but his body lost its looseness and his hands had became still.

'I was never able to make up my mind about them,' Howitt continued.

'So you never wrote the report?' Aitkin's tone expressed discomfort.

Howitt shook his head. 'I had no proof,' he answered uncomfortably. 'I never understood what made you so sure.' He poked at the fire with a stick.

'I wasn't.' Aitkin went back to his plaiting and they sat in silence for a few minutes, Howitt watched the flames weaving together in bright silky strands, seeing in his mind's eye the mossy rocks of the gorge and Aitkin holding up to him a child's skull.

A gunshot made them both jump.

Howitt was the first to speak again. 'They say they're dying out anyway, the natives, I mean. Survival of the fittest, as Darwin's theory would have it.' He wiped his palms on his trousers and picked up his mug.

Aitkin grunted in disapproval. They sat in uncomfortable silence. Aitkin steadily plaiting while Howitt stared into his mug of tea, his mind following a new tangent. He coughed and spoke. 'Tell me, what do you think of Darwin's ideas about evolution? You're an engineer and his theory is, in a way, about the engineering of species.'

Aitkin hesitated for a moment before answering. 'Bridges don't have souls. Same with kangaroos and all other creatures. What Mr Darwin overlooks, because he's so immersed in his pigeons, is the fact that human beings are different, separate, and cannot be a progression from other animals.'

'You've read his book?' Howitt asked in amazement.

Aitkin shot him a disgusted look and turned away.

'And it didn't persuade you?' He was like a dog with a bone sometimes, but his voice carried a small note of apology. He sipped his tea.

'I don't know what to make of it. At one level I suppose it makes sense, but I don't care for where it might lead.'

There was another gunshot.

'Sounds like we'll be dining well tonight.' He hoped Aitkin could sense his desire to appease.

ઌ

When he finally returned to the Cullyamurra depot, Howitt found the men had established a vegetable garden in the loamy soil around the edge of the waterhole that they'd fed with horse and camel manure. There was a patchwork of pumpkins, melons, radishes and beans. The ground about was thick with native clover and the air moist and full of autumn sweetness. The tents had been supplemented with humpies. 'So you've turned native in my absence,' Howitt joked with them.

His tent now boasted a branch-and-bark annex that cast cool shade over the entrance. Inside the tent, he checked on the boxes that held Burke's and Wills' bones, so aware of their symbolic and appeasing value. He heard Aitkin call his name. He carefully closed the lid on Burke's miniature coffin and went outside. A tall, imposing native had walked into the camp. His slender body was regally erect, his long hair captured in a net and his beard bound tightly to a point. When he saw Howitt, he gestured to his three companions standing further away at the edge of the camp, partly camouflaged by the straight dark trunks of trees. The three were moaning loudly and holding their stomachs.

'They've been stealing vegetables,' O'Donnell snorted. The garden was doused with arsenic sugar to deter ants. 'Serves them right.'

Howitt sighed and asked O'Donnell to make up a couple of quarts of soapy water. He sat the three natives down in a row away from the tents and indicated they were to drink the liquid. The sick men took their punishment and shortly afterwards vomited the contents of their stomachs. They continued to moan for some time, then realised they were cured and grinned widely at each other. The man Howitt took to be the leader had stood by watching anxiously, but he now smiled, too. He nodded his gratitude to Howitt and the group left.

The following morning, Howitt watched as the same four black men came towards him with a dead kangaroo slung between poles on their shoulders. Without speaking, they collected sticks from amongst the trees, dug a deep hole beside the white men's campfire, laid in the sticks and lit a fire. While they crouched at the edge of the pit Howitt fetched his journal and stool and sat watching them, writing up whatever they did. The other men gathered around him, also watching.

When the fire died down to coals, the natives lifted in the kangaroo and burnt the fur first from one side of the body, then from the other. They slit the beast open, removed its innards and filled the cavity with stones, stoked the fire, and covered the body thickly with branches. The leader gestured to Howitt to leave the kangaroo to cook—he pointed to where the sun would be on the western horizon when it was ready. Howitt rose from his stool and walked towards the man. He asked him his name. Mungallee, the man told him, his face impassive but not unfriendly. Howitt reached for his hand and shook it. Mungallee looked quizzically at his hand when Howitt released it, then beckoned to his fellows. They trooped out of the camp in single file.

Howitt had a stomach for anything, and they'd all eaten kangaroo before, but never so succulent and tasty. With fresh vegetables from the garden they could have been, Howitt announced, dining at one of Melbourne's finest hotels. The sun was setting and the trees appeared as black silhouettes, their leaves shimmering at the edges. More wonderful, Howitt thought, than anything Melbourne could offer. He poured each man an extra tot of rum, and topped up his mug of tea.

The following morning, after breakfast, he rode out alone along the Cooper looking for the natives' camp, and found it a few miles upstream. He had no fear of them, after their kind gesture, and a great desire to learn more about their way of life. During the night he'd recalled a conversation from a few years earlier with the pastoralist Angus McMillan. McMillan had suggested that Howitt might consider taking on the task of recording Aboriginal customs. It had been the time when he was setting off for his Gippsland expedition, and McMillan had offered his party a night of Highlander hospitality. Not long after, Howitt had discovered the bones in the gorge.

A pack of dogs barked madly at his approach. Howitt dismounted, tethered the reins to a branch, and looked about for Mungallee. Thanking him for the food was to be an excuse to ask questions. He walked towards a group of blackfellows playing with a ball, the dogs at his heels but harmless. The ball, he realised with surprise, was the dried and stuffed scrotum of a red kangaroo. There seemed to be more than two teams, so he couldn't quite follow the rules. One man pitched the ball into the air so that he could kick it, and the other players rushed up to be the first to grab it, some leaping lightly into the air, climbing up each other's bodies as if they were ladders. There were scrambles in the dust until someone emerged clutching the ball to his chest, then ran low across the ground until he had sufficient free space to kick it, aiming it in the direction of another team member. The players were young men, tall, fast and loose-limbed. There were shouts and laughter from the boundaries as the spectators cheered the game along. Taking his notebook and pencil from his pocket, Howitt quickly jotted down a dozen or so words to record the game.

He looked across to the camp, a little way off, where women

sat on skins around a fire. At their backs, set amongst coolabahs and bulky-trunked boabs, was a scattering of bark humpies. He would have liked to see what the women were doing, but was uncertain whether it was right for him to approach them.

Suddenly, Mungallee appeared in front of Howitt, greeting him as if there was nothing unusual about a white man showing up at his camp. He gestured to the game, explaining something that Howitt could not understand.

Mungallee nodded seriously at the questions Howitt asked in the Pidgin English he'd picked up during his dealings with other desert tribes. The native pointed to things around him, giving their names to Howitt like gifts. In return, Howitt offered his own words, only to have the native impatiently brush them aside like annoying insects. So Howitt conceded to listen, stumbling over the difficult combinations of sounds: *Yan-tru-wanta*, the name of the tribe; and *Barcoo,* the name for Coopers Creek. The man pointed to his chest and explained, through a sketch in the sand, that *Mungallee* meant lizard. He pointed to a teenage boy who was keeping the dogs under control, and introduced him as *Tchuku-ro*, meaning kangaroo. Mungallee pointed again to himself and said '*Pinnaroo*', implying headman. He called Howitt *Caliomaroo Pinnaroo*, which Howitt translated for himself as 'chief of the camp at the waterhole'. He jotted down the words in his notebook, wetting the lead of his pencil with the tip of his tongue and making stabs at the possible order of letters that would capture the strange sounds.

Mungallee led Howitt away from the game and towards the camp. As they passed the women, Howitt nodded and smiled his greetings, but they only followed him with their eyes for a moment before returning to their tasks. From one of the humpies, Mungallee collected a boomerang and a string bag, and walked with Howitt along the banks of the Cooper. They passed stone-and-reed fish traps set into the banks where the water flowed quickly and clearly, and stopped at a place where nets were strung above part of the creek. The native tossed the boomerang into the sky in a movement so quick that Howitt almost missed it. As the boomerang swung up and around, it made the sound of a whistling kite. Emu-wrens that had been pecking along the bank took fright and flew up into the nets. Howitt waded into the shallows with Mungallee to help him untangle the fluttering creatures, snap their necks and place them in the string bag.

He would write to tell his father of this; he'd be interested to learn of such inventiveness. In the comfort of England, his father was a supporter of native tribes and raged against the injustices of the Empire wherever it spread its grasping tentacles. He would seat the family around the dining table and quote at length from the book he'd written, *Colonization and Christianity*, instructing them in moral outrage. As the dutiful oldest son, Alfred could still recite whole tracts from memory: 'We pride ourselves on our superior knowledge, our superior refinement, our higher virtues, our nobler character.' The voice in his head was his father's, full of indignation, and he could picture him clearly, with his high collar and biblical beard, the open book balanced in his palm but hardly glanced at, his free arm gesticulating.

'We talk of the heathen, the savage, and the cruel, and the wily tribes, that fill the rest of the earth; but how is it that these tribes know us?' An eyebrow was raised in question, directed at Alfred sitting opposite. 'Chiefly by the very features that we attribute exclusively to them. They know us chiefly by our crimes and our cruelty. It is we who are, and must appear to them, the savages.'

As a child, and a British one at that, Howitt had never really understood, but he thought now of the bones in Gippsland. He looked at Mungallee, swinging his string bag full of birds. In his short stint in Australia, the only natives Howitt's father had met were the sad, dispossessed specimens that hung around the fringes of the diggings, dressed in rags and begging. Incapable of a day's work, he always said, showing little pity for their plight. He might have kept his faith in the noble savage if he'd met Mungallee; might have recognised that they had much in common. Mungallee was certain of his place in the world, just like Howitt's father, and a determined educator, from the way he showed off his boomerang and hunting skills just as his father showed off his learning.

Thinking of his father led him to Welch—the two disturbingly twinned in his mind—and he realised there was something in Mungallee's confident bearing that reminded him of the surveyor. He could concede, at this distance, that Welch might deserve his self-confidence, at least where his particular skills were concerned. Then he recalled Welch's departing look of contempt, and the familiar, more comforting dislike for the man returned to override any notion of pardon.

Howitt left the native distributing the catch amongst the women and rode back to his camp, his head spinning with what he had witnessed: the way the natives could be so languid yet so intensely attached to the land. It was as if there was nothing the land could teach them that they hadn't already divined and put to use, so that they could extract a healthy existence from the most slender resources. He'd thought them lazy and incompetent but he could now sense the timeless evolution of skills that lay behind such effortlessness.

As he rode back to his camp, he wondered about Burke. If the man had had more sense—more humility—and had sought the help of the natives, he might still be alive. But then, Howitt mused, I wouldn't be here.

# Chapter 2

The funeral procession plodded out of town. The main street of Bairnsdale, built wide enough to turn a bullock train, was clogged with buggies, traps, men on horseback, women and children in the town's only omnibus, even a couple of automobiles, all following the slow-paced plumed horses and black crepe-draped hearse. The procession passed hotels where men, lounging on rails—strangers in town—stood up straight and removed their hats. It passed the empty, shuttered shops, closed for half a day out of respect.

The town ended abruptly and the procession passed wide, cleared paddocks parched by summer heat. White dust kicked up by the horses settled on hat brims and parasols. Across the flat land the sheep wavered and the horizon blurred. Big black currawongs gave out their rusty calls from the boughs of gum trees.

He wasn't their native son—few his age were—but he was closely theirs, and he had achieved more than most of them ever dreamed of for themselves. Joining his funeral parade, men in sombre suits felt burnished by his successes; farmers' chests, barrelled and muscled, swelled with pride; women placed white-gloved hands on their breasts or the heads of their children and spoke of him in whispered, proprietorial voices.

When the procession reached the cemetery, Howitt's daughter May watched the swarm of people descending like crows on her father's grave. Their clothes gave off a mothball fug that hung in the thick humid air and made May's head ache. Waves of well-wishers flowed up to her, shook her hand and offered their condolences, their words indistinguishable one from another, then merged back into the crowd. She felt nauseous in her thick black skirt and jacket; the veil over her face was like a spider's web that she itched to tear away.

She watched as her brothers and sisters did a much better

job. Charlton and Gilbert, standing at the graveside in their black suits and high white collars, were shaking hands and accepting platitudes; Annie and Maude looked as if they did this sort of thing often. The four of them instinctively knew how to grieve, and knew what they grieved for. May longed to be back at Clovelly, under what had been her father's roof but was now probably her own. To be alone, her face towards the vacant blue bay, drinking in the cool sea breeze.

Annie came to her and took her arm. Although May was two years older, they could almost pass for twins, with their slim, straight bodies, dark hair and eyes, and pleasant, even features. 'Take a deep breath, here comes the Mayor,' Annie whispered.

The Mayor was full of ponderous condolence while he mopped his brow and the back of his neck with a starched white handkerchief. Then his mood lightened as he told them about the parkland the Shire intended to create adjacent to Eastwood, and how it would need a name.

May pictured the land, opposite the family farm where she had spent her childhood. The Backwater parted from the Mitchell River and curled around the property. When she was young, she would stand on the front verandah, watching across the Backwater towards the Bairnsdale Courthouse, waiting for her father to emerge. She would follow his black-suited form as he walked towards the bridge and across the river. Then he would disappear for a while, behind the banks of river gums, to re-emerge at the garden gate.

They weren't the only ones who lived there. Further along the Backwater the natives had camped on the land they had long considered to be their own, although it was part of Eastwood. The natives had been moved to the Lake Tyers Mission years ago. It was Gilbert's farm now.

'You could call it Brabrolong,' May offered. Annie placed a second hand on May's arm where it linked with her own, and the Mayor frowned uncertainly.

'Brabrolong?' He shook his head.

'It's the name of the land's original owners.'

The Mayor looked about, as if for help. 'We had thought,' he started hesitantly. 'That is, the Council would like to name the park after your father. The ladies in the Historical Society thought a bronze plaque would be fitting, something solid and substantial. They plan to run cake stalls to raise the money.'

'Our family would be honoured to contribute.' It was Annie who spoke in her clear, assured voice.

May looked down at her dusty boots. The Mayor gave a small bow and moved away, back to the knot of councillors standing on the other side of the grave.

'Leave me, Annie. I'll be okay.' She looked at her sister's worried face, so much like her own, and patted the hand still resting on her arm. 'I'll behave, I promise.' She tried to smile as she gently unlinked Annie's arm.

May walked a short distance from the crowd and stood behind a large white cross that was hot and rough under her gloved hand. There were tufts of grass at her feet that had survived the summer, and she kicked at them absent-mindedly as her eyes wandered over the tombstones, startlingly white against the mourners' black. She looked back at the hole in the ground where her father would soon be laid. Her mother's headstone was cool marble. Hers was the only name—Liney Howitt—on the large white slab; the engravers would return later to add her father's name.

The mourners had gathered into clusters. Around Professor Spencer buzzed the anthropologists, whose first knowledge of the Australian Aborigines was likely to have come from reading her father's work. Another group was made up of geologists and men from the Mines department who respected her father's contributions to their field of science, although there was less certainty now about his hypotheses. There were public servants up from Melbourne who had served under her father; and men who had been accused or defended in his magisterial presence, who came because of his fairness and justice. There were sharply dressed lawyers and solicitors; politicians (though Mr Deakin had sent his apologies); the Mayor and his gaggle of councillors. But most of the crowd was made up of ordinary people: locals and out-of-towners, who were here because her father would always be known to them as the man who discovered the fate of Burke and Wills and returned to Melbourne with the heroes' bones.

The church service had been almost unbearable: first the minister, so measured and heavy in his reverence, so certain of her father's entry to heaven; then the long drawn-out tributes from colleagues and friends. Her father would have relished the homage and gravitas, but he would have scoffed at the minister's meaningless words proclaiming his deserved passage into the afterlife. Or at least he would have scoffed to May when they were out of earshot of anyone else. Charlton had given the family eulogy, and he had done well, but it should have been me, May thought bitterly.

She had anxiously searched the crowd outside the church, but there was not a single black face. Did they stay away in protest? Or because of the hostility their presence might have incited? Professor Spencer and the other anthropologists would have ensured they came to no harm. They were, after all, Christians now. They could have stood on the church porch, she thought, hats in hands and heads bowed, as a mark of respect for the man who had strived to preserve their customs before they were lost forever. It seemed to her that the blacks had become indifferent to their own traditions, or perhaps simply resigned to their fate.

The crowd became silent and the minister read from his Bible, but May was not listening. She was still standing a little way off, watching two small boys slapping each other, listening to the sniffles and shuffling feet, breathing in the rich ordure of fresh horse manure. Overhead, three pelicans swirled in an updraft. May's eyes followed their circular path, and it was then that she caught a movement, half hidden by a towering stone angel with one hand grasping a dove as if to throttle it. It was Esmay: head bowed, shoulders shaking convulsively. Of course Esmay would come: she was the one Eastwood native who had remained close to the family. And of course she would have the good sense not to show herself. May longed to approach her;

someone coughed and she quickly bowed her head.

The first shovelful of dry earth hit the coffin lid, making May jump and startling a flock of sulphur-crested cockatoos into lifting raucously into the sky. Just as the minister was closing his Bible a south-westerly change swept across the paddocks bringing a cold wind with rain at its heels, sending the mourners scuttling to their conveyances. Annie's hand on her shoulder made May jump again. 'Time for us to leave,' she said gently. May allowed her sister to lead her back to the carriage, following the hunched shoulders of their brothers and sister. There was still the afternoon tea to be endured at Eastwood.

The rain started falling in swollen drops that bounced when they hit the parched earth. Annie raised her umbrella—how did she think to bring such a thing, May wondered—and the two women drew close together for shelter as they made their way from the gravesite. May turned to see the gravediggers, already drenched, rapidly tossing now-dark earth into the hole. She scanned the cemetery for Esmay but there was no sign of her.

'Don't look,' Annie cried, her sodden handkerchief clenched to her mouth.

❧

After the wake at Eastwood, and ignoring her siblings' protests, May drove the twenty miles home to Clovelly, alone in her horse and trap. With the cemetery dust on her boots, she stood before the bookcase in her father's study, scanning the shelves that were crammed with books and journals and dog-eared papers.

The house creaked in its emptiness. It was her mother's house, a gift from Papa. Or perhaps a compensation. Liney had named the house Clovelly after the village in North Devon where her parents had taken a cottage each summer. Not that there were many similarities. May had visited the Devon village with her father during their touring holiday. It was a clutch of whitewashed cottages perched on a cliff face, hemmed in by thick forest on three sides and the harbour below. The air smelt of salt and herring and was full of the noise of boat builders, fishermen and coal boat crews. There was the rattle of shingles as waves skipped along the shore, and the thunder of the sea breaking on the dry-stone quay wall. The village had a four-hundred-year head start on Metung. Here the land was certainly ancient: the bush that pressed in on the town, the bay as round and flat as a huge saucer of blue water, the far-shore sand barrier covered in tea tree, and the ocean beyond. But the newness of the settlement couldn't be disguised, despite the ramshackle fishermen's cottages and the few grand houses.

Papa's friend, the botanist Mr von Mueller, had argued with her mother about the garden. He wanted to fill it with plants that belonged. May could still see him, his face red with disagreement, his moustache drooping with the heat. 'Not roses,' he'd bellowed in his heavy German accent. 'They are for the old world, not this place. Look at the trees. Look at the light.' He'd waved his hands around, somewhat dramatically May thought. 'Definitely not a monkey puzzle tree,' he'd said in a disgusted tone. May had agreed with him, but neither of them were a match for her mother.

In her father's study, she walked her fingers along the spines of books until she found what she was looking for, the book fat with its own importance and heavy in her hand. She remembered when *The Native Tribes of South-East Australia* arrived in the post, still smelling of printer's ink. She had waited outside her father's study door and listened to the sound of pages being slit. Papa had been humming in that way he had when he was pleased with himself. She had been pacing, her footsteps muffled by the hall runner, until she smelt a burning and rushed back to the marmalade on the hotplate in the kitchen.

'I'm just popping out for a moment', he had called to May, who was still in the kitchen. 'Need to post a letter to Lorimer Fison. Tell him the book has arrived.'

As soon as he left the house May had slipped into his study where she had found the book lying prominently on his desk. Anxiously turning the pages of the Preface, she scanned the print for her name, hoping that perhaps, after she had finished correcting the proofs, he had inserted a sentence or two to surprise her. He thanked Annie King for her photographs, even though some of the photographs were May's. He thanked Dr Frazer, of course, for his advice, and many other people who had had only a fleeting influence on the work. She had spent months and months typing, correcting, even offering up her own research like a sacrifice at the feet of the Oracle. In London, while her father had socialised with his new academic chums, she had forgone sightseeing to spend day after day marking up the galleys and checking the proofs. But her name was not there.

When she flicked through the pages, she had seen that M E B Howitt was consigned to a handful of footnotes where he had acknowledged use of her work, whereas she had been able to read her presence on almost every page. All those words, hundreds of thousands of them, and he had wanted to be sure the world ascribed them all to him.

Words: that's what her father had loved most; words of law and justice; words that described the earth; that named trees and mountains. But especially natives' words, those strange sounds that expressed an even stranger world. *Dhadyan*: clever man.

He had loved her mother too, in his own way, although it seemed to May that he had appeared to be like a swan, gliding across smooth water, while her mother did all the paddling below the surface.

Her sisters had escaped into marriage, Charlton into his own family and career, and Gilbert had stayed on the farm at Eastwood. But May had followed her parents, like a loyal dog, to Melbourne when her father was appointed to the public service, and when he retired, to Clovelly in Metung. When her mother died—a sudden, wasteful death—May had, without question, taken up the role of below-the-surface paddling.

She might have been spared her mother's burden of raising five children, but she had different responsibilities thrust upon her: to nurture and coax and protect his thoughts from the moment they sprang into his mind to the time they were committed to the printed page. There were all the speeches that had to be taken down in her especially learned Pitman shorthand while he paced the room, and then transferred to neatly typed pages with two carbon copies; the black ink smudging her fingers and shirt cuffs. There were travel arrangements that had to be made, bags packed, words of encouragement to be delivered before he stepped before the lectern, applause to accompany that of his admiring peers. Lunch was to be on the table promptly at one o'clock so that his afternoons were free; his hat and coat to be brushed and shirts to be starched and ironed; the household accounts to be paid and the debts called in; the sumptuous dinners to appear as if by magic for visiting dignitaries.

Standing in her father's study, she lifted the book to her nose but the smell of printer's ink was long gone. She opened the book, knowing exactly where to find her name in the tiny six-point type of the footnotes, then slammed it shut. Her father was dead and buried.

She walked around the silent house, touching objects that still bore the imprint of his fingers. She picked up his pipe lying on a table beside the fireplace and breathed in the smell of him. She knocked out the spent tobacco on the edge of the firedog. The briar bowl of the pipe cradled smooth and round in the palm of her hand. He'd held it just like that, weighing it as he weighed a new idea. His was a life so full of vigour; she had thought, coming back into the house after the funeral, that there might still be some kind of a vibration, a palpable wave of energy not yet fully dissipated. Surely something would be left of the doggedness that towards the end of his life had given way to an urgency that was almost manic, like a fox that suddenly senses the hounds at its heels.

'Nearly everything is lost,' he told her over and over. The natives, he said, were losing their old customs so that nothing would be left for posterity and research. 'Shreds and patches, that's all. There is still so much to be learned of their marriage customs and totems, but there's hardly a black that can truly answer my questions now.' He was angry with them, but he accepted, too, that the fault didn't lie only with them.

Together, she and her father had spent the last few months answering correspondence and writing articles and letters to the editor of *The Argus*, defending his findings against arrogant upstarts. Her father was also eager to finish *A Message to Anthropologists*; he must warn his colleagues not to think that the way the natives now lived gave insight into their traditions. There were anthropologists who seemed unaware that customs were almost daily being modified or lost; they were making erroneous assessments, misinterpreting what they witnessed. At the end of each angry day, he would fall back into the embrace of the big wing-backed chair in the living room, open-mouthed, sunk into deep slumber. She would cover him with a tartan blanket, tuck it around his frail body, and tiptoe away.

She laid her father's pipe back on the table by the fireplace and went to the front door, calling to Borun, suddenly needing another life in the house. The dog bounded towards her, oblivious of everything. She crouched and held his brown head between her two hands; she could see her own tiny reflection in his amber-coloured eyes. 'Just us now Borun.' The animal wagged his tail. 'And you are welcome in my house.'

She stood up and looked out into the darkening evening. In the garden, the flame tree was in full flower, standing out blood-red against a sky still thickly purple with thunder clouds. The air was washed and crisp from the rain and she breathed in its coolness. Below the house, she could just make out the white-peaks of waves scuttling across the bay.

At forty-two she was an orphan—an orphan and a spinster: how grim. She shook her head against the self-pity and let the dog into the house.

ᔓ

The following morning, May walked down the hall and opened the door to what had been her father's bedroom. It was a room she had rarely entered, even when her mother was alive, and now she felt a sense of trespass. It smelt of hair oil and the slight mustiness of old clothes and slept-in bed linen. She drew back the curtains and the room flooded with light made blue from the bay's reflection.

There was so much to be sorted out, and no time like the present. She would start with the clothing. The massive oak wardrobe stood like an overbearing monarch in the room. It had been in her parents' bedroom at Eastwood, too, before they moved to Metung. When May, as a small child, had scarlet fever, her mother had laid her in the big bed during the day so that she could look out onto the garden and watch the birds. But she'd spent most of the time watching the wardrobe in constant fear that it would topple over and crush her, or that the door would spring open and a monster—hairy and horrible as she imagined a bunyip to be—would burst into the room.

The old fears lingered irrationally. She opened one of the doors tentatively and gasped. Inside were her mother's clothes, lined up like empty memories: she had forgotten all about them. Liney had been dead for five years and yet everything was so neat, as if just laundered and hung. That would have been Esmay's doing, she reasoned. Esmay, who had stayed loyal to her family; who had continued to travel from the Lake Tyers Mission to Metung to help May from time to time after Liney's death.

Her father was a man of remarkably few personal possessions, not counting all the rocks and fossils, spears and boomerangs, geological equipment, and books and journals. His own side of the wardrobe was almost empty: three day suits, an overcoat, two hats. Charlton had already claimed his gold watch and cuff links; Gilbert was to have his woodworking tools; Maude the von Guerard painting. Annie had asked for the sailing boat *Prelude*, for her children. Her siblings were happy for May to have his decorations: the Mueller medal; the cross of St Michael and St George; the various pins and badges of geological and anthropological associations in Australia and overseas. She would also keep the illuminated address that had been presented to her father by members of the Royal Society for the Burke and Wills relief mission. Her father had not put much store by it as a token of appreciation, but it was a beautiful certificate with gold-leaf lettering, swirling fine calligraphy, and jewel-coloured scrolls and lozenge patterns. Papa always said that he would rather have had money in the bank.

Emptying the wardrobe suddenly seemed impossible, as if she were throwing out her parents. She closed the door and leaned against it, looking past the bed and out through the window, her fingernails pressed deep into the palms of her clenched hands. She turned to the dressing table, still with her father's ebony-backed hairbrush and a silver-framed photograph she had taken of her parents, not long before her mother died. She picked up the picture and studied the image: her mother was seated, done up like a Christmas cracker in patterned taffeta, her father stood at her side with his hand on her shoulder. He was dressed, as always, in a dark suit, his beard an unruly white cloud around his face. As she replaced the photograph, May noticed reflected in the dressing-table mirror a large cardboard box on top of the wardrobe behind her.

She dragged a chair over to the wardrobe, lifted the box down and set it on the bed. She blew the dust from its surface, making the motes dance about her in the sunlit room. When she lifted the lid the smell of mothballs rose sharp and pungent, reminding her of the funeral, and bile rose to the back of her throat. She breathed deeply before lifting the items from the box and laying them side by side on the bed: the silk gown and the black velvet bonnet. The colours swam before her eyes: the scarlet gown lined with pink, the front of the sleeves turned back with scarlet buttons and cords, the gold tassels on the bonnet. She fingered the luxurious cloth, remembering her father's face shining with pride. And remembering, too, the pain she'd felt, as sharp as a splinter lodged under a fingernail, as she watched him kneel to solemnly accept his honorary doctorate.

It had been four years ago: 1904. She sat down on the bed, taking the gown onto her lap like a child, stroking the nap of the bonnet, running her fingers through the tassels. They had ridden in an open carriage through the cobbled streets of

Cambridge to Queen's College, pointing out to each other queer cottages and swathed banks of tulips. Papa had fussed with the long open sleeves of his gown and raised his hand to his bonneted head. 'I look more like a Beefeater than a doctor of science. What would our friends in Australia say? It is a pity you didn't bring your camera.'

She shrugged. She had been a good photographer; her work had been published in the pictorial pages of newspapers, in photographic journals, and in her father's publications. But her interest had waned as her passion for anthropology and writing grew.

The carriage had pulled up at Queen's College, and the building was more ancient and beautiful than she had imagined, its reflection trembling on the surface of the river. The trees along the far bank bore early green tracings of spring, and clumps of daffodils shone golden in the morning sunshine. May and her father were met by distinguished men in academic gowns: some scarlet like her father's; some black with hoods exposing their linings of scarlet, cherry and dove grey; some with the distinguishing addition of gold braid. They shook her father's hand and spoke in loud confident voices. A few nodded politely to May.

In the regal auditorium, Papa read his paper—'Group Marriage in the Australian Tribes'—to a large gathering of British scientists who then honoured him in responses that praised his scholarship. Lunch followed; even the Prime Minister Mr Balfour attended, although he spoke to neither of them. May was led into the dining room by a man who asked her politely about her sightseeing. 'Oh, you mean Windsor *cahsell*,' he corrected, as he deposited her in her seat.

She smiled at the woman next to her who was dressed in finely embroidered muslin: she was what an Australian would call mutton dressed up as lamb. May wore a sombre green woollen dress with her mother's cameo pinned at her neck. She felt frumpish and colonial. The woman was a professor's wife and talked without pause about her husband's brilliant career. After the rice pudding, with a skin so thick May judged she could have walked across it, she attempted to tell the woman something of Australia.

The professor's wife dabbed at her scarlet lips with her crisp linen napkin. 'It must be a truly frightful place, full of convicts and savages.'

May was taken aback. She had been describing the birdlife. She took a deep breath and replied stiffly. 'When I was a little girl I used to have nightmares about England, of rotting hulks and filthy dark streets. For me, it was the place where all the thieves and felons had come from.'

The surprise for May was that England was such an alien country. Oh, it was pretty enough, but she felt so out of her depth, when she had thought she'd step into the country as easily as stepping into the village store in Metung. Given the way it was spoken of in Australia, as Home, the place from which everything was inherited and by which everything was measured, she had thought it would be more familiar. She'd dreamed of stimulating conversations with like-minded people; instead, she met a subtle undercurrent that she couldn't fathom. At her lowest moments she believed the English possessed a secret code to deliberately exclude outsiders and so uphold their superiority.

Religion was another surprise. All the members of the Nottingham family with whom they stayed were kind and generous, but their Quaker way of life made them even more foreign. In her own childhood, her father had deferred to her mother's Quaker rules and did not question them being instilled in his children. But Australia had rubbed off the sharp corners of the tenets she'd carried away with her fifty years earlier, and it was to her father, anyway, that May had always looked for guidance.

May and her father had accompanied their Nottingham family to the Friends Meeting House for the Sunday meeting. May sat uncomfortably through the long silences on her hard, upright chair, trying not to fidget as the others waited expectantly for God's voice. There was nothing in the bare room with which to distract herself; even the windows offered only blank grey-day squares. Surreptitiously, she looked around the circle of faces, features in repose, hands clasped loosely in laps, and tried to imagine what thoughts were passing through their minds. Some faces bore quiet smiles: were they listening to the voice of God? Others frowned.

Suddenly a man spoke, making May jump, and the group of Friends opened their eyes. 'Friends, the British government is importing Chinese labourers into South Africa to work the gold mines. This is a return to slavery in everything but name.' There was nodding and murmuring.

'There is to be a demonstration in Hyde Park,' another Friend responded. 'How many Friends are able to attend?' Hands went up around the room. May watched, dumbfounded. This was as far from the church she knew as Australia was from Britain. She suspected there had been a subtle shift that had marked the end of the religious meeting and returned the Friends to more worldly concerns. Or had God been instructing them upon the glories of political activism? It was thrilling to witness such radical fearlessness as the Friends signed up for the demonstration.

'Won't you be putting yourself at risk?' she asked one woman who simply smiled at her and squeezed her hand. May didn't know anyone in Australia who attended political rallies. Even her father, with his strong ideals and beliefs, swam within the stream.

Thinking back to those strong socially minded people, so eager to act on their convictions, May recalled, by comparison, how poorly she had dealt with Dr Frazer. She laid the gown and bonnet back on the bed next to her, uncomfortable with the admission of how poor she was at standing up for herself. All the way to England, on the boat, she had practiced what she would say to him about his plagiarism; his failure to acknowledge his use of her work. But when she and her father were guests in his house in Cambridge, she had quailed. After dinner on the first evening, when the men rose from the table to retire to Dr Frazer's study to discuss anthropology, May had made to leave with them, as she often did in Australia.

Mrs Frazer had reached out and put her hand over May's.

'We shall have tea in the drawing room, dear,' she said firmly.

'For two years, Australian women have had the right to vote,' May told Mrs Frazer, apropos of nothing.

May and her father had spent the following day meandering along the Cambridge streets, their heads bowed against a wind that carried a knife's edge.

'Mrs Frazer thought to instruct me to put my butter on the side of the plate instead of directly onto my toast,' she complained to her father as she clasped her coat around her body with one hand and her hat to her head with the other.

'They're nice people, really, May dear.' But she could hardly hear him, his voice being whipped away by the wind. It was the day before the ceremony, and her father was as jittery as a cat.

'Here's what I've been looking for.' He motioned to a building they were approaching. 'We'll go in out of the wind,' and he led her through an arched doorway into the Museum of General and Local Archaeology. The high-ceilinged rooms were echoingly empty and their footfalls made an embarrassing noise on the polished parquet floors.

'This is what I miss, being burrowed away in Australia.' They were inspecting Fijian artefacts donated, the small slips of paper indicated, by Sir Arthur Hamilton Gordon. The room was as cold as outside, and May dug her gloved hands deep into her coat pockets.

'Burrowed away?' she reprimanded him. 'Where you have intimate contact with the Aborigines, have witnessed their ceremonies first hand, recorded their customs?'

But something else had caught her father's attention. 'Look, May, these are from Dr Frazer's very own collection. He does cast his net widely, doesn't he?' There were objects from all the British colonies, assembled alongside similar objects from Britain's own past. May objected to the display's inference.

'No, this is Dr Frazer's method of comparative anthropology, very admirable.' Howitt stood slightly bent over the objects to read the information cards, his hands clasped behind his back.

'It depends on what you choose to display, and what you compare. These baskets, for example.' May pointed to woven reed baskets that they both recognised. 'That's what the Aborigines still make at Lake Tyers Mission. And here they're compared to receptacles the English discarded thousands of years ago. To make the point, no doubt, about progress, rather than recognising a skill evolved over thousands of years that requires no further improvement. It is the Crystal Palace bragging, over and over.' She waved her arms about, taking in all of Dr Frazer's items for comparison.

'You might be right,' Howitt nodded distractedly.

'There are just so many hidden meanings.' May's eyes had welled with tears, but her father didn't notice, nodding vaguely at her indignation.

'You don't care, do you?' Her teeth were beginning to chatter with the cold.

'I do, but can't you enjoy this beautiful city, this wealth of knowledge, our kind friends, without finding fault with everything?'

She glared at him.

'May, you're my wonderful native-born girl and I'm proud of your very-Australian sentiments, but don't spoil this. Please. For my sake.'

May wiped her eyes with the back of her hand and bundled the gown and bonnet back into their box as she thought back to the grand ceremony at Cambridge, held in the Senate House. Howitt and his fellow honorands filed in, colourful as king parrots. The hall smelt of furniture polish and had warmed up with the crush of bodies, making her skin prickle inside her woollen dress. The oration was in Latin and after a while she forgot to pretend that she understood, and instead drank in the splendor and antiquity of her surroundings.

What would it be like, she wondered, to have her own work recognised thus, in this medieval place where tradition was as heavy as the stones from which it was constructed? The Vice Chancellor, dressed in black with gold trimmings, handed her kneeling father his honorary degree. She hadn't expected the rush of envy that assailed her as her father's hand went out to accept the scroll.

Following the ceremony, they filed out and stood in the cold sunshine that filled the old quadrangle. The air smelled of mown grass and coal smoke. May watched closely as her father basked in the congratulations of his peers. She felt a small tug of suspicion. Was Papa being too obsequious? He was more than their intellectual match. Was she being too sensitive, or did she discern hints of flattery where homage was due? He clasped every hand warmly and rounded his vowels a little more than usual as he conveyed his deep gratitude.

May put the lid on the box and carried it into her bedroom, closing the door, although there was no one else in the house. Removing her cardigan, she slipped the scarlet gown over her shoulders. The cloth flowed smoothly over her bare arms. With two hands she placed the bonnet on her head as if it were a crown.

In the corner of her room stood a full-length cheval mirror. She turned and stepped purposefully towards her reflection. Two steps from the mirror she stiffly nodded her head as she accepted an imaginary scroll of creamy parchment from her own reflected outstretched hand.

She tore the gown from her body and threw it on the bed where it lay like flowing blood. She tossed the cap on top of the gown and pulled her cardigan back on, mismatching the buttons and buttonholes. She would put the box with the pile of things to go to the church guild: dress ups for some lucky child.

❧

It took another day for her to summon the courage to start sorting out her father's study. In the dim light of early morning she felt his eyes upon her, those piercing eyes that missed nothing. She switched on the light to banish him. A yellow beam fell on his desk, still strewn with the papers he had been working on when he called her. He had been bent over his knees clutching his stomach, his face sweaty and grey, the Turkey rug awash with blood-flecked vomit.

There were framed photographs on his desk. The pictures were all her own work, documenting the Aborigines who lived in the halfway house that was the Lake Tyers Mission. She picked up a photograph of women weaving baskets. For the tourists, she thought bitterly, placing it back on the desk face down.

She shuffled the papers into an order of sorts and put them in a carton on the floor, then started on the books. As she cleared the bookshelves she came across a metal strongbox, locked. She'd wanted so badly something private, something that expressed his gratitude. From his Will she had inherited money over and above what was to be divided equally between them all. 'For her loving care' the Will had read, and while £500 would grant her some independence, it wasn't what she'd wanted.

She placed the strongbox on the floor—bare boards where the Turkey rug had lain—and knelt before it. In the top desk drawer she found a likely looking key. It turned effortlessly in the lock, and she lifted the lid. The box was full of letters: envelopes that bore the government's coat of arms, letters from her mother, and letters from her Nottingham aunt and grandmother. There was a pale blue envelope with unrecognisable handwriting, although clearly a woman's. She held the envelope to her nose. It smelt of dust. Slipping out the letter felt like trespass. It was from the sister of Henry Burrell asking for financial assistance for her brother who was in hospital and had no money. The letter complained that he'd never been properly paid for his part in the outback expeditions. And there was another letter requesting help, from a Mrs Ada Bartlett, asking Dr Howitt Esquire to support her claim for a pension having, she said, nursed a Sepoy named Dost Mahomed, 'until he was right as rain, through my careful ministrations, and went off on his camel to God knew where.'

'Camels,' she grimaced. Papa had always loathed them. Wouldn't even walk past their enclosure at the Melbourne Zoological Gardens when he took his children there. Remembering those excursions made her sit back on her heals and blush with guilt. He had been a good father, in so many ways. He'd made her life interesting and stimulating in more ways than she might have hoped. She crumpled the letters and tossed them into the waste-paper basket by her father's desk.

She came to a bundle of letters held together with a rubber band and recognised the handwriting. She pictured the writer, his tall frame stooped over a table crowded with photographs, his magnifying glass held to the eye without the patch. She'd never told her father of their association, but there'd been a day when he'd discovered some of Mr Welch's work amongst her own: beautiful light-filled landscapes that she wanted to learn from. Her father's fury had caught her unawares. He had threatened to burn the photographs if they ever again fell into his sight. His anger was so irrational and uncharacteristic that it had frightened her. She put the bundle aside; she might read the letters at some later date.

There was a tobacco tin that contained a lock of hair, too straight and coarsely black for any member of the family. It was a mystery that could also wait.

A great weariness had come over her. She came to the bottom of the strongbox: there was no envelope bearing her name; there was nothing else.

# Chapter 3

He would miss the departure of Burke's Victorian Exploring Expedition, setting out to cross the entire continent from south to north; to be the first to map a path through unknown country. It seemed that all of Melbourne planned to farewell the celebrity explorers from Royal Park. But it was turning out to be more mayhem than mission, Howitt thought. He had considered applying to join the expedition, until stories about Burke's character started to circulate. The man was a show pony, with not an explorer's bone in his body. And an immodest temper, by all accounts.

Instead, Howitt had accepted the role of leading an altogether different expedition, which would be leaving before Burke's. The Victorian government had run out of money, despite the taxes from the gold boom years, which had only just ended, and here they were in 1860, desperate for another rush to refill the coffers. Howitt was appalled by the profligacy of the politicians, but delighted that he'd be leading a prospecting party into the rough North Gippsland country. He would, he thought, prove himself to be quietly competent, in contrast to the attention-seeking Robert O'Hara Burke.

He had put together a party of men that included Henry Short, Alexander Aitkin and Weston Phillips: men he'd met on the goldfields in the fifties. They were hardy and cheerful chaps of such different sizes that they looked like babushka dolls when they stood together. Short was a nuggety, conscientious fellow with a migrating bird's sense of direction. Aitkin, of middling height, was as solid a companion as a man could ask for. Lofty Phillips was quick with his wit and strong as an ox.

Cameron was the only man in the party he didn't know. The red-faced, heavy-set Scot had been recommended by one of the expedition committee members—another Scot. Thick as thieves, they were. Howitt had agreed to take Cameron, only because they were going into Scottish territory and he thought it might be prudent to include a Highlander in the party.

Two hundred miles east of Melbourne they arrived at Bushy Park, the pastoral land of Angus McMillan. McMillan was respected as the region's pioneer, having ridden down into Gippsland from the Monaro high plains in 1839, greedy for all he saw. Now a parliamentarian, McMillan was helping the government to fund Howitt's expedition.

Bushy Park spread over the rich flats of the Avon River, cleared of its trees for sheep and cattle. 'Have we ridden all the way to Scotland?' Short asked, as they rode into McMillan's land. Lines of Scots pines and clumps of thistles had made themselves at home along the riverbanks. As the modest, squat homestead came into sight they passed a group of natives building post-and-rail fences. Phillips called out hello but none of them looked up from their work.

They were met by a man, perhaps the foreman, although Howitt had expected McMillan to greet them. The rough fellow showed them to the shearers' quarters where they were to bed down for the night. Without windows, the shed was dark and the air close, smelling of years of shearing: lanoline, old blood, urea, and men's sweat.

Thunder rumbled, and by the time Howitt's party made their way across the paddock to the house, heavy rain had begun to fall. The same fellow who had met them earlier directed them into a cramped and dimly lit parlour. Howitt and his men felt uncomfortable about being shown into the room before their host. They stood in silence, looking at their boots or the ceiling, rubbing their hands together and clearing their throats. A large stone fireplace at one end of the room sent billows of smoke into the room with each gust of wind. A man's room, Howitt thought with surprise, looking at the kangaroo skulls and bull horns mounted on the walls. He knew McMillan was married.

The door flew open and a man with a large head and remarkably short legs came into the parlour. Howitt stepped forward and the man held out his hand, introducing himself as Angus McMillan. McMillan's beard, Howitt noted as he shook the man's hand, was trimmed into the same biblical rim shape as his father wore, though he knew McMillan to be a Calvinist, not a Quaker. As Howitt introduced each of his men he watched McMillan closely. The man resembled a leprechaun but Howitt suspected that the cheerful bonhomie and glinting eye disguised a formidable determination.

McMillan explained to his guests that he was president of the Gippsland Caledonian Society and had invited his fellow members to join them for an evening of Highlander hospitality. As he spoke, they heard the sounds of horses and voices outside.

The Caledonians came into the room from the black night, dressed in kilts. Howitt saw Phillips place his hand over his smile and lower his head. The new arrivals were a rotund lot, a far cry, Howitt thought, from the gaunt crofters they might once have been, forced off their farms by their greedy Lairds. They shook the rain from their jackets and caps, stamping their boots on the rugs. 'A wee bit of moisture,' they commented as water sluiced down the windowpanes.

They settled down into deep armchairs, or stood with their backs to the fire, and McMillan handed out glasses of whiskey. The talk turned from the weather to horses, fat cattle and sheep dipping. The only book Howitt could see in the room was the Bible. The Good Book was set prominently on a lectern, a conspicuous show of piety that would never be countenanced in a Quaker household. He watched the way McMillan took in the room, measuring each man as he spoke.

'Come into my parlour, said the spider to the fly.' Howitt frowned, wondering at the aptness of the line from his mother's poem.

McMillan kept the ceilidh tradition alive and on this night was full of Scot's humour and storytelling. He waved his arms expansively as he related tales of discovering and settling Gippsland, practically single-handed. His language kept tipping over into Gaelic, cheered on by his fellow Highlanders.

'The hilltops lured us like sirens in those days.' He raised his glass of Glenmorangie in salute. 'The Cuillines hemmed us in on Skye, but these hills opened our eyes to vast vistas. Up around Numblaminjie we looked out over an Eden of verdant pasture all the way to the lakes and the sea.'

Aitkin leaned in towards Howitt and whispered: 'Making up his own hero legend.' But Howitt frowned and made the slightest shake of his head towards his friend.

'All there for the taking. Better than any gold rush,' added one of the Sgitheanachs who had sailed to the colonies on the *Minerva* with McMillan and now wore a large signet ring and gold-framed pince-nez eyeglasses. 'And we took it, by God. Not always easily.'

McMillan pursed his lips, as if remembering, but added nothing. Then he clapped his hands and called for music. The Highlanders had come prepared: a bagpipe was produced, a fiddle and a wooden flute. The men danced together in between the furniture, reel after reel, their kilts flying, toes pointing, bouncing on the balls of their feet and flinging their arms above their heads. The timber floorboards vibrated and the dogs out in the yard set up a howl. The dancers became red faced and short of breath. Phillips and Short clapped in time with the music. Howitt, standing with his back to a wall, tapped his toe to the rhythm to appear to be enjoying himself, but Aitkin, standing beside him, did not raise his eyes from the floor.

McMillan tried to push a glass of whiskey onto Howitt, but Howitt waved his hand to indicate he didn't drink alcohol. McMillan glowered and, holding Howitt's eye, took a large swig from his own glass, then turned back to watch the dancers. Howitt could not avoid thinking how foolish the men looked, stomping about and tripping over their own feet.

They sang *Scotland the Brave* and *Lochiel's Farewell.* They sang louder than the rain clattering on the corrugated iron roof. Howitt turned to Cameron who was slumped in a corner armchair, his face growing darker with each verse of the Culloden anthem. It struck him suddenly that Cameron was of a rival clan.

A young Scot called MacDonald sang *Sound the Pibroch* in a clear tenor, the others braying through the chorus: 'Tha tighin fodham, fodham, fodham; To rise up and follow Charlie.'

Cameron sprang to his feet. 'We were never disloyal,' he yelled out over the noise. The music died, the men stopped dancing, and all faces turned towards him. McMillan signaled to the fiddler to continue, but the man stood unmoving, his bow in mid-air.

'Our chief fought with the Prince at Culloden, no matter what lies are told.' Cameron moved towards the young MacDonald and poked his finger into his chest. 'Steadfast he was.' He peered around the room looking for disagreement. 'Not like the Campbells,' he muttered, his eyes falling on the bulky man who still held his flute to his lips.

'We don't fight amongst ourselves here,' McMillan spoke firmly. 'We're one clan only in this country, and that's Caledonian.' Cameron sunk back into his chair and McMillan nodded to MacDonald who took up his song again, without accompaniment. He looked directly at Cameron as he sang: 'No more we'll see such deeds again, Deserted is each Highland glen.'

Cameron was back on his feet, swaying. Howitt stepped forward and put a hand firmly on his shoulder. 'You heard our host. Time you turned in.'

'To St Patrick,' Cameron jeered, raising his glass to toast the monk who introduced whiskey to Scotland.

Howitt removed the glass from his hand and took his arm firmly. He guided him to the door and pushed him out into the night. Cameron, the fight gone out of him, wandered off into the rain in the direction of the shearers' quarters. There was just sufficient moonlight illuminating the clouds for Howitt to watch him go. Then he stood for a while under the dripping verandah, filling his lungs with fresh air. McMillan, as expedition sponsor, wouldn't condone the dismissal of a fellow Caledonian, no matter how badly he'd behaved. Howitt could hear him: 'What, you'd sack a man for just a wee dram and a spot of high spirits?' The saving grace was that once they were clear of Bushy Park there'd be no alcohol for months.

The parlour he returned to smelt of smoke, men, meat and

horses, and a platter of food had been delivered by a woman Howitt only saw leaving the room. Perhaps, he thought, it was McMillan's wife, though she retreated like a servant. The atmosphere was once more convivial. The songs had changed to tales of loving mothers and lost sweethearts. Howitt stood with his back to the fireplace where McMillan joined him, bending to light a taper in the flames and holding it to the bowl of his pipe.

'What is it that drives you into this country, young man,' McMillan asked him, 'if not to take it up for your own good?'

It wasn't only McMillan's beard that reminded Howitt of his father: he also had the same pulpit voice. It was six years since his father had returned to England, but listening to McMillan brought back the old discomfort, making him feel as if he were no more than a callow youth. 'As you know, the government wants me to find gold.' His voice was guarded.

McMillan waved his hand dismissively. 'But as you can't claim any finds for yourself, you must have another purpose, surely?' His eye had taken on a cool shrewdness.

'Curiosity?' Howitt shrugged; he still wasn't sure himself. He knew he relished the risks of trekking through uncharted country, and the challenge of keeping a team of men in line, but he kept these thoughts to himself. His eyes were watering with the smoke from the fire and he wiped them with the back of his hand.

The singing had come to an end and the others were listening to the conversation. They had sunk deeper into their armchairs, weighted down by the whiskey. 'Dr Arbuckle here,' McMillan pointed with the stem of his pipe to one of the slimmer men in the room who was wearing a large, hairy sporran and helping himself to a slab of lamb from the serving platter. 'He's an adventurer like you, but knows how to turn his finds into neat investments.'

Howitt started to speak, and stopped. He started again. 'I suppose I'm interested in mineralogy. It's a relatively new science; analysing rocks and minerals, finding fossils and layers of sediment that tell of the history of the earth.'

McMillan gave a harsh guffaw; there were echoing sniggers around the room. 'A rock, my boy, is a rock, not a storybook.' His voice took on a hard edge. 'The Bible tells us all we need to know about creation.' Howitt had already marked him as a man who might freely use those aspects of his Calvinism he found most suited to his ambition.

'And the market prices tell us all we need to know about the land,' added Arbuckle. A small cheer went up.

'The blacks,' McMillan offered after some reflection, 'are another matter.' He puffed a couple of times on his pipe, sending small billows of sweet-smelling smoke towards the ceiling, then pointed the stem of his pipe at Howitt. 'You might direct your curiosity towards them. There's God's work to be done there.'

Again, Howitt thought, it could be his father speaking: the same conjunction of religion and an interest in the natives. He shuddered at what he sensed to be a shrewd hypocrisy behind the words, or at least a salving of conscience, struggling to hide his unease from the watching audience.

'Money to be made, there, to be sure. Telling stories about the blacks and their savage ways. Titillate the public's imagination.' It was Arbuckle again. He had dropped into an armchair and spoke around a mouthful of meat. The man's mind obviously ran on tracks of coin.

ശ

'I can't believe those rumours about McMillan,' Howitt spoke to Aitkin later that night, their cots side by side in the shearers' quarters, but Aitkin merely grunted.

Howitt was certainly wary of McMillan, but they had finished the evening in good companionship and Howitt had come to believe his host deserved the benefit of the doubt. His stomach was full of roast lamb—not mutton, McMillan had insisted—and there'd been music and dancing, so rare in these parts. Even Cameron's drunken behaviour hadn't dampened the spirits of the ceilidh. True, there were uncouth edges to the hospitality: all that whiskey, and some of the talk about women and blacks had been unsavoury. McMillan's manner had at times troubled him, but men like that had carved their place out of absolutely nothing, which was bound to leave a mark.

The shed had filled with the sour smell of Cameron and his whiskey breath. Outside, the rain had stopped and frogs had set up a racket.

'He's a member of the Legislative Assembly, for heaven's sakes,' Howitt defended the Scot, raising his voice over the frogs and Cameron's snores. 'And a Protector of Aborigines.'

'Dens of thieves, both.' It was remarkable how Aitkin could speak in a soft voice and still, always, be heard.

'Fair go, Alex. He's known to be generous, provides the blacks with staples and blankets from his own purse. Bushy Park has become known as the Benevolent Asylum of Gippsland. The blacks call him Father.'

'The surviving few.'

He knew what Aitkin was referring to—everyone did—but there was no evidence and most men had the good sense to bury the past. He was prepared to see what Aitkin wouldn't: that this unwritten country demanded a shorter memory than older civilisations. The inappropriateness of Cameron's long-held grudges were testament to that.

Howitt turned away from Aitkin and pulled up his blanket to his ears. His mind turned to McMillan's suggestion about the blacks being an interesting subject for examination. The idea had merit. At the time he'd left England, London was a hotbed of speculation about man's origins. There were furious arguments between Unitarians like his father and those who believed races arose from separate blood pools. There were books and plays that mocked the idea that man had evolved from the apes; thunder erupting in the pulpits across the country. What might a study of this primitive race contribute to the debate? Could he make a name for himself in such a field?

Exploring was all well and good—in fact, for the moment it was his passion. But he could see that, in time, all the hidden corners of the land would be trampled over, named and mapped, their contours drawn in great swirling patterns of shape and substance. What then? What other notions of exploration might be possible?

'And then there's his piousness,' Aitkin's voice was bitter in the dark. 'It's not my God he prays to.'

'Leave it, Alex.' He felt a tremor of self-realisation that he didn't want to be bound by the principles that came with Aitkin's unwavering faith. Life was more complicated, demanding compromises, within limits, especially if you wanted to make a real go of it.

ɕɔ

They set off the following morning in bright, cold sunshine that foretold of winter's approach. Their horses' rumps bore the brand of the Crown and their reins were strung with bells in case they wandered off. Compass in hand, Howitt led the party across open pastures that quickly gave way to scrub, which thickened with each northern mile. Time and again they had to veer from their course, and Howitt's navigating skills were continually tested.

Over days, as the weather grew colder and wetter, they slashed their way through curtains of bush, sometimes on their hands and knees, and wasted hours shoveling rocks aside so the packhorses could pass. Their hands blistered, their faces became scratched, their clothes were heavy with mud. Their socks were so wet they squelched with each step and their toes froze inside their boots when they stood still.

From the top of Mount Birregun they looked across a range of tree-covered mountains, blue peaks stacked one behind the other, melting into the distance to the north and east. The beauty of the landscape was lost on Cameron. He sat slumped in his saddle, eyes on his scabby hands holding the reins, constantly grumbling that they should keep heading north. Howitt sat erect on his horse and looked into the distance. From time to time he reached into his pocket, withdrew his compass, and checked his bearings.

'And who's to say that gold lies only to the north,' Short

answered Cameron. He reached up to an overhanging bough to pick a spray of gum leaves and was rewarded with a dousing of cold droplets. Despite his loyalty, however, even Short was growing uncertain about their leader's motives for zigzagging across the country.

At the end of each day, as they set up camp, Howitt would leave them, pick and hammer in hand, and return some time later to unload a pile of rocks from his pockets. Sitting at the entrance to his tent, he would pick over what to keep, what to discard, before joining his men for a meal he had not contributed to preparing. Each morning he seemed to randomly pick a direction and lead them God knew where. The country had cleared a little, but the going was still hard work, the clay ground dangerously slippery and their path often blocked by fallen trees.

Short finally confronted Howitt, taking him aside as the others set up camp. 'You've brought me along as guide, but you chart a course of your own, that, I must say, I can't fathom.'

By way of answer, Howitt produced a handful of rocks from his pocket. 'Look at these,' he said with excitement. Short peered at the rocks in the gathering gloom of the bush. 'I'm starting to suspect that they are Upper Devonian. Do you know what that means?'

Short shook his head.

'They've not been identified in the colony before. They tell us in which epoch this part of the earth was formed. Devonian, as in Devon, England. From the Paleozoic era, known as the Age of the Fishes.'

'I thought we were looking for gold?'

Gold, Howitt would have liked to have told him, might bring short-lived wealth to a few, but this was science: the quest to find answers to the very origins of the earth. Short often demonstrated a genuine interest in the natural world. If he couldn't see the significance of the rocks—couldn't or wouldn't understand Howitt's passion—what chance did Howitt have of convincing the others? For a brief moment his anger flared: he was the one leading this party. But then his shoulders slumped. He'd sensed the growing restlessness amongst the men, sensed it and tried to ignore it.

'Lead on, Mr Short,' he said with resignation and an attempt at a dismissive wave of his hand. He watched Short walk back to the other men. The small clearing where the tents had been erected was surrounded by wattles that were in creamy flower, making the only points of lightness in the otherwise dull setting.

∽

They climbed into colder weather where the rain tended to sleet and food grew scarce. Howitt wouldn't admit, to himself or anyone else, that he had miscalculated. They would have already explored this northern area and been halfway back to the coast by now if he hadn't got sidetracked. He kept checking their supplies. There was nothing to supplement their rations: they hadn't seen a wild animal in weeks.

The men sat around a campfire that sizzled with wet wood. They had blankets over their shoulders, and clasped tin plates on their knees on which sat lonely islands of dried beef and soggy biscuit. The thick bush crowded in around them, blocking out the sky and further darkening their mood, and their unspoken accusations hung in the air with the heaviness of impending snow. Behind them, the horses whinnied and gave off their musky smell.

Howitt tried to be cheerful. 'Look at it this way: no white man has ever trodden this ground before. We'll return with maps that will allow the colony to be opened up all through this area.'

'No white man in his right mind would ever venture into this hell hole.' Of course, it was Cameron.

'Too wet for hell,' squibbed Phillips. He was sprinkling salt onto his bared legs to remove leeches that had grown fat with his blood. As the leeches shriveled from the salt and dropped to the ground, Phillips picked them up and threw them into the fire.

Cameron muttered something darkly.

'For heaven's sake, man, can't you take a joke?'

'Leave him, Weston,' Howitt cautioned. 'A fight won't improve his manners.'

The following morning, as they were preparing to depart, Howitt called the group together. He was struggling to contain his rage but he would not give the culprit the satisfaction of seeing it. The pulse throbbed in his temple.

'My rock samples are missing,' he informed them evenly, making sure that his eyes did not fall on anyone in particular. He'd been packing his saddlebags when he discovered his entire collection was gone. There had been rocks of every colour, from the palest cream to deep mahogany; granite specked with crystals; shards with deep veins of pink quartz. There were pale pebbles with dark patches like birthmarks; flaky brown shale and black lavas as porous as coral. And there were all his fossils, more precious than gold.

'I don't know who has taken them, and I don't want to know.' He kept his trembling hands in his pockets. 'But I do want them back in my saddlebag before we break camp in half an hour's time. Now I'm going for a walk.'

He strode off at a rapid pace along a wallaby track, so sodden and mossy that his heavy steps made no sound. The morning mist settled on his beard and in his hair, and his breath came out in damp white clouds. He'd like to send Cameron packing, or leave him behind to rot in the bush. Instead, he forced himself to slow down, to count to ten, to take deep breaths. He had to come at the problem with Cameron from a different angle. He wondered what his mother, who could always come up with a soothing solution, would have done.

When he returned, the rocks were back in his saddlebag. He said nothing, and left it to Short to give the directions. Before mounting his horse, Howitt scribbled some notes on a page he'd torn from his journal.

A few miles out of camp, the trees thinned and the land flattened, so that the countryside resembled an English gentleman's park. The men spread out, cantering across the broad space, cheered by sunlight that fell on the wet grass, making it sparkle.

Howitt rode up alongside Cameron and gestured for him to slow down. The man scowled as he reined in his horse.

'I need someone to be responsible for the packhorses and their loads.'

'You mean more work?'

Howitt inwardly sighed. 'No. Just to be in charge, to ensure that the loads are evenly packed and nothing is forgotten. The others will still have to do their share.' He had reasoned to himself that Cameron's bad behaviour might be due to his feeling unwanted by the group, but now, watching the man fiddle with his reins and scowl into the distance, he wasn't so sure. 'Here, I've written out a list of what needs to be checked each time.' He passed the list to Cameron who took it without comment and shoved it in his shirt pocket.

'So I can take that as agreed?' Howitt struggled to keep his voice even.

Cameron took the list from his pocket and thrust it back at Howitt. 'I canna read,' he said between clenched teeth before kicking his horse into a canter and riding away.

Howitt looked at the crumpled page in his hand, then screwed it into a tight ball and threw it after Cameron.

They rode back into heavy scrub and once again began to climb. When they stopped for lunch, Howitt left the men trying to light a fire with wet kindling while he scaled a higher peak to get his bearings. He held his compass and faced north towards an unending panorama of blue-grey trees. Turning slowly around, in the far distance to the south-east, he made out a string of lakes, long and thin like a lustrous snake winding along the coast, with the ocean beyond, extending to the far horizon. They would follow the watercourses that fed the lakes: rivers that might hold gold.

He breathed in deeply, the air chilling his teeth. Despite the poor diet and chilblains, the fleas that infested his swag, the rash breaking out across his unwashed skin and the thinning of his boot soles, even despite the failure to find gold, he was thriving on this life of adventure. His attempt to solve the problem with Cameron might have failed, but at least his mother would be proud of his effort.

As he picked his way down the icy slope his feet slipped from under him and he sat down heavily onto the gold-panning dish that swung from his pack. Suddenly he was shooting down the mountainside, tobogganing between trees and over rocks until he reached flat land. He came to rest in a muddy puddle, cracking its thin ice coating. His hands were red and grazed, and he'd torn a patch from his thick trousers. He slowly rose to his feet, checking each bone and muscle as it came to bear weight. The bush was silent apart from the sound of icicles dropping from gum branches. Good, he murmured in relief, no witnesses. He hobbled back to the campsite where the men appeared to be busy at their tasks: Aitkin mixing flour and water for damper, Short darning a hole in one of his socks, and Cameron skinning a snake he had killed. Nothing was said initially, until Phillips appeared with an armful of wood for the fire.

'Steep climb?' Phillips asked as he dropped the wood into a pile on the ground. The others kept their heads down.

Howitt was immediately on his guard.

'Quick descent, though, hey boss?' Phillips added. The others had looked up from their tasks and were trying to swallow their laughter in their beards.

Howitt had fined Phillips tuppence the day before for swearing, so he had to expect some payback.

'We thought that wee hill might be named Mount Howitt. Thought you'd christened it, like.' As he spoke, Phillips fed the sputtering fire with the drier wood he'd found.

Cameron tossed the snakeskin into the flames and grinned like a ghoul. Howitt harrumphed and stood with his back to the men and the fire, waiting for some warmth to defrost his battered body.

ꟹ

They turned south and trudged onwards. The ground was stony, with large rocky outcrops to which trees clung like limpets. They looked a bedraggled lot, with their lengthening hair and beards, and filthy clothes. Only Phillips whistled, or sang a bar or two from an opera in his tenor voice, regularly being told to put a sock in it. But he was the one who found the cave. He hollered, the others thinking at first that it was just another of his jokes, or another aria.

The cave was deep and dry, with the remnants of a fire and a pile of dry wood. Aitkin kicked in the ash and uncovered animal bones. 'Recent.'

Short stooped down and held up what looked like the skull of a wallaby. 'Better fed than us,' he said.

They built a fire that filled the cave with warmth and orange light, and stripped to lay out their clothes, along with saddles and horse blankets, to dry. Howitt was tired beyond reckoning. When he undid his braces, his trousers slipped to his ankles of their own accord. He was so much thinner than when he'd left Melbourne, and there hadn't been much of him to begin with. He pulled his clammy shirt over his head, holding his breath against the musty sour smell. Sweat from his armpits had left salty tidelines below the sleeves. The others, he saw, weren't any better, having suffered from diarrhoea and boils. Only the horses were in fair shape, there being plenty of feed for them.

The cave took on a rotting smell like silage, but no-one complained. They settled down around the fire and one by one dropped off into sleep. Howitt dreamed he'd returned to Melbourne and was being castigated by the expedition board for his failure to find gold. His inquisitors sat in chairs along one side of a long table, he on the other on a low stool. His rock samples had been laid out on the table, stretching in a line from one end to the other. McMillan was there, holding his bearded chin in his hand and narrowing his eyes as he looked Howitt up and down. He picked up a piece of granite and weighed it in his hand as if determining its worth, then finding it wanting, tossed it so that Howitt had no choice but to catch it. It turned into a nugget of gold. Howitt tried to tell the panel what he held in his hand, but no-one would give him an opportunity to speak, and when there was finally a gap in the questioning, he found he had lost both the gold and his voice. He woke sweating and panicky.

The following morning, Howitt was up at dawn, urging the men into action, telling them there wasn't a day to lose. Short shrugged his shoulders and stepped outside the cave into thick fog: a blank shifting greyness that he stumbled through to find the horses that had been hobbled beyond the rocky forecourt of the cave. He heard an odd noise and stopped to listen, peering into nothingness. Then a coo-ee, disembodied by the fog. Finally, a young lad, about fourteen or fifteen, stepped into Short's path. His clothes were ragged and covered in mud. His bristle hair stood up like a cockatoo's crest.

'Who the devil . . .?' Short stammered in surprise.

The lad waved his crook in greeting and then gestured behind him. Short peered as a small flock of sheep came to a bumping stop against the boy. 'What the . . .?'

'I've come from Master McMillan, who sends you these jumbucks, on account he thought you might be peckish, and he sends his regards, too. I've had the most trouble in the world getting 'em through the bush and findin' you. 'Specially in this fog. Wonder is that they have any meat left on 'em.' He lisped slightly, and even with his mouth closed, his buckteeth protruded through his wet lips.

Short called to the others, still in the cave. 'Over here,' he called again so they could find him and they soon appeared out of the fog.

'These, too,' the boy said, unaffected by the looks of amazement. He took a stack of old newspapers from the canvas sack slung over his shoulder. The outer pages were a pulpy mess, but the inner ones were still fine for catching up on what was happening in the world beyond the bush. Howitt could have hugged and kissed the lanky lad, despite his smell. Instead, he took the bundle of newspapers and paused over a headline.

'Ho, ho. What's this? Burke and Wills are overdue at the Coopers Creek depot,' he read, capturing the men's attention and feeling buoyed. 'Perhaps they're lost. I might have to go and look for them.'

❧

They made their way through the last of the thick bush and came to a clearing by the Dargo River. The river was in full spate and rushed noisily over boulders, creating wrinkles of white water and setting up silvery sprays that caught the sunlight and became rainbows. The horses were hobbled in shank-high wallaby grass and, taking advantage of the warm day, the men bathed in the river and spread their laundered clothes out to dry on the sweet-smelling grass. Howitt felt the crispness of a clean shirt against his clean skin and smiled. He gave his men the afternoon off and went exploring.

They had found gold in a tributary of the Wongungarra River, enough to satisfy the government and to start a new rush. He'd had the devil's own job keeping the men together, convincing them to fulfill the second part of their commission, which was to cut tracks through the scrub back towards Dargo for the hordes that would soon pour into the region. But they all had mining experience and knew that even when there was good gold, most miners barely scratch a living. They agreed, perhaps reluctantly, that the wages that would come from the government were more reliable.

The track-making had been heavy, mind-sapping work. The ground was either clay so heavy it made their boots too heavy to lift, or so rocky their picks bounced and sent shockwaves up their arms. Their axes sank into solid timber and became wedged, and trees fell unpredictably, giving them only seconds to escape being crushed.

But now the track was finished, and they were on their way home. Howitt watched as Short and Cameron headed back to the river with their gold pans until he lost sight of them behind a rise of land where the river entered a gorge. He wasn't thinking about gold, though. He constantly turned over the questions that had occupied his mind for the past couple of weeks: what was happening to Burke and Wills? What was the Royal Society doing about a relief expedition?

He climbed a steep incline above the gorge, scrambling

over boulders warm to the touch and coated in scabs of green lichen. In the sunshine, the gum trees expired eucalyptus-oil and he took deep breaths of the tangy mint scent. A rustle in the grass brought Howitt quickly to a stop. A snake slithered into his path: a glossy-black, four-foot long rope. It sensed Howitt's presence and rose into a striking stance, revealing its red underside. A cloud of tiny insects flew into Howitt's face but he dared not bat them away. He stood completely still, the bush's silence thundering in his ears. The snake lowered back to the ground, flattening its body and hissing before quickly slipping away between two large rocks.

Waiting for his heart to return to its normal rhythm, Howitt thought of the words from one of his mother's poems:

> And the Hydra down in the ocean caves
> Abode, a creature grim;
> And the scaled Serpents huge and strong
> Coiled up in the waters dim.

Reciting the words softly to himself as he resumed walking, he tripped over a rock and fell to the ground. On his hands and knees, he looked at the rocks around him. He picked up a stick close at hand and scratched around in the earth. With a rush of excitement, he uncovered a piece of slate that bore the perfect impression of a dragonfly: two pairs of outspread wings and a long stick body. He tried to think himself back into an unimaginably older epoch when a dragonfly had risen from the surface of the river—this very river rushing below him—wings flashing azure and crystal pink, to alight on this very rock. And then, in an instant, dead; entrapped and imprinted forever as a shadow on a grey surface.

> And the Dragons lie in the mountain-rock,
> As if for eternity!

More lines from his mother's poem: he shook his head at the strangeness of memory. For her, fossils could be no more than

6000 years old. Nature's capture of extinct animals tested her sorely, unless it was God who put them there. He'd brought her faith with him to Australia, still largely unquestioned, and when he'd sent his first fossil samples to Professor McCoy at Melbourne University, he'd been flabbergasted by the learned man's assertion that they were millions of years old. Millions of years! Coming to accept that the Professor was right had cost him dearly. Now he could only wonder at how his parents, most people he knew for that matter, could so easily reconcile a fossil with the Bible's teachings. Even the good professor juggled his learning so that his knowledge of an ancient earth did not compromise the Creation.

He walked back to where he could see Phillips stretched out in the grass. He crouched down by his side and showed Phillips his find.

'Very pretty,' Phillips responded, squinting into the sunshine and chewing on a stalk of grass, having barely glanced at the treasure.

They turned together at the sound of a shout from the distance, followed by Aitkin appearing, waving his hat above his head. 'Quickly, come and see what we've found.' Howitt thought first of gold, but Aitkin was too agitated for that.

Pushing through a copse of acacias, they came to the edge of the escarpment that dropped away in large mossy boulders to the river below. Aitkin indicated with a lift of his chin for them to look over the edge. There were piles of bones—human bones—scattered over the sloping ground. There were skeletons in grotesque postures, some tossed on top of others. There were tiny skeletons wedged between rocks, disconnected skulls, thigh bones, shoulder blades.

Howitt scrambled down the steep incline, taking hold of tufts of grass to control his rapid descent. Short was already there, turning over the bones delicately with the toe of his boot. Cameron kicked a skull and sent it rattling over rocks down to the river.

'Oh, for Christ's sake, man, show some respect,' Short told him sharply, then turned to Howitt. 'Looks like a whole family.

There must be twelve or fifteen bodies here.'

'Sheep stealers all of them; deserved their fate,' Cameron mumbled.

'And whose sheep, I wonder,' Short muttered, mostly to himself.

Phillips and Aitkin joined them. Aitkin picked up a small skull and shoved it towards Cameron's face. 'And you think this child—three or four years old—stole a sheep?'

'Killed by a rival clan, then.' Cameron stroked his long matted beard in a display of certainty.

A black crow flew across the sun and landed on a rock close by. It watched the party with its fierce yellow eyes. Cameron, seemingly disconcerted, wiped his hands on a clump of moss and climbed back up the rocks. His red hair was fiery in the sunshine.

'Will you report this?' Aitkin asked quietly, placing the skull back on the ground.

Howitt shook his head to clear his distress. 'I'll write a report when we get back to Melbourne. Nothing's going to happen in the meantime.' The crow gave a long mournful cry and flew off. Aitkin turned away from him and headed up the slope.

Howitt tried to picture what might have happened: the ancient battle cries of men on horses; the screaming, fleeing blacks; the stench of fear. He couldn't, or wouldn't, reconcile the man who had shown them hospitality with such a crime. He could just as easily picture the blacks attacking each other. He'd heard stories of the battles between the clans.

He dug in his pocket for his compass and held it in the palm of his hand without looking at the dial. His internal needle was swinging wildly, making it nigh impossible to set a course. He tried to think of someone he knew whose wisdom he could follow. Not Aitkin, who was too idealistic. Not his father, whose style was all indignant righteousness. His mother's goodness wasn't always practical. He could think of no-one. He polished the compass on his trouser leg and returned it to his pocket.

# Chapter 4

They drove up the mountain so fast Liney thought the buggy would fly apart. With one hand she held tight to the side handrail; with the other she clutched the cameo pinned at her neck. They jolted along rough tracks through tunnels of gum trees, so long and dark she thought they might emerge in China. Margaret, the servant girl they had brought with them from Bairnsdale, bounced wildly in the back seat of the buggy.

Every bend took her further from her girlhood. Her dress—pale pink and months in the making—was ringed with dust around the hem, and her bonnet had gone limp in the damp mountain air. There'd been nowhere to bathe for the past two days and she felt grimy within her layers of clothes. She turned away from Alfred, who was next to her clutching the reins, and sniffed at her armpit: did she smell? Alfred certainly did: a male muskiness that she supposed she would have to get used to. At the very least she needed to learn not to pull back when he leaned towards her.

They crested a hill and Alfred set the horses to a trot down a steep street. Liney's heart sank as she saw the town that was to be her home. The pot-holed street ran through muddy paddocks dotted with jagged tree stumps that looked like decayed teeth. There were a few clumps of gum trees still standing, and a line of hills to the north that might have marked the end of the earth. The dwellings were mean hovels and mud-smeared tents, set about in no apparent order. The only substantial buildings they passed were four hotels. There were men everywhere—most raised their hats as the buggy passed by. Liney could not see any women, or a church. She pulled her shawl tightly against the cold wind blowing down from the hills.

Alfred turned the horses onto a side path that led to a slab hut marooned in a sea of mud, like a boat that had gone aground and been abandoned. Please God, prayed Liney, don't let this be it. 'Home,' Alfred announced, pulling the horses to a standstill at the front of the hut and looking away from her. His ears, she saw, had gone quite red.

He jumped from the buggy and went around to help Liney down. She stepped straight into a puddle and the mud squelched up over her leather boots. Taking her hand, he walked her to the door, up a path that had been roughly gravelled, pushed it open and turned to lift her into his arms. She stepped past him into the room, already sensing the irrelevance of old traditions. The room was almost bare, but the fire had been lit and on the table a bunch of jonquils in a condensed-milk tin shone yellow and welcoming.

She turned to him frowning. 'Who would have been so kind?'

He shrugged his shoulders, trying to smile. She brushed her fingers lightly across his forehead and turned to inspect the room. It was makeshift: there was no getting away from that. The only window, opposite the door and above the table, faced the street. She crossed the room to look at the view. The glass was green tinged with a flaw running down its centre that made the outside world waver, as if she were looking through seawater. At the side of the cottage she could see a rough shed that Alfred grandly called the scullery. Above, smudged clouds drifted across a pale green sky. When she stood back, she saw how the light flowed across the table top in fluid ripples. She wondered if she would learn to love this play of light, or come to loath the way the glass distorted the world. There could be no room for doubt or self-pity, she reprimanded herself; she was grafted now, to this man and to this place.

Alfred joined her at the table by the window and placed a hand on the cool glass. 'The first house in Omeo to have a glass window,' he told her proudly.

A curtain divided the cottage into two rooms. She must not compare, but Liney could not help but think of the house she had so recently left: fourteen rooms; furniture, carpets and drapes imported especially from England; her father's library with its rows of gleaming leather spines; a kitchen large enough to prepare a banquet, and the servants to make it happen. From her upstairs bedroom, she had looked through clear glass to the rose garden, and beyond to the orchard. Alfred had warned her, she could not deny that, but not in her wildest imagination had she thought it would be quite like this. She pulled the curtain to one side to reveal a big cast iron bed that made her blush. 'What an adventure,' she said in a thick voice, running her hand over the raised pattern of the quilt. But when she looked up at him her eyes were shining with amusement.

'What's funny?' he asked, looking sheepish.

'I was thinking about the silver sugar tongs Betsy gave us for a wedding gift.'

He let out a hoot of laughter, then remembered: 'I have a wedding gift for you.' He held out his hand to her. 'Come on.'

She took another look around. At least it was hers and not her parents: there was a giddy liberation in that thought.

Outside the cottage, Margaret was directing a young lad to unload their luggage.

'Could we have tea, please, when we return,' Liney asked diffidently. The girl hesitated but nodded.

'You'll find everything you need in the scullery.' Alfred spoke with a voice used to giving orders. 'And space for your bedroll and other things.'

They walked across rutted ground towards a long timber shed with their arms touching. Liney's fine leather boots, part of her trousseau, made sucking noises as she stepped through the mud. He pointed to a solid-looking building on a slight rise above the cottage: his courthouse, he told her. It was odd, she thought, to have this house of justice almost at their door. Her father, a judge, travelled from home each day to his handsome Greek-columned courthouse in the centre of Adelaide town.

She stopped in panic as they approached the open side of the shed, which was in fact the stables, realising what was to come. A horse had materialised out of the shadows and stood at the rail tossing its head. It was taller than Liney, dapple grey with sharply pointed ears and a finely chiselled nose: a head like a sculptured piece of granite. It reminded her of the lions mounted on the gate pillars of her parent's home, as fierce as her father.

'Let her smell your hand.' Alfred moved towards the railing, and the horse gave a soft nicker.

'I can't.' Liney stood her ground and clasped her hands tightly together behind her back.

Alfred looked at her, surprised. 'You're frightened of the horse? But . . .' he waved his hand back towards the house where the young lad was unhitching the horses from the buggy. The servant girl Margaret was standing in the cottage doorway, hands on ample hips, directing the lad.

'I feel safe if I'm in the buggy. . . If I don't have to touch them.'

The sun went behind a cloud and the temperature immediately dropped. Liney shivered and wrapped her arms tightly across her chest. From a hook on the stable wall Alfred lifted down a side saddle and stood with it clutched to his chest. 'Liney, you can't live here if you don't ride.'

The sun reappeared and a magpie chortled. Light fell on the saddle, making the brown leather gleam. It wasn't new, but she could see where he'd had her initials embossed on the skirt: MBH, Maria Boothby Howitt. She went to touch the leather but could not, even when she saw the hurt in his eyes.

'Tell me.' His voice was like a croak, but he was looking firmly at her.

Suddenly, he seemed a stranger, this man she had married just a few weeks ago. Was this what marriage demanded: having to dig up and share your shame? She came from a household that kept its counsel. Her family was so large that remaining silent always seemed the easiest course. Now there was just the two of them. She looked towards the hills, her eyes following the wooded slopes up into the sky.

'I fell off, when I was young.'

'Were you badly hurt?'

She shook her head.

He replaced the saddle on its hook. 'Everyone falls off

sooner or later when they're learning.'

'It wasn't the fall.'

She stole a look at the horse. It took nothing to remember the terror as she told the story to her husband. The piebald gelding was called Soldier. He was new, and had never worn a side saddle. Her father had slapped Soldier on the rump and the horse had started to canter before Liney was properly settled. Her legs came out of the pommels and she slipped down the saddle and fell to the ground. Gravel grazed the skin on her palms; that was all. Then the animal had reared up above her, its hooves raking the air. When they came crashing down, they missed her by inches. As the horse reared up again, her father grabbed one of her arms and pulled her along the ground out of its way.

He left her on the ground and grabbed the bridle. With the whip in his free hand he lashed out at the horse until bright red slashes criss-crossed its rump. The animal screamed and tore its head against his tight hold. A stable-boy ran up to help but her father told him to keep clear: lessons had to be learned. When he turned his eyes on Liney she cowered, thinking he might whip her, too. Instead, he threw the whip to the boy.

'Get back on the horse,' he yelled at her, pulling the horse along so that he might reach her. The horse's eyes were wide with panic. She shuffled away from him on her bottom and hands, dodging his outstretched arm. Beyond him, her mother finally appeared, striding angrily towards them.

'Leave her.' She was a women made up of hard edges, from the coldness in her voice, to her sharp-featured face. She dragged her hair back so tightly into a bun that it stretched the skin at her temples and slanted her eyes.

Boothby was much taller than his wife, but he did not contradict her. 'Then take the snivelling little fool out of my sight,' he said.

He passed the reins to the stable-boy who placed a hand on the horse's muzzle and whispered into its ear. The horse stamped its feet a few times before allowing the boy to lead it away. Her father spat in disgust and stalked across the yard into the house. Her mother took Liney's hand and tugged her along in his wake.

A sour look had settled on Alfred's face. He shook his head as if to clear a bad memory. 'Why haven't you ever said anything?'

Liney felt like a foolish child all over again. She was twenty-one. Certainly she'd travelled from Nottingham halfway around the world—a monumental sea voyage, but one that almost everyone she knew had also taken. And apart from the long trip to Omeo, she had been nowhere other than Adelaide, done nothing with her life. Alfred was thirteen years older and had lived the life of an adventurer. He was an explorer and a hero. What an idiot she'd been, not to have seen what that difference might mean.

She hiccupped with old and new fear. 'I was a disgrace in our house. Everyone else rode so well. They would go out on riding picnics. I had to follow with the servants in the cart, bringing lunch.' She twirled the unfamiliar ring on her finger. 'I thought you might not marry me if you knew.'

'You silly girl.' He spoke gently and took both her hands in his. Behind Alfred, the horse opened its mouth wide, pulling its lips back to reveal its big teeth and pink tongue. Liney gave a small cry of alarm and Alfred turned sharply to the horse. He released Liney's hands and patted the horse's neck. 'Only a yawn. Not a pleasant sight, but a lot prettier than a camel.'

She tried to smile.

'Look at her Liney. Her name's Cloud.' A small brown bird that had been pecking at their feet flew off as Alfred bent down to pick up a handful of spilt chaff. The horse whinnied softly before taking the offering. Liney watched the muscles working along its fine nose as it made snuffling noises in Alfred's palm. 'You see how gentle she is?' Its nose was partly bald, revealing skin as pink as a human's. 'There's nothing like the feel of a horse's muzzle, soft as velvet.'

He looked at her closely. 'You can't be without a horse here. A buggy isn't always practical, and I want to take you riding through the countryside.'

She nodded, wondering where she might find the courage.

❧

Over the following month, as spring arrived and the weather cleared, Omeo looked almost pleasant, and Liney was learning to claim her place. On a clear but cool evening, Alfred wrapped a blanket around her shoulders and, carrying another, led her out into the still night. The navy sky was brilliant with stars, the moon no more than a sliver of silver. The only light was the square of their window. Alfred shook out the spare blanket and laid it on the ground and they lay down on their backs, side by side, looking up at the heavens.

Liney tried to recall if she had ever lain on the ground like this before. Perhaps in childhood, but her early years had been spent in Nottingham where most of the ground was paved and cobbled. In the big house in Adelaide, there had been garden furniture and hammocks: one would never have done what she and Alfred were now doing. She ran her hand over the lumpy grass at the edge of the blanket. Thank goodness her mother could not see her.

Alfred pointed to five bright stars. 'The Southern Cross,' he told her. 'The desert natives think it's the footprint of a wedge-tailed eagle.'

'But it's clearly a cross,' Liney said.

'It is to us. It all depends on how you see the world. We look at the four brightest stars arranged like that and it's a cross. And the cross reminds us of Jesus' death and the hope of redemption: stories that explain to us who we are. But these things mean nothing to the natives, they have their own stories to explain their world.'

'Because they don't believe in God?'

'Because they don't believe in *our* God.'

'But there is no other.' Her voice shook slightly. It might have been from the cold creeping into her body from the hard ground. There was a shout from down the hill in the town, followed by angry voices. It was a common sound and Liney hardly flinched. The voices faded away and silence returned.

'See those two bright stars?' She followed his finger down and to the right. 'They're the two ends of the eagle's throwing stick. Only, we know them as the front legs of Centaurus.'

Liney lay silently at his side. There were millions of stars, sparkling like raindrops on leaves after rain. Had she spent all her years with her eyes to the ground? She would like to reach up and pluck a star from the sky and give it to him. How silly he would think her if she told him.

'It takes some imagination, but eight of those stars makes up the figure of a centaur. Or so the Greek astronomer Ptolemy thought. '

Try as she might, she could not make out a pattern. 'What's a centaur?'

'Half man, half horse, from Greek mythology. That's what it must have looked like to the ancients when they first saw a man on horseback.'

She frowned into the dark night. 'And I must become a centauress?'

'A kentauride, you'd be called.' He paused. 'You'll soon be riding like a drover, I'm sure of that.'

They listened to the immense silence, the Milky Way massed above them. Liney felt unanchored, as if she might float away. She nudged in closer and rested her head on Alfred's shoulder. He rubbed his cheek against her hair.

'What's behind them?'

'Behind?'

'Behind the stars.'

'Ah. Nothing. It just goes on and on. Like a boundless ocean with the stars scattered like fish.' He passed his arm in an arc above them.

A mob of kangaroos went thumping past the cottage and a slight tremor passed through the earth. 'How do you know these things?' There was wonder in her voice.

He raised himself onto one elbow so he could look at her. Liney could see the paleness of his high forehead and the glint in his eyes. 'When I was a schoolboy, we played a game called The Universe. Someone, usually the teacher, would be the sun.

The boys would be planets whirling around the sun in their orbits, and the moons would race around the planets. I was usually one of Saturn's moons because I could run fast. The girls would stand on the boundaries as stars, twinkling their fingers. And there'd be stray comets and meteors flying about. It was all very chaotic but great fun.'

It was very different from her own schooling, at home with her sisters. They had a governess with bad breath and crooked teeth, straight-laced and boring, whose main activity was to put a ruler under Liney's chin and lift it roughly to make her sit up straight. Not for the first time it struck her that almost everything about her new husband was alien.

He lay down again. 'I've slept under this night sky more times than I can number. And relied on the stars, especially the Southern Cross, as much as I've relied on my compass. When we were out looking for Burke there was a comet, every night: a ball of white flame with a long tail blazing across the sky. I took it for a good omen.'

He slipped his arm under her shoulders and drew her close to his side. 'You can't help thinking that the answer to all we don't know about life is up there somewhere.'

Liney frowned in the dark. 'You mean God?' She shifted slightly to make herself more comfortable in the crook of his arm.

'His works have borne witness against Him.'

She didn't know what he was talking about, but she knew it disturbed her. She wanted to remind him that God made man after His own image but she sensed such words might make him cross.

'It's strange how looking into space frees you to imagine anything, and at the same time, makes you realise there are some things impossible to imagine. All that space, going on and on infinitely, whatever that means.' He was quiet for a few moments and when he spoke again his voice had changed, taken on an unexpected urgency. 'There's so much still to be explored and discovered. I want to be part of that, Liney, to learn to imagine the unimaginable; to make my own contributions to science. It's all so new and incredibly exciting.'

His ardency frightened her. She would have liked to tell him that contentment was holy. And she knew, in her bones, that science could be dangerous. But instead she asked: 'Were the Centaurs good?

'Not always. They were known to carry off nymphs.' He ran his hand over her breast and bent to kiss her.

'Alfred!' She gave a startled cry and pushed him away. 'Not out here where anyone can see us.'

He sat up and looked about theatrically into the empty night. 'You're right.' He stood up and she took his hands, allowing him to pull her to her feet. She wrenched free of his grasp, lifted her skirts and, laughing, ran towards the cottage, with Alfred close behind.

ග

It was the first decent night's sleep they'd had in weeks. The baby was still sleeping and Liney woke refreshed, but with a sense of self-reproach. As she performed the morning's tasks she kept picturing Mrs Soo Long as she'd often seen her in the town, scuttling along with her head down, a frightened mouse watched by cat-tongued women. Liney kneaded the dough with extra ferocity, flipping it over and ramming the heels of her hands into the soft mass. In the six months since Charlton had been born, Liney had felt unable to ask for help from the women in town. The miners' and the traders' wives were so different from any women she had known in her parent's circle, and she supposed they were diffident about approaching her, because of Alfred's position. It took Mrs Soo Long, an Irish woman married to a Chinaman, to understand her desperate need. Liney gave the dough one final thump, rolled it into a smooth ball and left it to prove.

After lunch the sun came out and a breeze blew up from the valley. As she put on her shawl and bonnet, she directed Margaret to wash the nappies, to take advantage of the fine afternoon.

Charlton would have to be carried all the way. She might

have used the buggy but she did not want to have to explain where she was going, or why. A perambulator stood in the corner of the cottage by the door, taking up more space than they could afford: a big, black folly from her sister Pip. It seemed to Liney to be more of an accusation than a well-intentioned gift. It was certainly evidence of her sister's inability to picture life in Omeo. The vehicle would look perfect on the streets of London—Adelaide at a pinch—but here? She could imagine the raised eyebrows; hear the sniggers that would follow her down the streets of Omeo.

Instead, she walked down the main street with the babe in her arms, and nodded her greetings to those who passed her. Out of the shade of the shops' awnings, the afternoon was warm and bright. The street became a track, orange and gravelly, that started to wind up the hill, and Charlton grew heavy and fractious in her arms. She rocked him and whispered to calm him.

'You see, the medicine has worked, like magic. You're such a good boy now. No more tummy pains, just like your Papa said.'

She hadn't believed Alfred. 'I don't care if she sells her potions to the Queen of England,' she'd yelled at him the previous evening in her fury and exhaustion, not caring if Margaret heard from the scullery. 'I'm not risking Charlton's life with that woman's green slime.'

But he had silently measured out a portion into a teaspoon, and taking the baby from her, had tipped the concoction into his tiny mouth. She had turned away and beaten her fists on the wall. Remembering her fury made her feel aghast. She hadn't known she had it in her to try to contradict Alfred so fiercely. It could have been her father, red-faced and boisterous with rage. And in the wrong.

'Your Papa always knows whom to trust,' she crooned to the now-peaceful babe.

She sat on a fallen log at the side of the track to catch her breath, resting the sleeping baby on her lap. It was the furthest she'd ventured since Charlton was born and she savoured a delicious sense of freedom. A gentle breeze pushed white clouds across the huge sky, and she held her hot face into its freshness. Fairy wrens scurried about at her feet, cheerful in their blue bonnets and collars. The tree canopies were full of the racket of currawongs, and other birds Liney was yet to learn to identify. Noisy miners and magpies had filled the garden in Adelaide, and starlings, imported like her.

The sound of a cantering horse caused her to turn towards the track ahead. She suddenly realised how foolish she had been not to tell Alfred where she was going. He never spared her from his tales of bushrangers. There was that terrible man who had chopped up his victims and put the body parts in his pork-pickling vat. Liney's stomach heaved with the memory of it, and with her fear. The gold coach now left with three police escorts after a spate of robberies, even the murder of a coachman. Mrs Evans, on her way to Bairnsdale, had been stripped of everything, down to her corsets. The bushrangers had laughed uproariously as they rode away with her clothes and wedding ring, and the gold.

The cantering changed note as the horse clattered across the wooden bridge over Livingstone Creek, so she knew the rider was just around the bend. Her heart raced and she clutched Charlton closely. Horse and rider appeared in a cloud of dust, just fifty yards away. She saw a big bay horse and, to Liney's immense relief, the stick-like figure of Michael O'Shea. He drew up alongside her. The horse bent its wet muzzle towards the baby and Liney reached up and gently pushed its head away. She'd long since lost her terror of horses. There was no room in this life for self pity, and old fears had been shunted to one side to make way for new, more pressing problems.

'You alright there, Missus Howitt?' O'Shea asked with deep concern, bending down towards her from his saddle, more like a praying mantis than a man.

'Just catching my breath.' Although, she thought to herself, I wouldn't want to breathe in too deeply this close to you, Michael O'Shea. How did his wife bear it?

'You're gettin' a bit near the Chinkies' camp.' He spoke in a cautionary tone. 'I had best escort you 'ome.'

Liney winced. Who was Michael O'Shea to pass judgement on the Chinese? A man who in a drunken state had pulled down his tent on the heads of his wife and children. 'Thank you, but I'm not going home.'

He raised his massy eyebrows so that they disappeared under the rim of his hat. His nose, his largest feature, shone red like a bauble. 'You can't go up there. Not alone; not with the babe.' The horse strained towards a patch of grass on the side of the track. O'Shea pulled sharply on the reins and the animal made a whinny of complaint.

'We are perfectly safe, Mr O'Shea.' She looked down at her son who had woken, his grey eyes watching her face.

'I think I should be asking Mr Howitt to come an' fetch you.' He lifted his hat and ran his fingers through his greasy hair, then rammed the hat back on his head.

'My husband is aware of my destination,' she lied, rising to her feet and waving O'Shea on his way with her free arm. The man hesitated, his horse doing small dancing steps from side to side. 'Good day to you.' She took some determined steps away from him towards the Livingstone Creek bridge. She could feel his eyes on her back but she kept walking. She was over the bridge before she heard him ride away towards the town.

The word would spread around Omeo like wildfire: that the magistrate's wife was visiting the Chinese. With her babe. There'd be mock horror, and small additions to each telling that might end up painting her as a woman who made pacts with the devil. Well, at least Alfred would not object when she told him tonight, and she was learning not to care so much about what others thought. 'A good Quaker,' her mother would routinely remind her, 'seeks guidance from the Spirit of God, not from gossip.'

Liney rounded a sharp bend in the track and the scrubby bush gave way to cleared land that looked like a huge scabby wound. The Chinese diggings were more barren looking than the township. There were no trees, hardly a blade of grass, and the baked orange clay made the place as hot as a desert. Liney turned onto the rocky pathway that led down to the camp and felt a sudden rush of anxiety. Mrs Soo Long was Irish, so would she be Popish? Or, worse, she might have adopted her husband's barbaric ways. Liney didn't know what they might be, only that God would disapprove. She looked at the child lying serenely in her arms and resolutely quickened her step towards the camp.

The place was a shambles: tents strung out like dirty washing; winding tracks over uneven mullocky ground that ended in piles of rocks and refuse. The clearing of the camp rose to a steep hill on one side and Liney could see water flowing down the hill into the tail races. There were dozens of Chinese men working the sluices and calling to each other over the noise. She stood near the first tent, her courage again deserting her. A dark-haired girl came out of the tent, and when Liney asked her, the girl pointed the way to Soo Long's place: a decent structure of calico and timber; better, indeed, than many a miner's tent in the town.

The hut was shielded on two sides by screens of boughs to protect its garden from the cutting winter winds. Mrs Soo Long was weeding amongst newly planted seedlings, and two small children were chasing each other along the aisles between vegetable beds that were green with healthy plants. Realising her presence, the children abruptly stopped their game and went quickly to their mother's side. Liney noticed their dirty clothes and grubby faces. They had their mother's brass-coloured hair and Chinese eyes; an odd combination, like a puzzle put together incorrectly.

The woman rose from her knees and wiped her hands down her pinafore, leaving muddy streaks the same colour as her hair.

'You shouldn't have come here.' Her voice was Irish and stern.

'I had to thank you.'

'It was nothing.' As she spoke, she again wiped her dirty hands down her pinafore before approaching Liney and gently pulling the swaddling away from the baby's face. 'He seems happy.'

'Oh, he is. It was like magic.' Liney blushed at her ill-chosen words.

'It was just a few herbs. I can show you how to make it.' She bent down and picked a leaf from her garden, crushed it between her fingers and held it to her nose before tossing it away.

Charlton started to cry, writhing inside his swaddling, his face screwed up tight and reddening. The Soo Long children's eyes widened in alarm and they looked questioningly at their mother.

'The babe needs a feed,' Mrs Soo Long said, but Liney kept her eyes on the crying baby, overcome with embarrassment at her stupidity of not planning her outing better.

'It's alright,' Mrs Soo Long reassured her. You can go into the house and feed him, and when you have finished I will make tea.' She gestured towards the hut.

The front door was a flap of canvas tied back with rope. Liney ducked slightly to enter a surprisingly large room with an earthen floor. There were neat bedrolls along one side, and a table made of fruit boxes with rough-hewn benches on either side. Along another wall ran a bench bearing bottles and caddies, a mortar and pestle, and a set of scales like those used by the gold clerk at the bank. The light through the canvas was milky and subdued, and there was a scent of something strange: cloves, perhaps. Agnes—Mrs Soo Long insisted Liney call her Agnes—bid her to sit, and then discretely went outside again.

As she nursed the baby, Liney cautiously looked about for icons, or signs of paganism, but the hut was unadorned and spotless. She wondered, annoyed with herself, what she had expected. A dripping horse's head? A baby in a bottle? It was because, she thought self-defensively, she'd had such a sheltered upbringing, her parents mixing only with people like themselves.

The familiar languidness settled over Liney. She could hear her new friend outside, encouraging her children in their game. A sharp laugh aroused Liney and she suddenly realised what she had forgotten. With her free hand, she quickly rearranged her clothing before carrying the baby to the doorway. Agnes was crouching down, showing something in the garden to her children: three red heads against a trellised row of green beans. She looked up and noticed Liney, and her distress. Coming into the house with the children in tow, Agnes went straight to a trunk and retrieved a square of white cloth and handed to Liney. Then she fetched a bowl of water, a flannel and a towel.

'I'm hopeless.' Liney's shoulders sagged. 'How did you know?'

Agnes' young son held his nose. 'Poooo,' he said, drawing out the vowel, and they all laughed. Liney let herself laugh too, feeling the luxury of the relief.

Once Charlton was changed, Agnes insisting that she would wash the dirty nappy, they sat on the seats. Agnes' children, Jim and Lucy, sat on either side of Liney, leaning into her and cooing to the baby. Liney, no longer noticing their dirty hands and faces, smiled at their pleasure.

'It's green tea, good for your milk,' Agnes explained as she poured what looked like dishwater into Liney's cup.

Charlton started to grizzle, his face reddening, and Agnes held out her arms to take him. 'He's a wee bit hot,' she said as she lifted him across the table and loosened the swaddling to let his arms wave freely. She held him against her shoulder and rubbed his back until he let out a huge burp, his eyes wide and startled. The children laughed. Softly, she started to sing:

Too-ra-loo-ra-loo-ral, Too-ra-loo-ra-li,
Too-ra-loo-ra-loo-ral, hush now, don't you cry!
Too-ra-loo-ra-loo-ral, Too-ra-loo-ra-li,
Too-ra-loo-ra-loo-ral, that's an Irish lullaby.

Liney tried to swallow against the swelling in her throat. Her mother had had plenty of experience—twelve children—but kept her advice to a few terse words in her letters, which were never timely enough anyway. For Liney, everything was trial and error. Alfred tried to help, but she grew exasperated at the way he thought there little difference between a baby and a foal. The midwife, with her pocked red nose and wild hair, had laughed harshly at Liney's enquiries, as if she were stupid.

There was no point complaining: in this place, most women had to manage without the help of mothers, the wisdom of grandmothers, the confidence of sisters, and the generosity of aunties. Immigration was a knife blade drawn through families, severing ties and traditions. Handed-down knowledge was for old countries where the generations piled up like the stones of a cairn; where you had the right to expect there'd always be family members to turn to. Here, even if you had family in Australia, the distances were so vast that they might just as well have been on the moon.

'There are other things you can do,' Agnes explained as she passed back the baby. Liney held the child up on her shoulder as Agnes had done. Agnes rose and took a small calico-wrapped package from one of the caddies on the bench. 'You can warm this and place it on his tummy.' Liney accepted the parcel with her free hand and held it to her nose: it smelt like the bush on a hot day.

'Is this Chinese?' she asked skeptically.

Lucy, tiring of Liney and the child, moved across into Agnes' lap. Agnes shook her head as she stroked the child's head. 'I learnt it from the black women.'

Liney dropped the parcel on the table as if it had burnt her fingers, and looked sharply at her new friend.

After a couple of moments of silence, Agnes spoke. 'They're here, you know. You might have seen them along the Livingstone as you came up today?'

Liney shook her head, not understanding. Lucy grew fidgety and Agnes set her down and went to fetch some wooden blocks. Jim joined his sister on the floor.

'The blacks,' she said, crouching with the children and looking up at Liney. 'It means the moths are not far behind them.'

'I must go. It's getting late.' Liney said, speaking quickly and rising to her feet. Her sudden movement jolted the baby at her shoulder and he woke up, but did not cry.

Outside, the sun had sunk behind the hills but the air was still warm, smelling strangely—a smell Liney assumed was opium—and vibrating with the thrum of cicadas. Agnes came to the door and patted Liney's arm in farewell. 'Your baby is thriving. You are doing a fine job.' She popped something into Liney's skirt pocket. 'For luck.'

The camp was busy now, the men returning from their diggings, voices calling and cooking pots being set upon fires. It seemed both utterly strange and domestically familiar, Liney thought, as she brushed a fly from her sleeping baby's face, cradled him in her arms and set off towards Omeo.

The bridge over Livingstone Creek creaked as it took her weight, and between the cracks she could see the white foaming water. She paused there and let her eyes follow the banks to a point where smoke was rising from amongst the trees. She thought she could make out black bodies on the shore.

She heard a horse approaching at a quick pace and as she made to move from the bridge, Alfred appeared on horseback.

'Are you all right?' he called to her before he reached her and reined in his horse.

'I suppose it was that Michael O'Shea who told you.' Her face was red with the heat, but she wasn't cross to see him.

He slipped from his saddle, his feet touching the ground with the spring of youth.

Charlton was hot against her, making her clothes damp and clinging. She passed him to Alfred and stretched her arms. 'I had tea with Mrs Soo Long.'

'That's wonderful.' He held the babe awkwardly. She lent towards him and settled Charlton more comfortably in his arms.

The horse gently nudged Liney's shoulder. She took the reins draped over Alfred's arm and put her nose to the animal's neck to breath in its horsiness.

Husband and wife walked side-by-side. 'Alfred, there are blacks, down by the river.'

'I know. They've come for the moths.' He was watching his son's face and not paying much attention to the concern in Liney's voice.

She wanted to yell at him: what moths? His habit of half telling her things, or not explaining at all, irritated her beyond endurance. Instead, she took a deep breath and asked her question calmly.

'Bogong moths: the blacks think they're a great delicacy. They come every year. There will be corroborees every night.' He changed the baby into the crook of his other arm.

'They eat the moths?' she asked him, screwing up her face in disgust.

'They're very good. Juicy, taste a bit like hazelnuts. They singe them in the fire to burn off their wings and legs, then mash the bodies to a paste.' He spoke with relish.

Liney put her hand on her stomach. 'Oh, stop it. You'll make me sick.' She took the baby back from him and passed him the reins of the horse. The sun had sunk low in the metallic sky, and their shadows were long and thin beside them. There was no breeze, and the laughter of kookaburras filled the still air. Alfred broke a small branch from a gum tree and used it as a switch to keep the flies away from his wife and child.

'I suppose it will be left to you to drive the natives on.'

He turned to her in surprise, slowing his steps. 'But they have every right to be here. We're the newcomers.'

She was taken aback, and looking at his face she saw that he was absolutely serious. The only natives she'd known had been civilised—if that was the right word for it. There were two young lubras in her mother's service, and the occasional native in Adelaide town. She rarely saw any in Omeo. She imagined those out here in the wilds to be savages.

'Omeo is becoming a proper town,' she told him. 'There's the church and the bank and the post office.' A terrible thought crossed her mind: 'What if they come into town without clothes on?'

Alfred quickened his pace again and Liney had to take a couple of quick steps to catch up with him, the baby squirming in her arms.

'If I know them, they'll keep to themselves. I'll have a job keeping the miners away from their women.' She looked at him with a raised eyebrow—at his language and the implication of his words. He turned away, embarrassed. 'They're nowhere near as bad as you think,' he added. 'They certainly won't harm you.'

She passed the heavy and restless baby back to her husband. Feeling in her pocket, she retrieved the gift that Agnes had given her and showed the small crescent-shaped biscuit to Alfred.

'A fortune cookie,' he informed her, trying to rock the baby in his arms. 'Break it open.'

She did as he said, letting the biscuit crumble to the ground as she walked, and withdrew a small square of dry pithy paper. It bore a message written in Chinese characters that looked like temples, and which she had no way of understanding.

ര

The weather had been hot and dry for a month. Alfred and Liney dragged through another interminable day and slept fitfully that night, the sheets twisted and clammy. In the early hours they were woken by thunder. White streaks of lightening flashed at the window, filling the cottage with a harsh glare. Then came deep-throated rumbles that made the plates rattle on the dresser.

'There'll be bushfires,' Alfred whispered in the dark. They listening to the rainless storm, then gradually drifted off to sleep once more. A few hours later he shook her awake. He was dressed and his face, close to hers in the dawn greyness, was creased with worry. 'I can smell smoke. I'll be back soon.'

She rose, pulled on her dressing gown and checked on the baby. Alfred had left the door open and she could see that the dawn sky was already a dirty amber colour, like a premonition. She closed the door against the smell of smoke and walked across to the window. With her finger she rubbed a hole in the shroud of fine dust. From across the road, a group of men was heading for the courthouse. In the glass's flaw, they looked like an approaching army of ghouls.

Charlton began to whimper and she lifted him from the crib

and sat in their one of their two armchairs. She pulled aside her dressing gown and nightie, and the baby suckled on her breast greedily while she listened to the men's voices, reaching her as incoherent shouts.

They were like children, the way they came to Alfred with their problems. As if Alfred, through one of his magisterial decrees, could put out the fire. But something had to be done; she knew enough that if the wind changed slightly to the west the town would be in grave danger.

Alfred came through the door as she was laying Charlton back in his crib. His face was pale and drawn. 'Jesus Christ but they are idiots.' He slammed the door behind him with his foot.

Liney covered her mouth with both hands. 'Alfred!' Her eyes showed shock. 'You blasphemed.'

For a moment he looked nonplussed, then annoyed. 'Do you seriously think God is listening? And if he is, that he'd be shocked by my use of his son's name? Given the circumstances?' He walked across the room and filled a glass with water from the jug on the table, drank it without pause, and wiped his mouth with the back of his hand. Liney wrapped her arms around her body. 'In fact, I hope he is listening and he does something about that damned fire. Perhaps he could send King Canute to lend us a hand.'

'I won't have such language used in my home, as if you were still outside talking to the miners.' She kept her voice calm and low, the way she remembered her mother used to.

Alfred's hand was clutching the glass so tightly it might have shattered. The vein in his temple looked like an angry worm. 'Do you know what they're saying?'

She glared at him.

'That the blacks lit the fires. Even though every one of them saw the lightning. Instead of preparing for the real threat, like rational human beings, they want to take their guns to the blacks' camp. I've had the d. . ., a terrible job trying to get them to see reason.'

'Even so . . .' She stood perfectly still.

'Oh, for heaven's sake, Liney.' He put the glass down on the table and pinched the bridge of his nose between his finger and thumb. 'I need to start organising men and water.' He turned towards the door and spoke to her over his shoulder. 'I just came in to say that you might pack some things in case we have to leave in a hurry.'

It was late in the evening before she heard the door latch lift. She had left a plate of Margaret's roast dinner for Alfred under a piece of gauze so the flies could not get to it, and had gone to bed. The curtain that divided the cottage was partly open and she watched him as he lit a candle and ate standing up, staring at the window. She could see the smoothly tapered candle flame distorted in the glass. He left his plate on the table and blew out the candle.

Liney closed her eyes when he pushed aside the curtain and entered the bedroom, where he undressed and left his clothes in a heap on the floor. He slipped into bed beside her and placed a hand on her shoulder. 'Liney?'

She would not answer him.

'I know you're awake. No-one lies that stiffly in their sleep.' His voice was gentle; she could tell he was trying to apologise.

'What about the children?' she asked, turning over to face him. She tried to read his face in the dimness. 'Not just Charlton, but the children that are to come?

He traced his finger along her cheek. 'You mean the fire?'

'What if you blasphemed in front of them?'

He groaned and fell back on his pillow, which brought all the anger rushing back into her body.

'You don't believe at all. That's the truth, isn't it?' The words were out before she realised. She had not thought she would have the courage to say what had rolled round and round in her head all day, like a huge bolder crashing around her senses.

He was silent, for so very long she thought he'd drifted off to sleep. She listened to his breathing, trying to control her own anguished, gasping breaths, and to the gusty wind rattling the shingles on the roof.

'I do believe, Liney. Now go to sleep.'

Neither slept. Alfred's mind spun around the dangers. The risk was spot fires: embers carried on the night wind into the trees around the edge of town. He'd posted lookouts and hoped they would stay awake. Constable Mullane was to do the rounds all night to make sure there was no drinking.

Alfred had managed to get the miners to focus on the fire and admit that the blacks were not responsible. The Chinese had dammed their aqueduct to provide an extra supply of water, and the hotels' empty barrels had been filled and placed on carts. But what use were buckets and barrels against a wall of fire that sucked oxygen out of the air and boiled blood even before the flames arrived?

The miners thought of the fire as a conquerable aberration, whereas it was as natural to the bush as shedding bark. He'd ridden up to Livingstone Creek to ask the natives for their advice on how to fight the fire, but they were gone. At the beginning of summer, he'd wanted to deliberately burn the grass paddocks to the north of the town, something he had seen blacks do to create a protective fire break, but the townsfolk would not agree, arguing that no-one in their right mind deliberately lit a fire.

Would the creek provide a safe haven if the fire swept through the town? If they covered their heads with wet hessian bags? Jack Armstrong had collected every hessian bag he could find and placed them in piles on the bank. Everyone knew where to assemble if they heard the church bell tolling. And he'd let it be known that anyone guilty of trying to muscle out the Chinese would be in the lockup as soon as the fire passed.

The one saving grace was that the miners had cut down nearly every tree in the town precinct to wall their mineshafts and feed their campfires. But he knew what was to come: he had seen fires so hot they burnt across bare earth. He had seen seed heads exploding in the crowns of trees, showering the ground with the germ of regeneration, even as destruction was upon it.

Had he thought of everything possible? He remembered a time in the desert when he and his party nearly died of thirst and knew how easy it was to overlook the obvious. What he couldn't think about was Liney and Charlton.

The clock on the mantel struck three and Liney was still awake. It was impossible to sleep with Alfred tossing about. Who was he, this man she slept with each night, who had once walked her to church along the quiet Adelaide streets, and sat reading her Bible while she stitched? She rose to check on Charlton, putting her face close to his crib to hear his tiny whistling breaths. Even the bunny rug smelt of smoke. Six hundred miles away, her family would be sleeping soundly between their crisp white sheets. She longed for her narrow bed in the room with the pale blue walls that she'd shared with her sister Pip. The Adelaide house was so big and cool. Its sandstone walls glowed at sunset and its garden smelt of lilacs and roses. She used to sit in the swing chair under the peppercorn tree on hot afternoons, reading and dreaming, and the black servant girl would bring her lemonade on a tray, taking slow, careful steps so as not to spill the drink on the lace doily.

When Charlton woke, she fed him, watching their joined shadow on the cottage wall and thinking, all the time, about Alfred. How he had come to her father's house carrying half the desert in his clothes and hair. She'd thought him such a hero. And when he'd scrubbed up, trimmed his beard and hair and dressed in her oldest brother's clean clothes, she had teased him, when no one else was listening, that he was the frog turned into a prince. She had laughed when he blushed.

He had regaled them with stories about how the Aborigines caught fish and birds; he described huge flocks of emus kicking up clouds of red dust; he spoke of flowers that, after rain, sprang from the sand to coat the desert in rainbow colours. She hung on every word, even when her brothers sniggered. In the garden, he had placed his compass into her hands—his most prized possession—and stood so close beside her that their arms had touched while he showed her how to read the dial, turning her around until the needle swung south of east. 'One day,' he'd said, 'I'll take you away in that direction.' It only occurred to her now that he had never mentioned God.

Once, behind closed doors, she'd heard Alfred arguing with her father. Or at least, she'd heard her father's voice raised in anger. That was nothing unusual, except that no-one ever dared answer Papa back. Had they fought over religion? She had certainly heard Mr Darwin's name spoken, and something about apes, but could make no sense of their conversation through the thick oak doors.

Their fathers—hers and Alfred's—had been friends in Nottingham: they were Quakers and ardent reformists who together thought they could change the shape and direction of the British parliament. At least neither she nor Alfred had inherited that obsessive zeal. But could it be that Alfred, even then, had doubts about his faith?

She looked at the peaceful, sleeping face of her son and ran her hand over the fine stands of pale hair that were damply plastered to his head. Please God, she prayed, keep the fire away from the town. She rose and went to the window, fearful that she would see an ominous orange glow. The night was black.

She laid the infant in his crib, and as she straightened she felt something shift, like a shiver down the spine. She stood stiffly, straining to hear what she'd sensed. The wind, yes, it was the wind buffeting the door. The candle flame was wavering.

'Alfred,' she called, running towards the bed. He was on his feet in a moment. 'Listen. The wind's changed.'

He paused. 'Yes. Yes, you're right. It's a southerly.' He took both her hands and skipped her around the room, whooping and singing: 'Blow the wind southerly, southerly, southerly.' She was reluctant to give in to him so quickly, but one crisis was over, and his relief was infectious.

She let him dance her around, and then she stopped. 'Hush.' She shook free and placed her hand over his laughing mouth, feeling his hot panting. 'You'll wake Charlton.' She clasped both his hands again and kissed them. It must be that he knew who was responsible for their salvation. She dropped to her knees, pulling him down with her. Together they lowered their heads, Liney stiffling a smile.

ഗ

Autumn had arrived, with rain, the dust settled and the air became cool and fresh. What grass there was, was tinged with green, and gardens that had been planted around the more substantial dwellings were still in flower. The climbing rose Liney had planted by the cottage door was smothered in the last of its full-blown blooms, and the vegetable patch was yielding fine crops of beans and carrots. Two glossy brown chooks pecked and clucked at a pile of potato peelings Margaret had thrown from the scullery.

On a Sunday morning of blue skies and gentle warmth, Alfred and Liney walked along the rutted Omeo street towards the church. Liney pushed the perambulator, which she had started to use after all, when Charlton had simply grown too heavy to carry about.

A group of natives came around the corner of the post office and walked towards them, draped in blankets and animal skins. They walked along the street, Liney observed, as if they owned it

'They're back,' Liney whispered with dismay.

Alfred hailed them as if they were friends. '*Gnowan ju*,' he called, beckoning them to approach.

She pushed the perambulator across the street to stand in the shade of the bank's verandah. She could smell them, even from a distance. Anger was bubbling through her as if she were a kettle set to boil. He was using their awful language, and there were women in the group who did nothing to hide their bosoms. One young woman, no more than a girl, was breast-feeding a child. Right there in the open. Standing close to Alfred. She thought of him, out in the desert, never a white woman in sight. She'd heard stories, even in the past few weeks, of white men with black women. She clutched the perambulator handle so tightly her knuckles went white. Suddenly, inside her bulky clothing, she felt fusty and weighted down.

Shortly after the natives had first arrived in Omeo, just before the fires, Reverend Griffiths had preached on just this matter, preparing them, she suspected, for the barbaric invasion. The Reverend was a callow, pock-faced man with huge ears, and in his high voice he had instructed his flock in the divine three 'Cs: Christianity, Civilisation and Clothing. Their responsibility as Christians and British subjects, the vicar insisted, was to lead by example. There was no salvation without shame. For weren't Adam and Eve expelled from the Garden of Eden and hid their nakedness which was their shame? 'Behold I come as a thief. Blessed is he that watcheth, and keepeth his garments, lest he walk naked, and they see his shame.' To be clothed was to be civilised, and in one's right mind, according to the Gospels of Mark and Luke. Even Liney had grown a little uncomfortable at the vicar's obsession with nakedness, but now confronted by the natives she agreed with everything he had said.

Alfred said his cheery goodbyes to the blacks and strolled across the street to rejoin her. The ironmonger and his wife walked past and they exchanged good mornings. Liney waited until they were out of earshot before she hissed at Alfred. 'That was disgusting. You should be ashamed of yourself.'

His equanimity disappeared and he looked confounded. He was about to speak when more people passed them, heading for the church. Liney smiled tightly at the families; Alfred greeted them by name.

'We'll be late for church,' she said haughtily as she gave the pram a small shove and strode off after the rest of the congregation.

They walked in silence, but when they reached the church, in plenty of time for the service, Alfred gave a surprised and gleeful shout and went up to a man whom Liney did not recognise. He looked more like a boy: clean-shaven, with curly brown hair down to his collar, and a clear-eyed, pleasant face. The men pumped each other's hands.

'Fancy seeing you here.' Alfred spoke first.

'Fancy seeing you here,' came the rejoinder, laced with irony, as the man waved his hand towards the church and the ragged congregation filing in for the service.

'Liney, come and meet Alex Aitkin.' He introduced the

newcomer as his friend who had been so indispensible on all of his exploratory missions. Aitkin looked at his boots, and Liney immediately liked him.

'So this is the heir,' Aitkin said, examining the babe and then the father. 'I can see the resemblance.'

Alfred beamed. 'You must come back with us after the service, to join us for lunch.'

The church was dim and smelt of sweat overlaid by Mrs Cross's roses, which filled a large vase on a table under the stained-glass window. Liney followed the two men into a pew near the front and parked the perambulator beside her. Reverend Griffiths had a large carbuncle on his chin; the string of boils so red and ugly that it made it difficult for Liney to concentrate on the service. She heard enough, though, to be pleased that he included in his catalogue of sins the matter of nakedness. Beside her, Alfred clenched his fists on his lap.

After church, as they walked back to the cottage, she listened in silence as the men relived past exploits. It was the first time since she came to Omeo that she'd seen Alfred drop his guard with another man. His work kept him aloof from the miners; his work and his interests which no-one here—if anywhere—shared.

'I see, though, that you have well and truly shaken the explorer from your bones,' Aitkin commented.

'Oh, no he hasn't, Mr Aitkin,' Liney answered. 'Alfred doesn't need any encouragement to be off, traipsing all over this wild country.'

'I don't 'traipse', as my wife puts it,' Alfred said with a note of annoyance in his voice. 'I have magistrate duties that take me to all the far-flung towns.'

As they walked through the town, Alfred started to tell Aitkin of his various interests.

'I've heard all about you,' Aitkin broke in. 'Police magistrate, mines warden, coroner, Crown Lands commissioner. Have I missed anything? It's quite impressive. And about your rock collecting and work with the blacks.'

'Oh? Where did you hear that?' Alfred asked in a puzzled

voice. He stopped walking and looked at Aitkin. A family walking behind almost walked into him. 'Sorry,' he muttered, lifting his hat in greeting and stepping to one side to allow them to pass.

Aitkin and Liney also stopped walking. 'Bumped into Edwin Welch a few months back,' Aitkin explained.

'How the devil would he know?'

'Alfred, please, it's the Sabbath.' But her words were automatic, her mind more concentrated on Alfred's surprised reaction to a name she had never heard before. She smiled and nodded a greeting to Mrs O'Reily, the church organist, who bustled past with her teenage children in tow, tutting at the obstruction to her path.

'I thought you must have kept in touch, which did surprise me,' Aitkin offered tentatively.

Howitt shook his head and they started to walk again.

'I've taken a job at Ramahyuck, the new Aboriginal mission at Lake Wellington,' Aitkin announced. 'You will have heard of it?'

'Indeed,' Howitt answered, but he was barely listening.

'I'm helping Reverend Hagenauer set it up. We've built the church already: a lovely weatherboard building with a corrugated-iron roof and a spire nearly forty feet high. Now I'm teaching the natives to build huts.'

'What a fine thing to do,' Liney said, smiling down at Charlton making gurgling noises in the perambulator.

Alex touched the rim of his hat and turned back to Alfred.

'That's where I caught up with Welch. He was there photographing the blacks. He's become quite accomplished.'

Alfred dug his hands deep into his pocket.

'He's creating a record so that Reverend Hagenauer can prove the changes that come over the physical features of the blacks when they convert to Christianity,' Aitkin went on.

'Is that possible?' Liney asked uncertainly, looking about to make sure that Reverend Griffiths was not close by.

'I'm not so sure either. But the blacks do take to Christianity. The Reverend calls Ramahyuck the Promised Land. Some of the natives are learning to read and write, even the women and children.'

'How amazing,' Liney said, her eyes shining with the validation of what Christianity could accomplish. She could do that, teach little black children to read their Bibles. The idea filled her with a sense of worth that might match the worldliness of the men.

'You would like it, Mrs Howitt. The natives play cricket; they're incredibly quick to learn and show great skill. And in the evenings they sit around their camp fires singing English songs.'

'Home Sweet Home?' Alfred said, so cynically that it made Liney wince. She felt the return of her anger: she could almost hate him sometimes.

# Chapter 5

It was as if he'd shed multiple skins. Howitt had seen plenty of evidence in nature: long black husks of snake skin crisping in the heat, or rough bark hanging in tattered streamers, exposing delicate pink trunk-flesh that was, nevertheless, firm and strong. He felt pared down to something new like that: to a hard, essential core, as if his body had known all along the life it wanted; it had been waiting for his mind and circumstances to catch up.

He had been on the road for over a week now, combining his judicial duties with geology and anthropology. He'd had the good fortune to meet up with the old Kurnai men Bungle Bottle and Master Turnmile, who had paddled him up the Mitchell River into country he'd never seen before: wild, lush, impenetrable bush; deep golden-walled gorges; and such utter silence that he often found himself holding his breath. His life was, he knew, blessed.

Last night he dreamed of the ticking of the grandfather clock, the one that stood in the hall in his childhood home in Nottingham, just to the side of the staircase. Panic rose in him, to think he was back in England, but he woke to the sound of pattering rain. His tent was no more than a canvas gunyah: a square of cloth slung over a rough frame of branches. He reached out to touch the rough canvas, to reassure himself that his Australian life was real; his damp swag helped to confirm the reality. The morning light was watery grey. From time to time a breeze passed through the trees above and sent a heavier shower of raindrops rattling onto his tent.

He sat up and pulled his saddlebag onto his lap, and felt about for the letter that had arrived for him just before he left home. It had remained unopened as he waited for the right moment. The handwriting was unmistakable: he had seen it scrawled across maps and in journal pages that pinpointed position and described the lay of the land.

He opened the envelope and tilted the page towards the light. It was not what he had expected: Welch wrote of his bad luck. He had a wife and sickly daughter, and a languishing newspaper that he published for an outback town in central Queensland, where the locals cared for nothing but the price of wool and the supply of shearers. He needed to make a move to Melbourne where he could start up a new rag.

Howitt felt his blood pounding in his temples. He wondered how Welch knew where to send his letter, then recalled Aitkin suggesting, years ago, that Welch was keeping tabs on him; a thought which unnerved him. Why couldn't the man just come out and say what he meant?

What would it matter, now, if Welch revealed that he had been the one to discover King? Nothing changed the fact that he, Howitt, had led the mission. But nothing changed the fact, either, that he had failed to acknowledge Welch's role. People would frown: was he not quite the man they had come to know and respect? He thought of the desert and of the scarecrow King, Welch standing over him protective as a mother.

It wasn't as though he'd profited hugely from any of it, Howitt thought angrily. He was granted the position of Omeo's Gold Warden and Police Magistrate in recognition of his efforts, which was a cheap payoff for the committee. When his duties were expanded and he moved to Bairnsdale—well, that was achieved through his own hard work.

He thought of the insult he'd had to bear at Burke and Wills' state funeral, for which he was chosen as a pallbearer but assigned to Wills' coffin, middle left. And then there was the monument. He had travelled the two hundred and fifty miles from Omeo to Melbourne for the unveiling of the Burke and Wills' statue. Liney, pregnant with Charlton, had stayed at home. He was grateful she hadn't been there to witness his humiliation.

The perfect autumn day had drawn a vast crowd into Collins and Russell Streets; there were frilly parasols and Homburg hats as far as the eye could see from the elevated stage. Howitt had stood on the podium amongst top-hatted dignitaries while Governor Sir Charles Darling delivered his address. The Governor was wearing his military uniform and his vice-regal decorations glinted in the sunshine. He spoke in an Imperial voice, and twirled his moustaches during well-timed pauses, giving the crowd time to cheer. Howitt stood behind the more important members of the official party, hands clasped firmly behind his back, waiting for the Governor to mention his name and thank him for the role he played. The Governor raised his eyes to the two huge bronze figures that towered over the crowd: Burke looked like an English scholar, Wills like a Greek god, or perhaps a supplicant. The Governor did not, however, gesture to the bas-reliefs at the foot of the monument that showed scenes frozen in bronze. One was a rendering of Howitt finding King.

Howitt grew increasingly uncomfortable as the Governor lumbered towards the end of his speech: '. . . the very form and semblance of those now celebrated men, whose great exploit has shed such lustre upon the records of exploration and discovery in this age, and engrafted so large a share of interest and glory upon the earlier annals of Victoria.'

The crowd cheered and Howitt swallowed hard. The government had spent £14,000 on the monument; he'd been paid £300 to search the desert for the hopeless wanderers.

Had Welch been in the crowd? When the throng finally dispersed did he approach the monument, running his finger over the bas-relief? Howitt did not wait to see. Not being able to bear the thought of afternoon tea at Government House, he had hurried up Collins Street until he reached the sanctum of his hotel.

And now, did Welch think that Howitt could snap his fingers and the powers-that-be would jump to any request? It wasn't as if he was Robert O'Hara Burke. He was the one who'd survived, which was not the way to go about becoming a hero in this land. You had to die out in the desert, Howitt thought bitterly, to have praise lavished upon your dry bones. His success, achieved through meticulous planning and leadership, was the very thing that denied him recognition and influence. Welch should know that. Even King, another survivor, had sunk into obscurity. All of his own achievements since then—at least he could say this—were his own. No-one had opened doors for him.

He'd have to think carefully about how he would reply to Welch's letter. He folded the sheet of paper and returned it to its envelope. He pulled on his dank trousers, coat and boots. Outside, his horses Wizard and Sam Patch were waiting under the dripping trees, their heads hung mournfully low. No chance of a fire this morning to warm him before the long ride; no tea laced with eucalyptus leaves to start the day. As he dismantled his tent, a pool of collected water soaked the bottom of his trouser legs and he felt the cold dribble into his boots.

He thought of what lay ahead: the triviality, the hostility, the irrationality of argument that awaited him in Dargo. It was a town full of men gone feral through disappointment and lack of society, veins running with as much alcohol as blood. They found insult and threat in the rise of an eyebrow or wink of an eye, and were too quick with their fists and boots. Howitt's job was as much to pacify as to pass judgement, to restore goodwill in a town too small to survive long-term animosity.

He practised the law in the only way he knew how, having never been formally trained. He'd simply been handed a gavel and a pile of legal tomes and thrust into the world of crime and justice. The fundamentals were easy enough: he'd had plenty of experience observing the workings of men's minds, pushing them through hostile country to the edge of their endurance and observing their behaviours brought on by ambition or fear. He always tried to look past the surface disturbances, and like a true Quaker, he still believed in the fundamental goodness of his fellow man. Even in this small outpost of civilisation he believed in justice.

His father's way had been to rail against institutions from the outside, battering on the door of the establishment with his Bible, wasting rivers of ink, trying to force the powerful to recognise the guilt in themselves and their social order. Australia's convict beginnings were proof of his father's impotence. A servant might steal a candle-snuffer from a master and be shipped off to the colonies for seven years; a master might run up debts of hundreds of pounds and strut about London in his fine new garb, head held high with disdain.

Howitt shook his head to clear the image of his father and London, and instead thought of Mrs Henty's scones. They'd be waiting for his arrival, fragrantly steaming under a checked tea towel. There'd be dishes of yellow butter and blackberry jam, and a pot of tea in its knitted cozy. The day wouldn't be all bad. He put Welch's letter out of his mind.

He swung himself up into the saddle, and Wizard picked up the track. The pack horse fell in behind, trotting along like a faithful dog despite its load of canvas and swag, tin plate and mug, books, geological kit of hammers and shovels, and box of specimen jars. The clay surface of the track slithered over its rocky base, but the horses were sure-footed as they followed the narrow trail through the thick, dripping bush.

He returned to his earlier musings. Gone were the bare bushman days when he could get by with the most basic kit; when he could go for months without needing a roof or a bath, with hardly a change of clothes, and, if no money, then also no debt. Now there were myriad calls on his time and his purse. These days he had a wardrobe of new skins: husband, father of five children—where did the time go? Magistrate, Protector of Aborigines, farmer. He even felt justified in granting himself the titles of anthropologist, botanist and geologist. He wasn't formally qualified, true, but his work was being recognised in British circles, which, no matter what he thought of the old country, was still the centre of the scientific world.

His father's letters had become more circumspect in tone. He seemed more inclined to recognise that his son had made a life for himself that could be, if not celebrated, at least acknowledged. His father's words hadn't reached the giddy heights of expressing paternal pride, but Howitt had long since outgrown the need for such approbation. The needling was still there, though. In his most recent letter, his father had transcribed an old saying that Howitt remembered from his youth:

The loss of gold is great,
The loss of time is more.
The loss of Christ is such a loss
That no man can restore.

The rhyme stuck in his head, keeping time with Wizard's metronomic trot. It was, no doubt, his father's intention that it have this effect. He'd never had gold to lose, and no-one could accuse him of wasting time. He knew what was meant.

So lost in thought was he that he hadn't even realised that the rain had stopped and a steamy sun was filtering through the canopy. The bush had come alive with birdcalls: the endless whoop-whoop-whooping of wonga pigeons; the rattling noise of wattlebirds; the call and answering lash of whip birds; the twittering chorus of fairy wrens and firetails. There were enough wings to lift the entire bush up to heaven.

It was his favourite ride, this journey that took him to court cases across the north-eastern region of Gippsland. From Bairnsdale, he crossed the Mitchell at Drover's Crossing and cantered across the river flats of Tabbaramunjie and Wombamunjie. The conjunction of English and Aboriginal place names could have been the threads of old and new worlds weaving together, but he knew it wasn't really like that, not at all. His brief time with Bunjil Bottle and Master Turnmile had only reinforced the gulf that lay between the cultures. He passed trees, Kurrajongs, which don't shed their bark and which still bore Angus McMillan's survey marks blazed into their trunks. The blacks would have taught McMillan about those trees, and much more besides.

Following the Angusvale run took him on to Judge O'Shea's old place where the swing bridge swayed wildly as the horses crossed the gorge. From the middle of the bridge, he looked down river to where a rainbow bled into the trees along the bank. On the far side of the river, he picked up a ridgeline that ran north-south and followed it through Tabberabbera, Cobbannah and on to Castleburn. Cobbannah was his favourite station, where he rode between stands of massive river red gums, across a shimmering bronze sea of wallaby grass that was as high as his stirrup irons. Cattle grazed on the rich native fodder, making them fat and glossy. The billabongs were alive with wild fowl that rose honking and quacking into the crystal air as he passed.

Rounding a bend, the world changed from grey-green bush to the dazzling colours of deciduous autumn-leaved trees, the golds and reds clashing brilliantly with the cobalt sky. The colours made his eyes water after two days of monochrome country. The tin roof of the hotel came into sight, and the barking town dogs—brown mongrels mostly—brought Mrs Henty out onto the hotel verandah to greet him, hands on her broad hips and a voice as loud as a bellowing bullocky. Howitt raised his hat to her and called Good Morning, although the sun was just reaching its zenith. She replied that the scones were about ready to come out of the oven, and disappeared back into the hotel.

A stable-boy led Wizard and Sam Patch away and Howitt climbed the steps, stamping his feet to force blood back into his frozen toes. He entered the empty lounge and walked straight to the huge stone fireplace. With his back to the flames, he felt his bones thaw and watched steam rising from his clothes. The room smelt of smoke, stale beer, sweaty men and roast beef. The timbers above the fireplace were blackened and the floorboards stained and sloping, but the beer taps and mirrors behind the bar gleamed.

When he could feel his toes, he crossed the road to the courthouse, bending to open the gate in the white picket fence that surrounded the building, making the place more homely than was appropriate. Inside, Constable Young raised his head from his pile of briefs and greeted the magistrate with respect. He was, true to his name, hardly more than a lad, and Howitt wondered how he coped under the command of Sergeant Hooper. The sergeant, who on this day was at home nursing a toothache, believed that the shape of his nose gave him a strong resemblance to the Duke of Wellington, and had he been given the opportunity, he would have led a similar life of honour. He modeled himself on his hero. He was reluctant to tell anyone that he'd come to Australia as one of Fitzgibbons' 'fifty men'—the group of London policemen who had spent their working lives on the city beat and on arrival in the colonies were dispersed to country towns. What Hooper lacked in knowledge of the bush and the men who lived there, he made up for in military bearing. It was a severe disappointment to him to have only Constable Young over whom to rule.

'Been out patrolling this morning?' Howitt jokingly asked Young.

Each morning, the unfortunate Young was required to stand with his horse at the gate of the police station while Hooper marched to and fro inspecting man and beast. Then the sergeant barked the order for the day: 'Patrol the track to Meerijig.' Young was never sure what he was supposed to be looking for, but he'd dutifully set off, alert and eager until the monotonous bush lulled him into daydreams of lamp-lit, bustling streets and women in brightly coloured gowns.

'Ten cases, I'm afraid, Your Worship, but nothing major. A few brawls; a stolen pouch of gold dust, although there's a question over whether it was gold; a couple of drunk and disorderlies; and Mrs Hyde's been neglecting to send her youngsters to school. Oh, and Trainer's accused of stealing a saddle.' Young pulled a face.

'Come on, Constable, Trainer's not such a bad beggar.' Howitt pulled his fob watch from his vest pocket, checked the time, and tucked it away.

'He's been up for every crime in the calendar. The Sarge loathes him, which doesn't help matters. I think Trainer deliberately tries to rile him.'

Although Young had lit a fire in the courthouse's small fireplace, the room was as cold as a dog's nose. The portrait of the sternly regal Queen Victoria hanging behind the magistrate's bench did nothing to add to the warmth. Howitt led the Constable back across the road to the hotel dining room where they devoured Mrs Henty's scones, and yarned until they heard the sound of horses and voices outside.

When they returned to the courthouse, it had filled with men who had seated themselves on benches that were arranged like pews. Cold sunshine streamed through the grimy courthouse windows and fell in long stripes across the timber floor. The men removed their hats and stood as Howitt climbed the two steps to his elevated bench. To his right was a somewhat rickety dock, to his left an even more dilapidated witness stand.

Young took his role as prosecutor seriously and frowned deeply as the miscreants pleaded their innocence. No-one bothered to be represented, the cost of a lawyer being beyond their means and far more than the fine they expected. The accused, knowing that there was only enough room in the lockup for the worst cases, nodded obediently as Magistrate Howitt cautioned them to behave better in the future, and fined them amounts appropriate to each crime.

Howitt had his head down writing when Young announced the second last case for the day, and Donald Cameron, charged with drunkenness, took the witness stand. Howitt looked up, and then down at his notes to check the name. Donald Cameron. He couldn't recall what the man's Christian name had been, but Donald sounded likely enough. He'd aged. Most of his face was covered by a grey beard, and greasy grey locks were tied back with a piece of greenhide. His shoulders were hunched and his stomach bulged over trousers that he had to keep hitching up. He would not meet Howitt's eye.

It was a shock to Howitt to see him—not just his presence in court, but that the man should turn up in Dargo, of all places, so close to one of Howitt's worst memories. He tried, generally, to keep his mind from the gorge just a few miles from the town. He shifted his position awkwardly on his elevated magistrate's throne.

Young read the charge. 'Do you have anything to say for yourself?' Howitt asked the accused, carefully observing the man's profile.

'I weren't drunk. My cart hit a log and I fell out. I got concussion, a numbness which caused me to fall down.'

Cameron kept his eyes down, his finger picking at the splintered wood of the witness box.

Howitt responded that such numbness seemed prevalent in the district. He found that as Cameron had already spent eighteen hours in the lockup he could go free. He warned him to be more cautious of tree stumps in the future. Constable Young stood dumbfounded, not understanding Howitt's unexpected leniency. Howitt waved his gavel at him to call the final case.

❧

At the end of the day, the hotel bar filled with men: local farmers and prospectors in clothes that might once have been of different hues but were all now uniform dishwater-grey. Their actions looked choreographed as they placed their weather-beaten hats on the bar, took their first long swills of beer, wiped froth from their mouths, and sighed deeply. The day's accused joined them; their appreciation of the first mouthful of beer was identical. Cameron was amongst them, already into his second ale. Howitt went up to him at the bar and held out his hand, which Cameron ignored.

'How has life been treating you?' he asked, raising his magistrate's voice over the din of voices. Dusk had fallen and Mrs Henty had lit the lamps in the bar, but still the room was gloomy.

'How does it look?' growled Cameron in reply, signaling Mrs Henty for another beer.

'I heard you were working for Mr McMillan. Before he died.' Howitt nodded to Mrs Henty's offer of a ginger ale.

Cameron glared at him. Was it possible, Howitt mused, for a man's eyes to get smaller? Cameron turned back to his beer and grunted.

'Nasty work it was, too. Cleaning up after that bastard.'

Howitt pulled back, shocked by the man's bitterness. He knew what Cameron was referring to. An image came back to him, of Cameron kicking a skull down into the gorge. He could picture Aitkin's face, creased in concern, expecting him to report the massacre.

'Same old ways: steal land and pretend you've always been an aristocrat.'

One of the miners came up to Cameron and put his hand companionably on the man's shoulder. 'Easy mate,' he cautioned.

Howitt turned his back on Cameron's hostility and faced the crowd. Joe Farley, a big man with an oval face who Howitt had fined and told to settle his debts, asked Howitt about his wife and children, and what was happening in the big town, meaning Bairnsdale. Howitt was grateful for the diversion.

'Ice is being made at Toonalook,' he told the man, who stepped back, agog.

'What, even in warm weather?' another man at Howitt's side asked, scratching the skin of his huge belly between the buttons of his shirt.

'The blocks are wrapped in hessian bags and used in the packing of fish bound for Melbourne. Already the fishing fleets are increasing, now that more fish can be transported quickly.' The two men nodded sagely. Others at the bar had stopped talking to listen, though Cameron didn't seem to care. 'And the ice is used to cool the beer in the Bairnsdale hotels.' This brought a small cheer.

'They say you're growing hops now, Mr Howitt.' It was the man with the big belly who spoke. Howitt remembered his name: Ted Paine. Other men standing at the bar hooted and said it was a good thing.

'Never been grown in your parts before, isn't that so?' Paine raised his beer in a mock salute.

'Yes, Ted, that's right. They're shooting up like beanstalks.' Only hours earlier he'd issued Paine with a fine for drunk and disorderly.

'Won't be much good in a drought, Your Worship.'

'Oh, they're hardy enough. Like you, Ted.'

'No, Mr Howitt, Ted couldn't survive a drought.' It was Mrs Henty who spoke from behind the bar, wiping her big red hands on a towel, and the men laughed again as Ted nodded and lifted his pint of warm beer to his lips. Howitt looked at

Cameron out of the corner of his eye. The man was slumped on the bar, taking no part in the laughter.

*

In his saddle bag, wrapped in an oilskin, were his sketchbook and pencils, and Rosenbusch's latest volume of *Mikroskopische Physiographie der Mineralien und Gesteine*. Howitt's schoolboy German was still sufficiently good for him to understand most of what he read. He turned Wizard's head in the direction of home. The horse knew what was expected of him: to keep to the track while Howitt swayed in the saddle and read.

Liney wouldn't expect him home for couple more days, giving him time to explore the region for further additions to his geological map of northern Gippsland. She never begrudged him time for his research. She was so efficient and practical; he could leave almost everything to her. He hoped she hadn't forgotten that the teams had to be arranged for hops picking. It was early days, but when the time came there was a rush for labour across the district. Chinese and Italian pickers were easy enough to muster, and Tulaba would put together a motley crew of blackfellows. But there were still the overseers to organise, and men to lay and rake the hops in the kilns. He'd meant to call in on his neighbour Stan Sullivan before he left for Dargo. Would Liney think to ask Stan to rustle up a team?

Returning his book to the saddlebag, he spurred Wizard to a canter and rode down the mountain for some distance, over what he'd already classified as Upper Devonian rocks, since endorsed by the geological academy. He thought about the immensity of age that separated this day from the land's formation. How wonderful it would be to be able to speed up time, to witness the great convulsive shifts. The broiling sea washing over the land; the land masses rising; the eruption of volcanoes with outpourings of white-hot lava cooling to brilliant red and flowing across the undulating terrain. The great crashing of trees and tumbling of boulders. Ash filling the spaces where rivers had flowed, firming into wide plains. Then the torrential rains: rushing water digging deep into the land, splitting it apart again into deep valleys and rivers with plunging gorges. The earth, holding the memory of those earlier trees, sending up new shoots to hold and shade the soil, to provide a canopy to shelter the bracken and ferns and delicate orchids: the beginnings of new life. The story of all of this was enshrined in the rocks he collected, and in the imaginative leaps he made to connect one event to the next through the specks of crystal and granite he examined under his microscope. Darwin called such observation the eye of reason, which was different from the eye of sight. He'd taught himself how to see in that way: to use his reason to make the leap from the obvious to the possible.

His work was well regarded, his scientific findings as well as his magistrate duties. But then he thought of Welch and the letter in his saddlebag. Along with his achievements there were also failings. A failure of character, he thought with self-disgust, was more damming than if he merely misclassified a rock. What would he say to Welch? Offering Welch any assistance would seem like an admission of guilt, a caving in to his subtle attempt at blackmail. The Lord knew he didn't have the money to set the man up in business, if that's what he was asking.

Then, thinking about Cameron and McMillan, he recalled Arbuckle. The man had made a fortune from subdividing land and was known to be a keen investor in new ventures that advanced the colony, or at least advanced it in the direction that best suited him. The memory of Arbuckle and of that night at McMillan's was accompanied by a sour taste, but perhaps he would be interested in taking on Welch's proposed newspaper. Not that Howitt had any inkling of whether Welch's writing could be said to benefit the wealthy. He sighed deeply. He would write to Welch as soon as he returned home, making no promises. And he would write to Arbuckle, although that would also require a good swallowing of bile.

He thought of asking Welch for the photographs in return for his efforts: those desert images of which he'd always been so jealous—he could admit so much to himself. As far as he knew Welch hadn't published them. But he knew he wouldn't ask.

The trail down towards Bairnsdale was a tunnel of white-limbed gums. Where the trees thinned, he could see across the plains back to the mountains. Sheep grazed in paddocks of grass polka-dotted with dandelions, and there were occasional rough-timbered huts with blue smoke snaking out of chimneys into the clear sky. The breeze, no more than a whisper, carried birdsong, the sharp tang of eucalyptus, the distant barking of a dog.

He stopped for lunch by a gravelly shoal on the banks of the Wonnangatta and lit a fire. With warm sunshine on his back, he drew out his sketchbook and sat hunched over a clean page, a mug of billy tea cooling at his side. He could sketch the trees, the huts, this river, the mountains, but how to capture what really moved him: the smells, the sounds, the mystery of the place? If only it were possible to draw in some extra-dimensional way that caught an all-encompassing experience of place.

The sound of a cantering horse broke his thoughts and he looked around, up the track along which he'd come, to see Henry Anderson approaching. He stood up to greet his friend.

'I've been trying to catch up with you all morning. I called into Dargo for breakfast, and Mrs Henty told me you'd made an early start.' The Reverend smiled out of a face so weathered it resembled a piece of bark.

'Not as early as yours, by the sound of it. Where have you come from?' He took the reins of Henry's horse and patted its nose.

'Grant. A christening and a funeral in the space of three days.' Henry dismounted and took his lunch from his saddlebag.

'And how were the good people of Grant?' Howitt asked, tying the reins to a low branch close to his own horses.

'Dismal, and ever-diminishing, now that the gold has just about run out. Those left won't stay long. Old Mrs Walker the post mistress spends her days writing letters to mail to herself, to keep the post office looking useful.'

'Any good finds while you were there?' Howitt poured Henry a mug of tea as he spoke.

'I didn't have time to look, I'm afraid.' Reverend Anderson, too, was a collector of rocks. He took the tea and blew gently across its surface. They stood side by side, facing the flowing river. The only sounds were from the chatter of water over the gravel shoal, and the horses pulling at grass.

'If you have time now, I was going to do a little prospecting here before heading down to Tabberabberra for the night.'

The two men walked along the riverbank with their hammers and picks, kicking over stones, stooping to inspect the flinty ground. Anderson's eye fell on what looked like a prize, and he dug it up and turned it over in his hand. It was nothing and he tossed the rock aside. They stood in silence for a while, watching a platypus appear on the opposite bank, gaze about in its near-sighted way, then slip into the river without so much as a ripple.

'Mr Darwin's jigsaw puzzle,' Henry offered good-humouredly.

'No, my friend, that would suggest design.'

Howitt chipped away at lava-shale and unearthed a perfectly preserved outline of a fern frond, caught in the act of unfurling. He carefully excavated around the fossil and brushed the loose soil from its face. After inspecting it closely, he handed it to his friend and watched Henry's face break into a look of wonder. It was exquisite; worth sending to Professor McCoy at Melbourne University. It might lead to another paper, something to make those academic geologists sit up and take notice.

'What do you see, Henry?'

Anderson traced the frond with his finger. 'Such perfection.'

They both looked at the specimen in the minister's hand. 'You see nothing else?'

Anderson sighed and handed back the fossil. 'I'm not the man of science that you are, Alfred. I collect to see the mystery of life, not to find fault with the Bible.'

Sometimes, Howitt wanted to shake his friend—and Liney too, for that matter—but not today. He suspected that part of being happy in this life was being agreeably deluded, and who was he to judge, he thought uncomfortably, having so recently been reminded of his failure to denounce McMillan, and his poor treatment of Welch. What he wouldn't admit to either Henry or Liney was that sometimes he felt like a blown egg.

ᔓ

In the late afternoon Howitt and Anderson rode through cleared country and into the McGenty's yard at Tabberabberra. Two men came out and hailed them in their soft Gaelic voices. The bachelor brothers ran an inn of sorts, where you could get a dry, if not always clean, bed, and a meal.

Rabbits hung from hooks by the fireplace waiting to be skinned, and although the house smelt of stale smoke and tobacco, the table was scrubbed and the room tidy. Soon Howitt and Anderson were sitting over tin plates piled high with a rich brown stew and potatoes freshly dug from the garden. A mug of grog was set before each man. Both knew the rules: that you paid for the meal, and offered a little extra, but not as payment for the grog, as the brothers didn't have a liquour licence. It was the sort of offence that Magistrate Howitt and Reverend Anderson easily overlooked. It wasn't that Howitt was a drinker now, but nor was he a strict teetotaler. He took a sip of the grog, not wishing to offend.

The McGenty brothers took their own meals out onto the verandah, and when Howitt and Anderson had finished eating, they lit their pipes and went out to join them, sitting on a bench with their backs against the cottage wall. Anderson asked the older McGenty brother—a big, shy man who spoke little English—to play his bagpipes. Agreeing, he retrieved the instrument from the cottage. The tartan bag was meticulously patched, two of the wooden stocks had split and were bound with greenhide, and the drone cords had been replaced with rope. McGenty stood with his back to the view, tucked the bag under his arm, closed his eyes and rested the fingers of his big hoary hands delicately on the holes of the chanter. His breath filled the bag, releasing an initial discordant noise through the drones. He steadied his breathing against the squeezing of the bag and played his fingers along the chanter to set free a tune of longing and loss that drifted out through the silent trees.

Howitt shifted uncomfortably on the bench as he remembered the first time he'd listened to Scottish music in the antipodes, from another epoch it could have been. All my devils coming home to roost, he thought cheerlessly.

The brother playing the bagpipes was lost in his music and it seemed to Howitt that the younger brother, who was staring out into the night, might be seeing a different countryside; wet and green, where the hills rose vertically and trapped the thick white clouds for days on end.

'Did you know Angus McMillan?' Howitt asked Henry in a whisper, so as not to disturb the pipes.

'Heard of him, never met him.' Henry puffed on his pipe, filling the air with the smell of sweet tobacco.

They sat listening to the music for a few moments. 'He found gold at Crooked River, after me, and much more of it,' Howitt offered. 'Started another rush. All his men deserted him. At Moroka River his horse rolled on him, injuring him badly. He got as far as Iguana Creek, south of here, almost spitting distance from Bairnsdale.' Howitt pointed in the general direction with the stem of his pipe. 'But he died at Gilleo's Hotel, penniless and alone after all that he'd had. I don't know where the money went. His wife couldn't afford to bury him, so a few of us chipped in.'

'There were stories about him,' Reverend Anderson mused. He stretched his legs out in front of him. 'Used to be passed around like dirty secrets. I never knew whether to believe them or not.'

Howitt grimaced in place of an answer, but Anderson wasn't looking at him. He was watching the bagpipes as they swelled and deflated under the player's arm.

'Anyway, it seems the stories have died with the man. He's on his way to becoming a pioneering hero.' Henry puffed on his pipe, his toe lightly tapping to the music.

'The blacks,' Howitt spoke cautiously, looking into the bowl of his own pipe. 'Died largely of disease.'

Reverend Anderson nodded.

‘And the battles between the tribes, their culture so broken down they fought and killed each other.’

‘That too.’ Anderson took a breath as if about to make a comment, but instead took another draw on his pipe.

‘McMillan was good to me, you know,’ Howitt said. ‘I think he must have spoken on my behalf, helped me secure the job of leader of the relief mission.’

Howitt rubbed his back against the rough timbers of the cottage wall and thought back to when Aitkin had come to see him, bringing him his first news of Welch. A good man, Aitkin; he’d travelled all the way to Omeo. They’d had lunch and Howitt had led him towards the courthouse, intending to show him around. But Aitkin had come with a purpose. He’d brought up McMillan as soon as they were out of Liney’s earshot.

‘I can’t get out of my mind what happened to them, especially now I work with the blacks. I think it should be called for what it was: massacre. Or murder.’ Aitkin had spoken the words evenly. ‘I think there should be an inquiry, even if no-one is brought to trial.’

Howitt had responded abruptly: ‘You can’t be serious. McMillan is a powerful man. Any hint of accusation or incrimination would end my career and see you off Ramahyuck before you could say corroboree.’

They had reached the courthouse but had paused on its steps.

‘I heard you had become chummy with McMillan.’ Aitkin had tried hard to keep his voice steady.

‘Neither of us can stop the tide of their extinction . . .’ But Howitt was, by that time, talking to Aitkin’s departing back.

The bagpipes released their final notes like a dying moan. The silence brought Howitt abruptly back to the present. That business with Aitkin had happened over a decade ago and still he felt the shame. Anderson clapped enthusiastically and Howitt joined in with a more desultory applause. His father’s battle cry had been to ‘Speak truth to power.’ How had he forgotten that? McGenty took a swig of grog and started on another haunting tune.

# Chapter 6

The racket of the birds signalled the coming day, even though it was still dark. Margaret must have lit the lamp in the scullery. Liney smiled, imagining how the birds might have woken suddenly, shouldering each other along the roost as the lamplight reached the trees. Quick, we've missed the dawn. First a solo, then a duet, then the bush-cracking chorus: enough noise to wake the dead. Breakfast birds, the locals called them; they were called laughing jackasses in Adelaide.

When the kookaburras stopped to draw breath, or realised the trick that had been played upon them, Liney could hear Margaret rattling the griddles in the stove. She'd be blowing her sour morning breath onto the flames to coax them into life and heat, her lank hair falling into her eyes. Then followed the clash of the kettle hitting the hob, the rattle of crockery and cutlery, and more laughter from the trees.

Liney yawned deeply. Five children. Five children, three milkers, a dozen chooks, four pigs, one goat (because cow's milk gave Annie hives), the dog, the cats, the pet magpie: all those living creatures dependent on her care. And Alfred. No wonder she was tired.

And yesterday, that awful disagreement with Mrs McLeod.

Liney rolled over in bed and looked out the window—the glass was mountain-stream clear compared with the wavering ocean she'd grown so fond of in the cottage in Omeo. A pearly light was seeping across the garden and home paddock, and more birds were joining the dawn chorus: untuneful individually, they collectively created a lively composition that seemed to offer encouragement for the day ahead. The back door slammed and Margaret came into view, buckets in hand, her footsteps leaving a trail on the dew-laden grass, on her way to the cows. She had matured into a solid, heavy-footed women, of few words and fewer smiles, but a good worker, none-the-less. Turk, Alfred's dog, came into view, and bounced along beside Margaret with a stick in his mouth. She paid the dog no heed.

The morning was cold. Liney pulled the blankets up to her chin and thought of her first months at Eastwood. It had been summer when they moved to the farm—how long ago? Charlton was nearly twelve now, so it must have been some ten years ago. Already hot at dawn, she would drag her tired body out of the tangle of clammy sheets and pull on her layers of clothes, all the time willing the morning sickness to stay down. While Margaret set about preparing the kitchen for the day, Liney would collect her pail and stool, and walk out into the steel-blue morning, the grass snapping beneath her feet. She'd been wary of the cow, of its bulk, despite its ruminating calmness, and would approach the animal tentatively, placing her hand on its rump so it would know to let down its milk. That much her neighbour Mrs Callaghan had taught her. It would take her half a morning to fill the bucket. The smell of the animal and the hot foaming milk made her stomach heave. When the nausea settled, or more often, when she'd been sick in the grass, she'd drop her head to her knees and cry. Cry for the wretchedness; for the shortness of money; for the loneliness when Alfred was away; for her mother who never visited to lend a hand; for the fact she had not a clue how to be a farmer's wife.

And yet, looking back, they were good years: the move from Omeo, the bigger house, and the birth of children without mishap. If she were to wish for a different life, she couldn't imagine what it might be. They had this magnificent piece of God's earth, so abundant in its yields most years. The Mitchell River Backwater wound like a protective arm around the property, and the air was so fresh after the smoke of Omeo and the stench of sewage when the wind was from the nor-east. She could no longer recall the fetid fumes that used to belch from the Nottingham factories. To the south of the farm, the township was a patch of buildings beyond the river, and the mountains rose blue and solid to the north. All that, and a good marriage, when all was said and done. She saw women doing heavy work that should be left to men; women turned tinder dry by poverty; women publicly belittled by their inebriated husbands. Alfred might not be a saint, but he was a gentle, trustworthy husband, a caring father, and a good provider; she knew her good fortune.

It was Tulaba, however—Alfred's man—who helped her most. Black as coal and good as gold: that's how she privately thought of him. In their second autumn at Eastwood, the pear trees that the previous owner had planted had borne so much fruit they'd had to use timber props to prevent the branches from breaking under their load. It was Tulaba who had brought her help for the picking and bottling. He appeared at the back door with three Brabrolong lubras from the river camp, each dressed in cast offs of faded cottons that did not fit any of them particularly well.

He told her their native names, and she shook her head. 'You,' she pointed to the youngest, a girl of about twelve, pretty in her scrawny, native way. 'You will be Esmay.' She pointed to the next, an older woman with a mass of curly hair. 'You will be Gladys.' The third was a woman in her early twenties, shyly standing behind the other two. 'And you will be Polly.' She stepped back as if to admire her work. 'Now, how do you like your new Christian names?' They glanced at each other and made no response.

'Do they speak English?' she asked Tulaba. He shrugged his shoulders: a little.

She gave them each a large basin and led them to the orchard, which was perhaps a rather grand name for what was then just a handful of trees surrounded by open paddocks. 'You must handle the fruit carefully so that it doesn't bruise,' she instructed. 'And pick only those that are this ripe.' She showed them a sample of what she needed. They poked their fingers gently at the fruit. The morning sun was already hot; they must work quickly while the fruit was still cool. 'Go on, go on,' she urged them, shooing them as she did the chooks, before walking away to the house.

Half an hour later she returned to the orchard. From a distance she could see the women lolling under one of the trees. When she came closer, she saw that they were eating pears. Around their heads buzzed clouds of flies frenzied by the sweet juices. The basins lay in the grass, empty.

'No, no,' she ran up to them in a rage. She grabbed a basin and pulled a pear from the tree. 'Like this,' she placed the pear in the basin. 'And this,' she tore another pear from its branch and added it to the basin, and another. The women watched her without emotion. The one Liney had named Gladys wiped her hands on the grass, slowly rose to her feet and held her hands out to help the other two. They started to pick the fruit.

'Faster.' Liney flapped her hands at them. 'Surely you can work faster than that.'

The girl she called Esmay held up the pear in her hand to show that it was unmarked and of perfect ripeness, and placed it with slow, infinite care into her basin.

Liney, almost in tears, swished her skirt around her and went off to find Tulaba. She brought him back. 'Tell them they must work faster.' But their basins were now brimming with the butter-brown fruit. Tulaba smiled at the women and turned to Liney with his hands open to her.

She caught Esmay's eye. The girl hung her head to hide her mirth.

'You cheeky girl.' Liney put her finger under the girl's chin and lifted her face to scold her. But the sudden flash of fear in the girl's eyes caught Liney by surprise and she quickly withdrew her hand. The girl dropped her head again and Liney had to stop herself from apologising. Her mother had instructed her during those rare moments of training in household management: 'Be fair but firm.' Well, that was her mother all over. 'Never let them think they are your equal,' she insisted. 'They'll only take advantage.'

And now here it was, another year and the last of the pears to be picked. Lying in bed, Liney imagined she could smell the cloying scent of windfall fruit, and could hear the drone of insects drawn to the juicy spoils. Each afternoon, the native women collected the fallen fruit, placing each pear gently in their gathered up skirts—even fruit that had been pecked by the birds—to carry back to their camp.

She did her best with her blacks. There were misunderstandings and sometimes disagreements, but they'd found a way—she and the native women—of working out where the line was drawn. She was proud of her supervision, but also knew she needed them, with so much work to be done around the home and the farm. She would never go as far as her neighbour Mrs McLeod, who locked up her gins in a tiny cell when she went out, the key swinging from a ring attached to the sash around her waist as if she were a gaol warden. The woman had instructed Liney not to let the blacks touch meat her family would consume, and only those vegetables and fruit that were to be thoroughly cooked. But instead, Liney had taught her charges to wash their hands and hold them out for her inspection before they prepared the meals. The demanding tasks were left to Margaret.

Yesterday, Mrs McLeod had dropped in for afternoon tea. Her broad, rough-skinned face bloomed with a purple bruise just below her right eye, which Liney made a point of not noticing. Her neighbour had told her in the most conversational way, with Liney bristling at every 'aint' and dropped aitch, how the previous evening she'd found a pan that had not been properly scoured. She was a great one for inspecting every nook and cranny of her scullery.

'So I took hold of that gin and pulled her over to a candle and held her hand over the flame until she begged for forgiveness. This morning she was all teary, and I told her she'd get more of the same if she didn't wipe the pout off her face and get to work. Great big watery blisters, there were, on her hand. Serve her right for being such a slattern.'

Liney had felt sickened. She pictured Alfred standing beside her, red faced and ready to explode: don't stand for their ignorance. He'd told her that, time and again.

'I don't think cruelty works,' Liney said quietly, fiddling with the handle of her teacup. 'It just makes them more rebellious, don't you find?'

Mrs McLeod had picked up a cookie and taken it half way to her mouth, but she put it down on her saucer and narrowed her eyes at Liney. 'You can't afford to give them an inch. Kindness would be wasted on them, or make them behave above their station.'

It wasn't so different from what her mother had advised, but coming from Mrs McLeod, it was loaded with loathing and ignorance that made Liney fume.

'You speak as if they were not human beings.' Liney's voice shook slightly.

Mrs McLeod stood up abruptly and looked about for her basket. Liney sat for a moment longer, then went to fetch the basket from the floor by the door. She held the door open as Mrs McLeod swept past, hat askew, head high as royalty.

Another neighbour offended. Liney sighed. She supposed she'd have to find a way to apologise, but not today. If only Alfred were here. He was so certain about these sorts of things, whereas she had not argued well, and then vented her spleen on the eggs. Mrs McLeod had brought a couple of duck eggs wrapped in newspaper. 'The only eggs for a sponge.' Liney mimicked aloud the woman's rough voice. After the neighbour had left, Liney had taken the eggs outside and thrown them at the shed wall. The yolks burst and oozed yellow and viscous down the planks and into the grass. The cats would find the mess so it wasn't a complete waste.

She glanced at the clock on the bedside table: five more minutes and she would have to get up. To take her mind off Mrs McLeod, she thought about the trees that now filled her beautiful orchard: the pears and pomegranates, apples, apricots, plums and citrus. In springtime, the orchard was a misty cloud of pink and white blossom; in summer and autumn, coloured fruits hung thickly like baubles. She even loved the twiggy bareness of the trees in winter, and then the daffodils bursting from the ground around their trunks to herald a new season.

There were also the vegetables, lined up like soldiers in the black silty soil. She was proud of her magic, the way she produced such bounty. Out of dirt and water and a handful of seeds she conjured all they needed and some besides that she gave to the natives. The pantry smelt of earthy potatoes and the shelves were crowded with bottles of jewel-coloured fruits and vegetables, marmalades and pickles. They represented her work, but also her care.

And the black women, she thought with a sigh, they too were in her care. She included them in her prayers each night, that God grant her patience, and the strength to teach them Jesus' love. They came at the end of her prayers, after she'd prayed for the safety and health and happiness of her children, for rain and good crops, for family all so far away, and, especially, most fervently, for Alfred, that he find his way back to God.

She'd written a special prayer for him, with Reverend Anderson's help. They had sat together through a long, wet afternoon when Alfred was away and she was particularly gloomy. Henry ate his way through a whole pound cake while she told him more than she meant to, feeling the prick of disloyalty even as the words left her mouth. Henry had nodded and munched, and then taken a small notebook and pencil from his pocket to craft the prayer. She had since edited it back to something that might be achievable. *Dear God, please save Alfred from his curiosity; let him not question that You created the world and all that is in it; please God, don't let him lose his way.* She kept the prayer close at hand in her Bible, along with Agnes Soo Long's slip of rice paper with the cryptic message that she had never been able to decipher. But she never again asked Henry for advice.

The rising sun was burning off the dew and a misty halo hovered over the grass: it would be a glorious day. From the bedroom window, she could see the garden with its autumn flowerings. The dahlias in front of her window were too garish, she now realised, for this mellow time of year; their bright reds and yellows belonged to the brasher days of summer. But the pink and white salvias melted into the soft morning light, and the windbreak poplars were clothed in leaves the colour of butter.

Beyond the garden lay the farm. They had a lot of land now, gradually acquiring more acres, all of which had come under her care. Alfred, gone to the towns up around Dargo this time, had been away four times in the past six months on magistrate rounds, each time for weeks on end. Despite his cheerful words over his shoulder as he rode away, the farm work could not be put on hold for his return. The land was like another living creature, demanding and impatient. She'd learnt so much; what couldn't she do? She couldn't shoe a horse, or shear a sheep, or round up cattle, but that was about the extent of it. She could probably round up cattle if she had to.

She recalled the first time he'd left her alone at Eastwood. 'How long will you be gone?' she had asked him, alarmed at the idea of his absence. Their cottage was surrounded by so much empty space in those early days. She was in the early months of pregnancy with their second child, her friend Agnes Soo Long still lived in Omeo, and she had only the sullen Margaret for company. It was before she'd come to rely on Tulaba, when she still felt uneasy about the blacks in the camp further along the Backwater. The closest white neighbour was over a mile away.

'About a fortnight. Not long.' He didn't look up from the papers he was sorting through on his desk. 'I've asked Reverend Anderson to call on you from time to time. He's good company.'

'He won't help with the milking though, will he?' she said crossly. He turned a worried face to her, which made her feel ashamed. 'It's all right, Alfred. I'll manage.' She understood, better than him, how much they relied on his wages.

He'd kissed her warmly before swinging up into his saddle. She'd stood at the gate, one arm raised in farewell, the other lying protectively over her belly. Alfred hadn't even turned around, his mind having already fled Eastwood. He'd always be an explorer—she'd come to realise that years ago. It was as if the time he spent in the desert, searching for Burke and Wills, had cast a spell on him that he would never shake off. Rider and horse disappeared into the hazy summer light: a centaur, she had thought watching him go; a man who belonged on his horse.

With a sigh she rose and sat on the side of the bed, shuffling her feet about on the mat until she found her slippers, her mind returning to Mrs McLeod. The problem was that most people agreed with the woman. Even the ladies at the church guild said the most unchristian things about the blacks. Mavis Carmichael didn't have any blacks in service but that didn't stop her passing judgement. She was another gossip, that Mavis. Would they call her a nigger lover? Liney had heard the term used often enough. Or a traitor? Did she care?

As she washed and dressed she thought of the day to come. Gladys and Polly, who were such good workers now, would do the laundry. Esmay would pick fruit and keep an eye on the youngest children. Margaret would take the buggy into town to buy groceries—Liney made a mental note to write a list—and pick up the stock feed Tulaba needed. Charlton would have to be nagged to fill the water cistern and bring in the firewood. There would be butter to make; if she made it early, the girl—Margaret had really long been a woman—could take it into town. And a hen would have to be slaughtered for dinner. She would do that, too. The cold water on her face dashed away some of the tiredness.

Sitting down at her dressing table, Liney looked at her face in the mirror, grimacing at what she saw. She picked up her hairbrush and pulled it through her hair—once so richly auburn but now the colour of dried leaves with grey streaks. Laying the brush down again, Liney looked at the blotches and scratches on the back of her hand and turned it over so that it was face up. With the forefinger of her other hand, she traced the lifeline that ran across her palm. It was a bold, deep crease, a line that told of determination and resilience. But how far along the line, she wondered, was this moment in time? She followed it to its end and her finger ran off the edge of her palm. Alfred's parents had turned to spiritualism to seek answers: all that mumbo-jumbo started by the Fox sisters in America, who claimed to have made contact with spirits from the afterlife. The creed had taken off like wildfire, even in Australia: mediums and clairvoyants, séances, mesmerism and hypnotism, faith healing and levitation, claims of multiple heavens and multiple hells. As if one of each wasn't sufficient to deal with. Her parents-in-law, she understood, were probably attracted by the informality of the movement and the fact that the spirits were reputedly sympathetic with the Quaker testimony of equality for all humans.

The previous year, a 'trance lecturer' had come to Bairnsdale and Liney would have liked to hear her speak just to know what all the fuss was about, but Alfred would not see money wasted on frauds. Liney wondered what it would be like to have definite answers to contradict her husband's incredulity. She sighed as she twisted the long tress of hair into a bun at the back of her neck, pushed in pins to hold it in place and rose to start the day.

᠅

After breakfast, as Margaret cleared the dishes and scrubbed the table, Liney set her other workers to their various tasks and went down to the dairy to churn the butter. It was her favourite place, because it felt like hers alone. Alfred had promised to build the dairy years ago after she had wept copiously over a batch of butter gone rancid with the heat. Initially full of enthusiasm for his project, he had sketched designs at the breakfast table, letting his porridge go cold while he shared his ideas with her. Then he'd wandered off into his study 'just to check something' and hadn't emerged until she called him for lunch. She had banged the rolling pin on the table as she rolled out pastry, and slammed the kettle on the stove. Margaret kept out of her way; even Turk the dog, usually asleep on the backdoor mat, had slunk away. When she took his morning tea to his desk and set it down so hard that the tea slopped into the saucer, he barely looked up, just grunted what might have been a thank you. She looked at the book he was reading: Lyell's *Principles of Geology*. Of course! After lunch he had put on his coat and hat and set off for the courthouse. 'Don't worry,' he'd said, mildly annoyed, as he stepped out the front door, 'it will be built.'

Eventually, Tulaba had taken the building in hand. He excavated into the slope that led down to the riverbank, retaining the exposed earth with beams cut from gum trees. He built timber walls and lined them with hessian, and crafted a roof of shingles. He left an open vent above the back wall, like a chimney, so that the air that swept up from the Backwater was drawn through the dairy, keeping it cool, even in summer.

The shingles and timber walls were now weathered to a silver-grey and the hessian fibres held a permanent sour-milk smell. Liney lifted her face from the churn to let the cool river air flow over her hot skin and rolled her shoulders to ease the ache that always came from continuously pounding the paddle up and down. From the doorway she could see the children playing in front of the dairy. Beyond, the fence and gate to the Backwater kept them in check. Gilbert and Maudie, the youngest children, were playing together, pretending to be horses; Annie, the middle child, was lining up her dolls for tea. And May, the second-born, was, as usual, in her own world, poking a stick about in the garden to find creatures to examine under her father's microscope.

There was a family of ducks waddling along the bank on the far side of the garden fence: two adults and six ducklings in a neat row. They made families look so easy.

When the butter was made and cut into creamy yellow blocks, the buttermilk put to one side for cake baking, and the dairy scrubbed clean, she returned to the house, calling to the children to join Esmay in the orchard. May ran ahead, and Liney watched as Esmay stopped picking fruit to see what May held out to her, their heads together as they earnestly discussed May's find. It would be a ladybird beetle, or a witchetty grub, or a grasshopper, or some such. It never mattered: life in any form fascinated May. Esmay, Liney knew, would be telling May some story about whatever creature she held in her hand. Esmay was happiest playing with the children: teaching them to imitate the calls of birds, to identify tracks in the dusty earth, to hop like a kangaroo. The children laughed and clapped their hands. 'Show us again,' and she'd hop about. It was funny, but there was dignity in it, too.

She was quick and clever—Liney had found it easy to teach her to read and write—but she could also try the patience of a saint. Only yesterday Liney had to scold her because Esmay could not take seriously the need to sweep into the corners of every room. In frustration, Liney had grabbed the broom and swept furiously, showing her how to do the job properly. 'You's sweating, Missus,' Esmay laughed behind her hand, causing Liney to sweep all the more vigorously. The dust rose and settled on the furniture.

Liney collected the axe from the shed and laid it in the grass beside the block, then went to select a suitable hen. Turk followed close behind. When she closed the door of the coop behind her the hens rushed up to her and pecked around her feet and at her skirt. Outside, Turk ran up and down, his nose to the chicken wire, barking and wagging his tail. The chooks were like people, each with their own personalities: bully, leader, slinker, hen-pecked. She had to resist giving them names because it made eating them so much harder.

From the middle of the crowd she picked out a three-year-old bird that she knew was going off the lay and caught it by the feet. Hanging upside down, the hen squawked and flapped for a few moments, then subsided into silence as if already dead. She stepped back out of the coop, carefully closing the door. Turk pushed his nose into the chook bringing it back to life again with more squawking.

Liney tucked the bird under her arm to free her hands. 'Come here, Turk,' she said. The dog, knowing the fun was over, put his tail between his legs and head down, allowing himself to be chained up to a post by the shed.

The hen once again hung limp in her hand. She wished they wouldn't be so easily taken to their death. The bird allowed itself to be laid out with its neck extended over the block. Liney quickly grabbed the axe and in one swoop, chopped off the hen's head. Only now did the protest begin. The headless bird flapped its wings madly, racing about in circles until it ran into the shed wall, just out of Turk's reach, and keeled over. A low keening from the shadows of the nearby peppermint tree told Liney that Esmay had been watching. The children were still at their games.

'For heaven's sake, girl, you've seen it done a hundred times.' Liney wiped the axe blade on the grass.

The girl stood with her arms held tight across her chest, rocking her body.

'It's no different from what you do to a goanna. Why is a hen so different?'

Esmay wriggled her fingers, racing them about in circles, her eyes following her hand, wide with horror. Then she turned and ran away.

Liney sighed, picked up the hen by its feet and took it into the kitchen where Margaret had set a pot of water to boil. She dunked the headless bird in the water to scald it, then lifted it out and laid it on the kitchen bench. When it was cool enough to handle, she rubbed her hand up and down the carcass to remove the feathers. The downy under-feathers clung to her fingers and stuck to her sleeves and apron. They even stuck to her face when she wiped the sweat away. She dipped the naked bird into the boiling water again, and laid it on the bench, covered with a tea towel, ready for Margaret to prepare and roast when she returned from town. She would instruct Esmay to clean up the mess of feathers.

Tulaba had left a wheelbarrow full of cow manure by the rose bed at the side of the house and after lunch, Liney took her trowel and started weeding. The children followed her to play. Charlton, having finished his chores, joined them this time and was showing his young brother how to set a hoop in motion and keep it rolling with the aid of a stick.

The soil was rich, black river silt that went down forever. Everything Liney planted grew dense and luxurious, but so did the weeds. The couch grass they had planted, selected to survive the droughts, sent its roots deep into the soil, and long runners sent up shoots to invade the garden beds. The shoots held on with all their might when she tried to pull them out.

She sat back on her heels on the edge of the garden to

watch as Margaret drove up the driveway, met by Tulaba who unloaded the cart. Beyond them, Gladys and Polly were taking the washing from the line. They both wore old cotton dresses that had once been hers, standing bare-foot in the cool grass with the blue sky around their heads. The older woman, Gladys, lifted a corner of a white sheet and held it against her dark mouth to test if it was dry enough to be taken from the line, yet still damp enough for ironing. I taught her that, Liney thought. Gladys must have sensed her watching. She turned around and smiled and waved, then bent down to lift the heavy laundry basket onto her hip.

The autumn sunshine was warm and Liney wiped the sweat from her brow with a dirty hand before returning to her weeding. Yellow-breasted robins hopped about her, waiting for worms unearthed by her trowel. Turk, off his chain again, slept at her side chasing rabbits in his sleep: legs, tail and eyelids twitching madly. 'You're a fickle creature,' she said to the sleeping dog. 'Happy to be with me now, but you'll desert me the moment your master returns.' She ran her hand over the chocolate-brown coat and the dog's body relaxed.

Annie and Maudie started to squabble, arguing over who would be Mother.

'I'm the oldest,' Annie told her sister haughtily. Maudie gave her a push and Annie returned with a stronger shove that sent her sister toppling into the garden.

Liney stood up and brushed soil from her apron as she walked towards the girls. 'Annie,' she rebuked her while looking about for Esmay who, having unwillingly cleaned the kitchen, was supposed to be watching the children. Maudie was howling for all she was worth. Liney picked her up to soothe her while she spoke crossly to Annie. 'You stand right there, young lady,' and in the next breath, in exasperation, called: 'Esmay, where are you?' She wiped Maudie's eyes and nose, and telling the child she wasn't hurt and had nothing to cry about, set her down on the grass and fetched a couple of toys. She then took hold of Annie's hand and towed her towards the house, still looking about for Esmay. That lazy girl would be hiding somewhere, asking her ancestors to find the chook and reconnect its spirit head to its spirit body.

Even so, when Liney returned to the garden having sent Annie to her room, she expected to see Esmay comforting Maudie. Neither was in sight. She looked about and saw the gate open, the one in the garden fence that led down to the river. The gate she always insisted remained closed. She turned about: Gilbert was there, still enthralled by Charlton's hoop, and May, but no sign of Maudie. She lifted her skirt and ran through the gate and down to the water's edge, calling Maudie's name.

The ducklings, placidly foraging in the grass, took fright and waddled rapidly towards the water, quickly becoming camouflaged by the mottled green light on the surface. The drake followed the ducklings, but the mother duck hung back, dragging its body along the ground and flapping its wings. When Liney paid it no heed it moved closer and made shrill calls of distress, dragging a wing along the ground as if it were broken. Liney ran away from it, along the bank, the duck lifting into the air and flying to its brood still paddling frantically across the water.

This could not be happening. She tried to tell herself nothing bad had happened. She forced herself to slow down, to think. Where might Maudie be? Just because the gate was open . . . Liney heard a splash that made her spin around. A swan had landed on the river; circles of rippling water were spreading out towards the banks. She took great gulping breaths, her eyes roving across the water's surface. The river ran slow and silent; the family of ducks had found shelter in the reeds on the opposite side.

She picked up her skirt again and ran further along the bank to where a row of young willows trailed their branches across the surface of the water. She slashed the branches aside and looked deep into the dark, slick water. Running further along she tripped over a tree root and put her arm out to save herself, catching her sleeve on a branch and tearing the fabric.

Please, dear God. Please, dear God. She ran along the bank

in the opposite direction, to a place where Alfred had tied a long rope to a branch so that the older children could swing out over the river. She looked under the jetty and disturbed a black snake. A snake, she thought with horror.

She realised someone was calling her name and looked back towards the house. Esmay was at the gate with Maudie on her hip, waving her free arm.

'You lazy gin, where were you?' Liney started to berate Esmay as she ran towards her. When she reached Esmay, she wrenched Maudie from the girl's arms and held her child tightly. 'Why was the gate open?' Liney spoke between gasps, trying to catch her breath. Maudie began to cry. 'Hush,' she told the child curtly and turned back to Esmay who kept her head lowered and refused to answer Liney's question. 'You hopeless, unreliable darkie . . .'

'Maudie's safe.' Esmay spoke grumpily so that it took Liney all her willpower not to hit her. Instead she sent her to sit with the hens in the coop. Half an hour of terror would serve her right. 'And stay there until I say you can leave.' She glared at Esmay's back as the girl dragged her feet towards the hen house. At the coop door, she stopped and looked back at Liney, probably hoping for a reprieve, but Liney waved her in.

Maudie put her finger in the tear of her mother's sleeve and made the hole bigger. Liney swatted her hand away and the child started to scream. 'Oh, Lord in heaven.'

She walked up and down the lawn shushing the child in her arms until the crying turned to hiccups, then sat her on the ground with her toys and went back to her gardening.

Liney's hands shook as she shoveled cow manure from the wheelbarrow and tossed it around the base of the roses, so roughly that most of it got caught in the thorny branches making the end-of-season bushes look even more bedraggled. Maudie had come to sit by her with her small watering can and was making patty cakes with the manure, trying to feed them to the dog. Turk turned his head this way and that, as far as possible, to avoid her offers. The child was filthy, with dirty trails down her cheeks where her tears had been. I'm no better myself, Liney thought, feeling the damp patches under her arms that would have made dark half-moons on her dress.

Suddenly Turk pricked his ears; he gave a bark and ran off, almost knocking Maudie over. It could mean only one thing. And here am I, smelling like a cow paddock.

'Quickly, your father is home,' she called to the other children. They dropped their various games and raced away to meet him, disappearing around the side of the house in Turk's wake. Annie ran out of the house, letting the door slam.

'Annie,' Liney scolded the girl, but this time there was no anger in her voice. She wiped her hands on her apron and gathered up loose strands of hair, coiling them quickly into the bun at the nape of her neck, just as Alfred strode around the corner of the house, Gilbert on his shoulders, Turk and the girls bouncing alongside, Charlton trailing behind. Liney caught her breath: he looked more like a bushranger than the burgher he was supposed to be.

'Do hush May,' Liney said as she walked to meet her husband, gently chiding her daughter whose questions rained on her father like hailstones. Alfred placed Gilbert on the ground and put his arm around Liney's shoulders, gave her a squeeze and kissed her cheek. She breathed in his smell of horse, stale sweat and earthy clothes.

'Your horses, father,' Charlton spoke hesitantly. 'I could see to them if you wish me to.'

'It's all right. Tulaba will do that.'

Liney felt a stab in her heart. 'I'm sure Tulaba would be grateful if you gave him a hand.' She tussled Charlton's dark curls before the boy sprinted off. She always felt vaguely uncomfortable about Alfred's returns, at the need to reopen the space that had closed over in his absence. 'Maudie's awfully grubby,' she apologised as Alfred lifted his small daughter into his arms. She looked to see the state of the other children, as if they were the measure of how well she had managed in his absence.

He snuffled into Maudie's neck and took a deep breath. 'Phew. 'You're not a little girl, you're a poddy calf.' Annie sidled up to her father, putting her arms around one of his legs and he patted her head.

He lent across the children to Liney. 'I missed you,' he whispered into her ear.

'Mother, mother,' May pulled on Liney's sleeve. 'You forgot about Esmay. She's still in the chicken coop.'

'Don't ask,' she warned Alfred when he looked enquiringly at her. 'Go and tell her to help Margaret in the kitchen. Remind her to wash first,' she directed May, but vaguely. She felt nonplussed, suddenly aghast at her own capacity for cruelty. Was she her father's daughter in temperament as well as blood? Alfred set Maudie back on her feet and knelt down, one hand caressing Turk's head, the other on Annie's shoulder as she showed him the cat's scratch on her arm.

Liney could imagine Esmay's terror; it only took the memory of a horse raking the air with its raised hoofs, her father yelling at her. She would make it up to the girl, in some small way.

---

A tiny fist held tightly shut: that's what the fossil looked like; a fern frond on the point of opening. 'Perhaps a million years ago,' Alfred explained, cradling the rock in his hand. The children sat around the large deal table in the kitchen, now scattered with bits and pieces from Alfred's pockets: seed pods, a tiny bird's skull, leaves dried to pink and mauve, a rock with specks of fools gold. He ran his thumb over the polished surface of a river pebble, as unblemished as his children's flesh, then put it down and picked up another stone of black and white speckles.

May, thin and serious, her fringe falling into her eyes, examined a rock bearing a fossil that looked like a worm, tracing the raised pattern with her finger. 'That's for you,' her father told her. Liney, sitting across the table from him, inwardly sighed. She didn't believe in having a favourite amongst the children, but May was the apple of Alfred's eye. They were so similar in temperament—equally curious and quick—which was fine for Alfred but goodness knows what it meant for May's future.

Charlton picked up a small animal thighbone marked with patterns. 'That,' Alfred explained, 'was given to me by an old Brayakaulung man. It's meant to have secret powers.'

'I wish you wouldn't bring these things into the house,' Liney complained. But what a losing battle that was. He winked at the children and they grinned conspiratorially.

He had walnuts, too, that he had gathered from amongst the fallen autumn leaves in Dargo. He sent Charlton to fetch the hammer while he pushed his collection to one end of the table, and Liney laid out newspaper. Margaret stamped into the kitchen bearing a basin of just-picked peas. She grumbled that her table was not her own, and where was she to prepare the vegetables. 'That chicken smells wonderful,' Alfred assured her. The roasting bird, spitting and spluttering in the oven, filled the kitchen with a rich aroma.

'Well,' Margaret replied, 'You had better not spoil your appetites with those there nuts.'

Seated around the table again, the children listened as their father told them tales of his journey and cracked open the shells, distributing the kernels between them. From time to time he passed a whole walnut under the table to Turk who sat panting at his feet. The dog dropped down with the nut between his front paws and crunched the shell, leaving bits all over the floor.

Amongst the nuts was a boat-shaped pod. He held it out in his hand to show them. Liney, standing with her arms crossed, observed her husband's dirt-engrained hand, the fingernails that needed cutting.

'The seedpod of a Kurrajong tree on the upper Mitchell River,' Alfred said. 'That's where I met up with Bunjil Bottle and Master Turnmile, two Kurnai men. They took me in a bark canoe, what they called their *gri*, up the river. That canoe was no triumph of naval architecture, but it floated well enough and Master Turnmile made it slip through the water, paddling with a square of bark in each hand that he called *wraeel.*

May leaned her elbows on the table and rested her chin in her hands, waiting for the story she knew would follow. The other children leaned in around their father, also enthralled. Alfred ran the seedpod along the tabletop, a canoe making its smooth passage along a quickly flowing river. Liney turned her back on the story and stood at the kitchen bench to help Margaret pod peas.

'We turned into Dead Cock Creek and it was like entering a long green tunnel, the lilly-pillies were so dense and dark. After a few miles we dragged the canoe ashore and, on our hands and knees, crawled behind a rushing waterfall, a *doogooroo*, into a mysterious cave.' His voice took on a ghost story-telling timbre; the children were mesmerised. Liney turned to admonish him, but he and the children were bathed in the last of the afternoon's sunbeams coming through the kitchen window, making even Alfred look too angelic to scold.

'We climbed over a flowstone and found a still pool of black water that soaked up our whispers. Stalactites glowed faintly in the eerie half-light, like long gnarled fingers reaching down to grab us. We heard a low murmuring, like a moan, coming from the depths of the cave and Master Turnmile grabbed the sleeve of my coat; I could hear his teeth chattering in my ear. I kept my back to the damp cave wall, trying to peer into the dimness. Bunjil Bottle whispered to me that it was the Narguna.' He stopped and looked around at the children. 'We were in the Narguna's den. His *nrung*.'

'You might at least speak English,' Liney scolded, over her shoulder, forcing peas from their shell.

'What's a Narguna?' Annie whispered.

'The Narguna,' he said, lowering his voice as if the monster might hear him, 'is a wicked ogre that haunts the valley of the Mitchell. It is a loathsome stony creature, all lumps and bumps and rocky edges—*Wallung* the natives say—with a human breast and human arms and hands. Hands to snatch small children who wander unawares into its den.'

He beat his hand on the table and the children jumped. Liney turned around again and he caught her eye. Before she could complain, he gave her his best winning smile. She shook her head, her mouth a straight line.

'Did you have your rifle, father?' Charlton asked.

'No point. If you fire a bullet, or throw a spear or a boomerang, the Narguna will turn your weapon back on you.'

'Did you see it?' May asked wistfully, as if she wished she had been there.

'I felt something grip my heart and I heard its heavy footsteps coming towards us.' He banged his hands on the table in a slow measured beat. Liney tut-tutted and shook her head. 'I could feel its power, trying to drag me into the depths of the *nrung*. I clung to a rock.' He grasped the side of Annie's chair. 'Hand over hand over the rocks we dragged ourselves away from the evil force, back to the cave entrance, and fled. Bunjil Bottle and Master Turnmile had that canoe, their *gri*, back in the water before you could say Jack Robinson.'

'Alfred,' Liney snapped, turning to glare at him. 'Your father is very naughty to bring silly stories home with him.' Liney and Alfred looked at each other over the children's heads. And you children, she might have added, you're as bad as Turk: you only have eyes for your father when he's home. When you have nightmares tonight, though, it will be me you call for.

'I brought something back for your mother,' he told the children, getting up from his chair so he could reach into his trouser pocket. He produced seeds in a twist of paper. '*Acmena smithii*,' he informed them, 'Otherwise known as lilly-pillies. They'll make a good thick hedge.' Liney looked doubtful. 'No, really. Glossy leaves, fragrant white flowers and purple berries. The birds love them. And they'll block the sou-westerlies that you say make you scatty.' He placed the seeds in Liney's hand.

And who will plant this hedge, she wondered, looking down at his gift.

Later in the evening, when the children had been put to bed, their prayers heard and their candles extinguished, they stood together in the kitchen, and he held her face in his hands. He ran his thumbs over the dark circles under her eyes. 'Tell me the news: what you've been up to. How the children have behaved; how the hops are ripening; what letters you've received from Home. I'll make us tea.' He had bathed and changed into clean clothes, and she had trimmed his hair and beard. He was her Alfred again.

'What, billy tea with eucalyptus leaves? I doubt you remember about kettles and cups and saucers.' But her voice was happy as she lifted the boiling kettle from the hob and filled the teapot.

She turned back to him, her eyes sparkling, remembering. 'I was at the McPhersons when they were rounding up the turkeys. It was the funniest thing. There were hundreds of them, turkeys I mean; they herded them through tar so that their feet would survive the walk all the way to Port Albert where they put them on a boat for the Melbourne market.'

'So now you want turkeys at Eastwood?' he asked her, amused.

'Oh no, they're so stupid.' She swirled the pot in her hand and set it on the table. 'Young Samuel had to go ahead scattering corn on the track. They'd only gone a hundred yards or so when the sun went in behind a cloud and the turkeys thought it was dusk. Those silly birds flew up into the trees to roost. The dogs were barking madly around the trunks and Bert McPherson was raging up and down, flicking his streamers at them, his face turning puce. There were so many birds on one branch it broke and sent them squawking and flapping to the ground.' She wiped the corner of her eye with her sleeve. 'Then the sun came out and they set off again at a trot, making the most unholy noise. Just think, having to put up with that all the way to Port Albert.'

'They'll be weeks on the road. And Bert's not the happiest man at the best of times.' Alfred chortled, sitting down at the table and letting Liney pour his tea.

'Peggy tried so hard not to laugh when the turkeys fell out of the tree. You could tell she wasn't sorry to see him go.' Liney caught the look on his face and put her hand on his arm. 'It's lovely to have you home.'

# Chapter 7

Each year, the heat of the sun shrank the slab walls of the oast house, leaving gaps that had to be covered before the new-year's firing. Howitt was standing on a ladder, the sound of his hammering ringing through the clear air. From the corner of his eye he saw Tulaba coming up the bank from the Backwater. The native's silent, barefoot steps could still send a shiver through Howitt.

Tulaba shielded his eyes against the sun as he looked up at Howitt. 'Boss, come to tell you I'll be going away on Sunday business.'

'Those hops aren't far off from harvesting,' Howitt responded, looking down on his man from his great height and waving an arm towards the river flats where the vines swayed greenly on their tall poles. They both knew that the hops would be long in before the *Jeraeil* began. It took months of exchanged message sticks to called the tribes together.

'A big ceremony, Tulaba? Initiation?' Howitt asked as he made his way down the ladder. He could feel his pulse quickening.

On his last ride to Gelantipy, the flooded river at Buchan had caused him to take a higher trail through the back of the town, past the timber mill that filled the air with the sharp resin smell of newly cut timber and sweet smoke from burning sawdust. As the handful of timber millers' cottages petered out, the track narrowed to a path that wound between straight-trunked trees. The trees came to an abrupt end and he found himself in a clearing: a circular rut worn into the ground. He'd heard of these bora circles but had never before seen one. He dismounted and walked around the mound that marked the circumference of the great ring. It was an arena with two openings like stage wings, but hollowed in the centre, pounded down, he thought, by centuries of stamping feet. Its mystery had rekindled a long-held desire to witness that ceremonial dancing, and all that took place within the secret circle. The idea of attending a *Jeraeil* had stayed with him like an itch, but as a white man—an uninitiated white man—there seemed to be no chance. The practice was dying fast; he hadn't heard of a *Jeraeil* being held in seven or eight years. But that only intensified his desire to capture the wealth of cultural information such an event would reveal. What a contribution to science it would make.

'Any chance that I might go with you?' He tried to keep his voice casual. Tulaba was a respected elder of the Brabrolong tribe. He had belonged to his father's brother, Bruthenmunjie, the last great *Gommera* before the coming of the whites. As well as the work he did around the farm, Tulaba was Howitt's main informant on tribal customs.

Welch had written to him recently; it was an odd letter from that odd cove, full of praise for his work on native customs and Cainozoic rocks. Welch had finished with an offer to publish any article Howitt might care to send him. His work would add prestige to the newspaper's reputation, which, Welch claimed modestly, was already considerable. If the offer was genuine, he might use Welch to disseminate his ideas to the general public. It would be a fine thing to be publishing beyond the closed circle of academics and serious amateurs.

The paper Howitt considered submitting was titled *Native Witchcraft and Sorcery*, a topic with popular appeal, he thought. It was a starting point from which he could work up to the more complex—and provocative—customs of the Aborigines, which most people found difficult to fathom or believe. The witchcraft information he'd learned mostly from Tulaba. The native was like a vast lode of ancient knowledge waiting to be mined, and Howitt considered himself the miner. He extracted the stories and stored them away for safe keeping into the future.

But now the old man was wrinkling his brow, as if the prospect of a white man at their ceremony was distasteful.

'What you want to come for?' Tulaba fingered the buttons

on his shirt, which was one of his boss's castoffs.

'I'm interested to see what you do. To understand more about your witchcraft. No cause for you to be *dyinagan*. Certainly, I'm not afraid of your *baan*.' But he was afraid of his own desperation to attend. He worked at keeping his face passive.

Tulaba would only say that he would talk to the other elders, but said it in such a way that suggested he had no intention of talking to anyone about his boss's request.

'You have my word, my *kanti*, that I will use what I learn for the good, the *launman*, of your people.' Tulaba merely nodded and walked away. Howitt glared at his back, wanting to command him to stop, to turn around and promise to do what his boss was asking.

Patience was needed, and Howitt waited a week. Tulaba came to him from time to time about farm matters, but did not mention the *Jeraeil*. Through the night, he'd lain awake, Liney complaining about his tossing and turning, working out a scheme. Attending a *Jeraeil* was the opportunity to fill the biggest blank space in his research. Darwin's theory of the survival of the fittest hung like an axe over Howitt's work, aware as he was that the blacks would soon die out and with their extinction would go all their ancient ways. Thoughts of extinction made him uncomfortable, recalling his own complicity when he'd discovered the bones on the Dargo River. The memory had formed an inerasable watermark on his mind, but it did not prevent him from finally devising a plan. It gave him some cause for disquiet, but there was a more important issue at stake.

The following day he rode to Tom's Creek. The main road was deserted apart from the occasional buggy or rider. Ahead, he could see clouds massing in the west, foretelling a storm, but the sky above him was clear and he rode through alternate pools of light and deep shade cast by trees. In the paddocks beyond, farmers were scything their crops and building stooks. When Howitt reached the Tom's Creek bridge, he dismounted and walked along the bank through low scrub and late-flowering wattle. The creek ran narrow at this point, with water spooling into deep holes in the centre. After about a quarter of a mile's walk Howitt saw the small spiral of smoke he'd been hoping for. He looped the reins around a branch of a wattle tree and left his horse to graze. Soon he could make out Turlburn, alone as usual, wearing his red postman's jacket. The old man raised his hand in greeting and Howitt squatted at his side by the fire. They had met like this many times: after Tulaba, Turlburn was Howitt's best informant on Aboriginal customs.

The wind had strengthened and clouds dark and flat as slate filled the sky, turning the light a dirty yellow. There would be a storm, Howitt thought. From the strength of the wind he calculated that the front would hit Bairnsdale by mid-afternoon. He would have to be quick.

'I've brought you some tobacco, Long Harry.' He handed over a small pouch and they sat in silence while Turlburn pulled apart the strands of tobacco and packed his clay pipe. Howitt picked up a small burning branch from the fire and handed it to the native. Together, they sat in silence and watched a pair of long-legged moorhens scratching about in the reeds along the riverbank. Turlburn pointed to a kingfisher: a sapphire and fire-opal jewel that shone out against the drab bush. The bird sat motionless on a low limb, watching the water. Suddenly it dived, making a small splash, emerged with a writhing fish and darted back to its perch.

'*Wudhur warngun*,' Turlburn said quietly, describing the quick action of the predator bird.

Howitt took a deep breath. 'Tulaba tells me there's to be big Sunday business soon.' The old man nodded, not taking his eyes from the kingfisher.

Howitt stroked his beard, trying to look deep in thought, waiting for the man to respond.

'Tell me about the *Turndun*, Long Harry. What's its secret?'

The old man looked at Howitt sharply, frightened, and shook his head vigorously.

'Just between us, *werna*.' A fish jumped close by, making a soft plopping noise and leaving rings on the surface, but the kingfisher remained motionless.

The old man poked a stick at the fire making the flames leap. From time to time he snuck a sideways look at Howitt, as if hoping he had disappeared. Howitt waited, but he felt a sense of panic rising in his throat. He took another deep breath.

'Your fishing line?' he asked Turlburn, pointing to a stick dug into the bank from which a string hung slackly into the creek. 'Good fishing today?'

Turlburn shook his head. Another long silence followed, Howitt's impatience mounting.

'Remember that time, Long Harry, when you were *muraty* with the sweating fever? Remember how I brought you medicine?' Howitt watched the old man's profile closely.

'Not sick. *Brewin. Mulla-mullung* scare away, better than *loon* magic. Him *dhadyan*, clever man.' Turlburn grumbled, shaking his head.

'Remember, *gullendan*, when you were having trouble with your *bulamirnda's* brother and I sorted it out for you?'

'Him a *tinban* man. No good.' He laid his pipe on the ground as if he had lost interest in it.

'Yes, but it was me who settled the disagreement.' This wasn't going as planned. Howitt picked up a stone and tossed it at one of the moorhens, which shrieked and hurled itself towards the water. The kingfisher took flight.

Turlburn hung his head lower and fiddled with the buttons on his postman's jacket. Suddenly the fishing line went taught and he sprang to his feet. He hauled ashore a good-sized perch, but he left both fish and line on the bank. He turned and looked down at Howitt for an uncomfortable minute of silence, then beckoned to the white man to follow him into the dense black-wattle bush behind them. *'Bugdee budgee mul,'* Turlburn hurried him. Howitt rose immediately to his feet and followed the man. Turlburn let him pass, his eyes darting around, and he gave Howitt a small shove to push him further into the scrub.

The first drops of rain made the leaves tremble and released the smell of dust. Lightning forked across the black sky, followed by rolling thunder. Turlburn looked up at the sky and then at Howitt. He was sweating, running the palms of his hands up and down his trouser legs, but he told the white man the secret of the bullroarer, the voice of the Great Being. His voice was low and rumbling, and Howitt had to lean close and strain to catch the words, to learn the mysteries passed on to young initiates. Turlburn revealed tribal secrets that, by doing so, put his life at risk.

The native finished abruptly, as if a guillotine had come down on his words. He turned and stumbled back to his campfire and did not look up when Howitt called good-bye. By the time he reached the bridge the rain was pelting down, spattering the surface of the water with pockmarks and fading the light to a deep gloom.

※

The hops were maturing beautifully, their dark green elongated cones hanging in bulky, spice-smelling clusters. Howitt knew that all his efforts, when he wasn't in court, should be going into preparation for the harvest, but thoughts of the *Jeraeil* filled his mind. It infuriated him that he knew the secret but couldn't find a way to use it to press Tulaba for an invitation.

Then came his chance. A week after he'd extracted the secret from Turlburn, he was walking home for lunch from the Bairnsdale Courthouse, along the Backwater towards the house. A movement startled him, causing him to stop and take a step backwards. A group of six natives waited for him, half-hidden amongst the river gums. Howitt relaxed when he recognised the men: elders of the Brayakaulung tribe, his informants about the customs of their tribe further to the west. They'd never been to his property before, and now they stood about, shuffling their feet in the grass. He greeted them and was surprised that they answered him sullenly.

'What's the matter? Have you come for the teeth, the *nerndowa*?' he asked, his mind working madly.

Without looking at him, the oldest man Mirriart spoke. Howitt knew he was a *Birraark*, a man who has communion with the spirit world. Mirriart told him that the boys had taken ill, just as he had predicted. He ran his fingers along the wrinkled grid-like scars on his chest. Another elder—Wurngunna—pointed angrily towards the house.

The previous year, the Brayakaulung clan had made Howitt custodian of teeth extracted from novices. He'd put the teeth, wrapped in cloth, into his collection bag, which caused an immediate outcry. It took him some moments to understand that the piece of crystal quartz already in his bag—a rock the natives had earlier given to him— would put a curse on the teeth. It was all bumpkin, but they were obviously still upset.

He guided the group of men through the gate and around to the back of the house. He left them at the foot of the verandah steps while he went into his study. As he was walking back through the kitchen, he asked Margaret to bring them tea on the back lawn. The woman scowled without looking up. Liney, helping Margaret with fruit bottling, looked at Alfred in exasperation and said, with some bad grace, that she would do it.

He returned to the elders with a tobacco tin and, removing the lid, showed them the teeth lying on a scrap of calico. 'You see. Not with the rocks. Quite safe. Not make the boys *muraty*.' He handed over the tin to the *Birraark* who took the teeth out, one by one, and checked them, holding them close to his eye.

Liney brought cups of tea outside and set them on a table under the great arching boughs of an oak tree. The tree was changing colour and littering the ground with autumn leaves. She tried to usher the men towards the tea, to sit on the chairs, but they ignored her, making their own way to the table. Standing, they shoveled spoonfuls of sugar into their cups. Alfred saw the expression on Liney's face. He could read the way she was trying to judge the mood of the men. She raised an eyebrow but he nodded to her reassuringly. The natives were drinking their tea and inspecting the leaves of the oak tree, talking quietly amongst themselves. Liney returned to the house.

He asked the elders about their journey and they told him it had been difficult. 'No much *wadgan* to eat, not much *jirrah.*' The sugar was making them jovial. One of the men, wearing a *bridda-bridda* around his waist, the fur mangy and foul smelling, was trying to tell a story but Howitt was having trouble following his rapid-fire speech.

'*Grangalloo dindin . . . Ngalko mrart . . .* ' The man filled a spoon with sugar and ate it as he talked. '*Gunyeru.*'

Howitt seized on the word *Gunyeru*, their word for corroboree. 'You will be coming to the *Jeraeil*?' he asked them, keeping his voice calm.

Mirriart looked startled and placed his cup firmly on the table.

Howitt spoke in a low voice, revealing his knowledge of the *Turndun* in a way that suggested he was already an initiate. The elders exchanged nervous looks, and spoke too quickly to each other in their own language for Howitt to follow what they said. He opened his hands to them: he had nothing to hide.

Wurngunna was angry. He raised his fists and his voice and kept talking until Mirriart held up his hand for silence, touched the bone through his nose and sucked in his breath, making a whistling sound through his widely spaced teeth. Howitt watched his face closely, ignoring the scowls of the others.

The old man looked sternly at Howitt as he told him the ceremony was to be held at Wuk Wuk. One of the others tried to interrupt him, but the elder continued. He spoke the names of those to be initiated and told Howitt he would receive word when it was time to attend. The old man's voice was strained with ambivalence, yet he spoke seriously as one *Gommera* to another. Howitt nodded with an equally serious expression.

Before the natives departed, Howitt went into the house and returned with packets of tobacco, sugar and flour. They accepted the gifts without comment and, without saying goodbye, made their way around the house, through the gate and down the slope to the Backwater. He followed them to the gate and watched as they walked along the bank in single file towards the native camp, where they would stay for a few days with Tulaba and his people before returning to their own country.

He turned away from the gate and started to walk slowly up the path towards the house. From his pocket he retrieved his pipe and tobacco tin and packed the bowl. He would write to Fison immediately and tell him of his triumph. Reverend Lorimer Fison was his friend and colleague in anthropology; he would be envious of this breakthrough, though he might wonder at Howitt's tactics. And Tulaba would be put out, but he must learn to accept that times had changed. He knows his traditions are running away like water down a plughole, Howitt mused. I want to do this for him.

He scratched a Lucifer against the sole of his boot and lit his pipe. After puffing reflectively for a moment, he took the pipe out of his mouth and inspected the bowl. The blacks would still turn out to help with the harvest, of course, otherwise they'd miss out on the harvest feast.

Those armchair ethnographers in England who can only hypothesise: they'll have to sit up and take notice, he smiled to himself, thinking about the first-hand account he would write of a *Jeraeil.* Not the part that involved the women, that had already been documented, but what came later: the secret men's business, the initiation of the boys: it had never been done before.

The ceremony could take up to a month, he knew, but he could request, at the most, two weeks leave from court. He would have to ask the elders to cut it back so that he didn't miss the most important elements.

The bees thrummed in the last of Liney's roses, and on the cool breeze springing up, he caught the tobacco smell of dying flowers. The Quakers had a test for determining the value of an action. His mother's voice came unbidden into his mind, asking him: is it true; is it kind; is it necessary? He felt decidedly uncomfortable as opened the back door and entered the house.

Tulaba did not help with the hops harvest. Those natives that did join in the picking were slow and moody. The Chinese workers picked three bushels of seed cones to every one of the blacks'. And the natives worked in silence, whereas normally they sang along with the Italian pickers. Even the glorious autumn weather, blue and mellow, the air scented and the land green after rain, did not lift their spirits.

Howitt drove the dray between the rows of hops, listening to the opera tunes the Italians sang as they worked. It reminded him of Phillips, all those years ago, his Figaro echoing around the North Gippsland hills. The pickers slung their full baskets up onto the cart and he drove the load towards the oast house.

Away from the activity of the workers, and despite the good feeling he had about the crop, the unease he had felt earlier seeped back into him. That morning he had found a *Gule-wil* on the back step. He'd almost tripped over it, and hesitated before picking it up. The wood was smooth, as if it had passed through many hands, and the etched patterns had been recently refilled with colour. Howitt didn't know what portent the patterns told, but he knew the blacks believed the *Gule-wil* carried the evil intent of the sender. He took it into the kitchen and threw it into the stove fire. The dry wood crackled and quickly turned to ash.

'Mr Howitt?' One of his neighbours, a lad with carrot-coloured hair and a freckle-covered face, was calling to him; he might have been doing so for some time. Howitt realised he had reached the oast house and had been sitting motionless in the cart when he should have been helping to unload the baskets. Others were heaving them onto their shoulders and carrying them into the oast house. He climbed down from the cart and stood for a moment, scanning the house verandah, but there was no sign of Liney. He walked the short distance to her dairy and looked inside, but she wasn't there, either.

Returning to the oast house he picked up a rake and set about helping to spread the hops across the slatted floors. It was like working in an oven. The heavy work made him sweat profusely, and the smell made him queasy. On the vines, the cones smelt sweet, but once picked they reeked like dirty old clothes. Already his face and hands were starting to break into angry red weals, the rash itching so that he wanted to tear at his skin. It happened every year—the price of the harvest.

The work was finished by the late afternoon. The sun was

low in the west, turning the sky pale pink, and the air was cooling quickly. Howitt lit a fire on the ground floor of the oast house, and the hot air and smoke passed up through the floors and out through the cowl in the roof. The extra heat made his eczema rash scream and he buried his hands deep into his pockets to stop himself from scratching. Liney, he thought, would know where she'd put the cotton gloves she'd made for him to wear at this time of year.

The long table under the oak tree on the back lawn had been set up for refreshments. He saw Margaret appear from the house, carrying a tray of drinks. Behind her, May followed with another tray, far too heavy for her. He sent the carrot-haired lad to give her a hand.

'Where's your mother?' he asked as he walked towards May.

His daughter was flushed and panting, and wiped her hands down her mother's apron which she wore over her pinafore. 'She's not well, papa. She asked me to help Margaret.'

He went past the crowd of pickers gathering around the table, stopping himself from breaking into a run, and entered the house. He found Liney in the bedroom, lying down, the curtains drawn.

'Liney?'

'I'm sorry, Alfred. I felt faint.'

He put his hand to her brow and removed it in alarm. 'I'll send one of the men to fetch Doctor Cunningham.'

'No, it's nothing. A small fever. I just need to rest for a while.' She pushed the heavy blankets away from her.

From the pitcher on the washstand, he poured water onto a flannel, his hands shaking. He placed the soaked flannel gently on Liney's brow.

'I mean it, Alfred. I do not need a doctor. Just some sleep.' She lifted his hand away and held the flannel herself.

Her loosened hair spread out on the pillow around her head. For the first time, he noticed the grey streaks. 'But why didn't you tell me earlier that you were unwell?' She gave him an odd look that he couldn't read. 'You must rest, at least for a day or two,' he added in his magistrate's voice, but his mind had gone back to the *Gule-wil*.

He would say nothing to Tulaba, or better still, ask him to tell him about its powers and be scornful of his fatuous explanations. Tulaba might be more civilised than most of the blacks, but it did no harm to remind him from time to time of the superiority of rational thought.

ൖ

Although Wuk Wuk, the site of the *Jeraeil*, was not far from Eastwood, Howitt retrieved his compass from his jacket pocket to check his direction before setting off. The familiar action gave him comfort, as did the weighty brass object itself.

Liney came out of the house to see him off. She was pale and had lost weight, but she assured him that she had recovered from her illness. His concern for her health added further to his unease.

The sky was densely overcast, the bush lifelessly grey as he rode out of Bairnsdale along the back road, then turned into open country and dug his heels into his horse's flank. The speed, the biting wind: they helped to clear his mind.

When he reached the site of the *Jeraeil* he dismounted at the periphery, leaving his horse tied to a tree, and walked towards the clearing. He wanted time to get a sense of the mood as he approached, but the *Wirnum* had seen him and walked quickly towards him. The man was dressed in woollen trousers and a coat that seemed to have been fashioned from a blanket, gathered at the waist by a thong of woven reeds. He was a tall man with a clipped grey beard, so unlike the unruly black beards most of the native men wore. Scowling and poking his sharp finger into Howitt's chest, the headman immediately demanded that Howitt prove he was truly initiated. Other natives gathered around, young and old, dressed in an array of ragged shirts and trousers. The grey day turned darker with their mood.

Howitt bid three of the older men to follow him, past the gunyahs the natives had built for their sleeping shelters, into an area of thick black-wattle scrub. The wattle flowers had long-since died and scarified seed pods clung to the branches in brown clumps, each tiny seed outlined in its case. Howitt broke off a branch and tossed it away. Female bowerbirds, greenly speckled and raucous, squabbled amongst themselves on the ground nearby. He stopped at a point where he would not be overheard by the women who were working close by. They were clearing twigs and leaves from a large open circle of land, and laying out blankets and animal skins. The circle, Howitt recognised, was the large *bora*, the outside circle that represented the earth and that was not secret, being open to the mothers of the initiates and the old women of the tribe.

When he stopped in a small opening amongst the trees the Aboriginal men gathered around him. He realised, suddenly, that Tulaba had silently joined the other elders. When Howitt nodded a greeting, Tulaba's eyes slid away, as if he, too, was ashamed.

Anger towards Tulaba flared in Howitt, but he fought to suppress it as he addressed the *Wirnun*, telling him what Long Harry had told him about the bullroarer, the *Turndun*, without giving away his informant's identity. He knew the *Turndun* to be the special symbol of the messenger's mission; that its power accompanied the message sticks that were carried from tribe to tribe calling them together for a secret ceremony. One of the elders put his hand on Howitt's shoulder and pushed him roughly, demanding to know what wicked man had betrayed the secrets of the *Jeraeil* and the *Turndun*. But Howitt, remaining calm, intimated that he'd learned the mysteries from attending the *Kuringal* ceremony of the Murring tribe, and this silenced if not satisfied his inquisitors. Tulaba stood off to the side, erect and aloof, watching the squabbling birds. Howitt shifted uncomfortably inside his heavy clothes and stiff new boots.

He asked after some of the natives missing from the group, but the headman spoke disparagingly: 'These half-castes have nothing to do with us.' Then Howitt casually enquired about Long Harry and was told that the old man was too ill to travel. Too afraid, Howitt thought to himself grimly.

❧

It was days before the ceremony began, as they waited for the clans to gather. Howitt spent his time interviewing any of the natives who would talk to him, or he went walking in the bush, looking for botanical samples. Finally, one afternoon when he returned to the clearing, the rehearsal for the ceremony was underway. He stood watching the old women as they instructed the novices, the *Tutnurring*, in their performances. The elders left him, moving off into the trees on the other side of the clearing. The *Tutnurring* sat cross-legged with their eyes on the ground and practised moving their bodies sharply first to the right then the left, keeping time with the old women drumming their yam sticks on folded rugs to created a muted yet insistent sound.

The boys were then joined by their appointed *Bullawang*—their male protector—at the site the women had cleared: the large bora ring. A distant rhythmical noise preceded the arrival of a procession of men led by the *Wirnum*. Their bodies were smeared with charcoal powder, and strips of white bark were bound around their waists, arms and heads, and stuffed with tall waving tufts of grass. Howitt noticed with annoyance that the men still wore their trousers.

He sat on the perimeter of the circle, his back to a tree trunk, his notebook open in his lap. While the young women cared for the children, the old women and the men circled around and around the novices, making periodic cries of *Yeerung*, which was meant to send the boys to sleep: they would go to sleep as boys and awake as men. At first Howitt wondered how anyone could doze off with such a commotion going on, but as it dragged on and on, he found the monotony of the noise lulled him into a weird vacancy. The children, at first mesmerised, dropped off to sleep in their mothers' laps.

In the evening there was a huge campfire, and roasted wallaby for dinner. Howitt stood apart, balancing a tin plate in one hand and eating the succulent meat with the other hand. When he'd finished, he handed the plate to one of the women and returned alone to his post by the tree. A middle-aged woman in a man's jacket, unbuttoned to reveal her large, drooping breasts, approached him. Without speaking, she fingered the eczema weals on his face. She took his hand and studied the raw rash, lifting his palm to her nose to sniff it, then dropping the hand. She tutted.

'It's a bit of a mess, I agree,' he told her good-naturedly. She shook her head and walked away.

After the meal, the dancing began. Howitt knew the natives to be great mimics, but was taken aback when the dances morphed into what were quite clearly settler stories. He watched the drama of a shipwreck unfold, and there were horse and cattle dances with prancing, cud chewing, scratching and calf licking. There was even a parody of the hops harvest, and an imitation of a man who looked a lot like himself, reading intently and scribbling notes. Were they, he wondered, telling his history while he recorded theirs? A full moon had risen and was tracking across the sky, its light adding to the oddness of the atmosphere, making Howitt feel strangely dislocated. His notebook lay untouched in his lap. The natives laughed and called out to the dancers.

When the dancing was over, the women covered the *Tutnurring* with blankets, then everyone else retired to their gunyahs. In the moonlight, Howitt went to check his horse, which stood with other horses in a roughly corralled area beyond the camping ground. They were mostly Eastwood horses—he had made that concession to his best black workers. He ducked under the branches that served as a fence and gave a low whistle. Wizard came straight to him, whinnying softly, and Howitt ran his hand along the horse's familiar, cool coat. The horse nuzzled his neck and continued to nicker.

Feeling that at least one creature loved him, he returned to his tree. As he was shaking out his swag, Bobby McLeod, one of the men from Tulaba's clan, approached him. Bobby was a big man and a good worker on the Eastwood farm, but whenever Howitt asked him for information about customs, Bobby always just shrugged. Now he handed Howitt a sheet of bark bearing a watery clay mixture. He told Howitt that one of the women had made it, and that he was to smear the paste on his rash. Howitt lathered the concoction onto the eczema on his hands and face. The coolness gave him immediate relief. Bobby grimaced and told Howitt he looked like a *Nyol*; it was a word Howitt knew: a little man who stole people's memory, for good or evil.

❧

Dance and song filled the following evenings, but nothing much seemed to happen during the days, except that it became pleasantly warm with a breeze that carried the smell of the bush and rattled the leaves along the ground. The men hunted, with little success, and the young women and children collected bush foods from the surrounding area. The old women and *Bullawang* continued to tutor the *Tutnurring*, watched closely by Howitt. He was desperate for them to continue with the initiation and muttered to himself about the blacks having no concept of the value of time. But he was in no position to urge on the *Wirnum*, and wouldn't dare ask Tulaba, who still ignored him.

He sat on his saddle on the ground writing up his notes. In the branches above him, a family of apostlebirds pecked insects out of the bark, occasionally sending down showers of seedpods onto his page. Twelve of them, there should be, he mused. Biblical Apostles they were sometimes called, or Happy Families. He sketched one of the birds in his notebook, a mitre on its head and a crosier under one wing. Christianity might be something that happened on another planet; so incongruous did it seem in this setting. He thought of Liney and hoped desperately that she was well.

Then, just before dusk after a day that had seemed no different from any of the others, the natives stirred into activity. Bobby led Howitt to a smaller bora circle, concealed from the women and children by dense tea-tree scrub. It was the clearing that represented the sky and was the men's secret place. This time, Howitt was invited inside the circle. The young initiates sat in the centre, fidgety and scared. Howitt sat cross-legged and straight-backed like the other observers around him; an alert chronicler.

The tall, neatly bearded headman impressed on the *Tutnurring* the need for secrecy, 'You must never tell this. You must never tell this,' he repeated over and over in a monotone that sounded to Howitt like a Mass, with the same mix of authority and mystery. He opened a fresh page in his notebook and wrote down the words.

The *Wirnum* raised himself up to his full height and began the revelation of ancestral beliefs. Howitt, from his position inside the circle, licked the lead of his pencil. He looked across to Tulaba sitting on the opposite side of the circle and found that the native was watching him closely. Tulaba was so scrawny out of his cast-off farm clothes. His chest was crisscrossed with scars, his black skin hung in old-man folds. Howitt raised a hand but was not acknowledged. Fair enough. In this setting, Tulaba was royalty, Howitt merely one of the subjects.

'Long ago, *mulbitthunga*,' began the *Wirnum*, his face creased with solemn purpose and concentration, 'there was a Great Being, Mungan-ngaur.' He went on, winding the story around a myth that seemed to Howitt uncannily similar to a Bible story. Mungan-ngaur had lived on earth; he'd given the Kurnai their names and shown them how to make implements. He had a son Turndun, who was charged with conducting the original *Jeraeil.* A tribal traitor revealed Turndun's ceremonial secrets, and in retaliation Mungan had filled the whole space between earth and sky with fire and water. The men went mad with fear and speared one another; many drowned when the sea rushed over the land. The few survivors became the ancestors of the Kurnai, but others were turned into animals, birds, reptiles, fish. Mungan left the earth and ascended into the sky, where he still remains.

Howitt noted the fear and reverence that passed in waves across the boys' faces. These were the same youths who the old men despaired had turned wild by their contact with whites, losing respect for their elders and customs. When the men stood in a circle around the naked youths and swung their sacred bullroarers the boys hunched down, as if to escape the fierce and frightening thunder of Turndun's voice. With every swing of the bullroarer, the novices were severed, sinew by sinew from their mothers until total cleaving freed them to enter the community of men.

Howitt, too, was intimidated by the booming *Turndun*, the ancient voice of their god. As old as a fossil, he thought. Much older than Jehovah. It dawned on him—almost took his breath away—that not that much separated their culture from his. There was in each a fundamental human craving for understanding and purpose. Didn't the philosophers, from the earliest Greeks to Descartes, from Copernicus to Newton, dedicate themselves to just these very same questions? Howitt felt a wave of vertigo as the two worlds that he had always held apart concertinaed into each other. He touched the ground beside him as if its solidity might offer him anchorage.

On the farm, wherever he sank his spade and turned the earth, he brought up stone tools: axes mostly, or basalt shards to scrap the flesh off animal skins. They were the discarded implements of a people without pockets, he always thought. He'd considered the simple, unchanging shape of the tools as one more confirmation of the primitiveness of the Aborigines, but suddenly he wasn't so sure. One might see continuity as abidingness, the lack of need for constant change, and there might be a strength in that, no better or worse than the strength and fascination he found in science and progress.

The formal part of the ceremony was over and in its place a game had begun between the initiates and the young men, with much clapping and cheering. Howitt, busy with his notes, looked up vaguely. He noticed that the elders, not participating in the game, had become old men again, their ceremonial paint running with sweat, their tufts of grasses wilted and broken, their faces haggard from effort. He felt a sudden stab as he grasped that he might have just witnessed the very last Kurnai *Jeraeil*—ever. The realisation rocked him. The initiation ceremony, performed for every Aboriginal male child for thousands of years: how many men might that be? Then to be suddenly snuffed out in one generation. In another generation even the memory might no longer exist. He tried to imagine what it might be like to lose the cornerstone of your culture, something that told you who you were and why you belonged. It would be like Christianity dying before his own children reached adulthood. He felt grief as keenly as if the loss were his own.

He might have discarded his faith, but it had been his choice, a singular decision that sent not so much as a ripple to disturb the solid edifice of the Christian church. But his musings on religion brought to mind his father's insight and courage to see that Christianity could be a scourge, the way it marched into new lands and declared itself the victor, taking no prisoners. That's what was happening here, right under his nose, and he felt a shudder of recognition at his own contribution—his very presence in this country—to the demise of the native customs.

The laughter of the game no longer reached him as he remembered how he was complicit in other ways. He looked at the natives around him and thought of the piles of bones.

His journal still lay in his lap. He flicked through the pages of notes he'd written over the past few days. They were nothing but flat, passive squiggles, as if the English language had become flimsy in the presence of so much meaningful activity. The words lacked the colour of the dance, the roar of the *Turndun*, the strutting steps and sweeping gestures, the moods of fear and elation, the command of the *Wirnum*.

The game ended and the natives began the work of packing up. The magic was over, too, and Howitt felt himself emerging from a trance. His legs had become cold and stiff, and he stretched them out before him. What nonsense he'd been thinking. It was like theatre, where you could lose yourself in the drama, but sooner or later the curtain went down and the actors retired. You had to acknowledge the end of the play, and return to the real, complicated world. He looked at his hands. The clay had dried and cracked, and underneath, the eczema had all but cleared up.

# Chapter 8

Why did they have to draw attention to themselves? May was watching the man across the aisle from the corner of her eye. He was playing a mouth organ; the mournful music rose over the clatter of the train and filled the hot carriage. She looked down at his feet: they were protected by cardboard cut roughly into soles and bound by twine around what remained of his shoes. The carriage was stifling, the air muggy with human smells. The windows were closed tight against the coal smuts that flew about like black snow. May folded the letter she'd been reading and returned it to her purse. She took out her handkerchief and held it to her nose, closing her eyes and breathing in the sharp-sweet scent of *Eau-de-cologne*.

The man started to sing, sitting there in his grimy jacket, his mouth organ in his hands that hung limply between his knees.

> Melbourne was happy, we must all confess,
> Til this depression brought such distress.
> Now we are silent, sadly we roam,
> Wandering onward – no friends, no home.

Another man, a couple of seats further along the carriage, joined in. May could just see his hat, the crown darkly stained, the rim partly detached.

> Will no-one help us in our despair?
> Borne down by sorrow, weighted with care.
> Each day we suffer hunger and pain
> Waiting the sunshine after the rain.

The singing was neither boisterous nor rebellious; it was a resigned, tuneless strain that carried defeat in every note. May squirmed, sitting there in her new green skirt and matching hat.

She still felt the shock of seeing people begging on the streets; families living under sheets of cardboard; filthy scrawny children with wild hair and wilder behaviour. Now that Papa was a senior public servant with the Mines Department there was no shortage of money at home. Their house in Malvern, with its overcrowded rooms that her mother so loved, was like a brick fortress against the poverty, the drought, the queues of men waiting for jobs they had no chance of getting. Even her young brother Gilbert, who had stayed behind in Bairnsdale to manage the farm, was doing reasonably well.

The train lumbered past the backyards of cottages. There were sagging back porches, chicken coops and vegetable gardens, and clotheslines strung with sheets and shirts that flew horizontally in the strong northerly wind.

A hot wind like this had been blowing, and there had been another drought, all those years ago when her father had come to tell her there was no money for her to continue her schooling. She was on the swing that hung from one of the boughs of the oak tree on the back lawn. Except it wasn't lawn: the drought had withered every blade of grass to brittle brown, the wind whipping off the home paddock soil. She had dragged her booted feet back and forth through the dust, not caring about the scuffs. Her father had stood before her, holding his jacket closed around his body with one hand, his empty pipe in the other. She had heard her parents talking that morning; she knew what he had come to say.

'Charlton, too?' she had asked. Charlton didn't even like school, but her father told her to be reasonable. The opium poppy crop had failed, and there was no money for her to return to the Presbyterian Ladies College in Melbourne.

Drought-stricken poppies had invaded her dreams ever since, their dry stalks clacking in the wind like a native message of warning. She still carried the grievance. She was smarter than Charlton—much smarter—and he had gone to university, had married, had children, while she stayed at home with her parents, a spinster as withered as the drought-struck poppies.

The train made its half-shunting motion as it approached

the Melbourne Terminus. May kept her body rigid to avoid bumping up against the large woman next to her who had spent the journey constantly mopping the sweat from her face. May inhaled from her handkerchief again before returning it to her purse, from which she took a coin. The train shuddered to a stop and May stood up and took a few steps. She held the coin out to the man with the mouth organ, too embarrassed to look at his face.

'Thank you, lass.' It was the same resigned voice he'd used in his singing.

Looking straight ahead, she made her way along the aisle and stepped out onto the platform. The gusty northerly flung the smells of hot metal, coal and oil into her face. It was already so hot, and it wasn't yet ten o'clock. A sheet of newspaper wrapped around her skirt before breaking free and lifting towards the river. May clutched her folio and purse to her chest with one hand, and with the other held on to her hat. She bowed her head into the wind, left the station and walked briskly up Swanston Street.

There were men sitting on the pavement with their backs to the shop windows, smoking and staring into space, oblivious to the pedestrians who had to dodge around their extended legs. The street was hectic with horses and buggies and cable trams; young men on bicycles with packages balanced on their handlebars; men sharp as crows in their black suits and hats; women in smart outfits, already laden with shopping bags, hurrying on their way to morning tea.

May paused at the sight of a man who had slumped onto his side against a shopfront, his small brown and white dog asleep in the crook of his arm. She had to resist the urge to frame him, to hold up her hands, her fingers and thumbs creating an open square in which to capture the story: hopelessness and trust. Instead, she stepped around him and entered a building that was dim and hushed when the door wheezed closed behind her. She climbed a broad staircase to the first floor, a rabbit warren of corridors and closed doors with brass plaques that spoke of all manner of trade. After the third turn, she came to a door with a plaque that read 'Australian Photographic Review'. She knocked and without waiting for a reply, opened the door and entered. The room was large and lit through grubby windows that looked down onto Swanston Street. A man wearing a green shade was bending over a long table covered with photographs, examining one with a magnifying glass. He did not acknowledge May's presence, and she stood, clutching her folio, waiting for him to finish.

He picked up a wax pencil and made some marks on the photograph he was studying. May breathed in the smell of his oily hair tonic and the faint mustiness of the room as she shifted from one foot to the other. When he had finished with the photograph, he stood up straight, putting his hands in the small of his back to stretch. He was a big man and wore a patch over his right eye. His suit was clean but shiny with age.

'Good morning, Mr Welch.' May spoke a little warily because she was never sure of the mood in which she would find him. When he was in good spirits he was the best mentor a person could have.

He smiled at her. 'Good morning, Miss Howitt. Atrocious weather.' She nodded. 'And how is your father? And your dear mother?'

'Father is well, and mother frantic because Mr Deakin is coming to dinner tonight and she doesn't trust the cook.' She picked up some of the photographs from the table and examined them as she spoke. Her parents' connection with Mr Welch was hazy in her mind. Mr Welch had been with her father in the desert, but beyond that, their relationship was a mystery. There had been that awful occasion when her father had seen some of Mr Welch's photographs, which May had taken home. His fury had been unfathomable. From then on, she had hidden the photographs and refrained from mentioning his name.

'Ah, Mr Deakin. Your father does move in illustrious circles these days. Deservedly so, deservedly so,' he muttered, nodding his head. 'Anyway, young lady, let's see what you've brought me today.'

Welch had given up editing Arbuckle's newspaper, ground

down by the man's demands for economy and a toady tone in every story. Editing a photographic journal was like a picnic after all those years of politics, misfortune and crime. He pushed the photos into a pile at one end of the table to make room for May's folio.

She untied the leather thong and opened the wings of the case. The top photo was of a building site.

Welch picked it up by its border. 'What's this?' He peered closely at the photograph.

May put a gloved finger under her nose to sponge off beads of nervous perspiration. 'Stonnington Mansion, close to where we live. It is being built for Mr Wagner and his wife.' But that wasn't really the story of the photograph. For May, it was a study of the men labouring on the site, of their worn faces and straining muscles. The man in the foreground, a timber beam balanced on his shoulder, was looking her way. A moment later he had spat on the ground and told her to clear off; a lady should have better things to do with her time.

That was also her father's attitude. Papa didn't mind when she took photographs of the family. He even asked her to take photographs of the natives to accompany his papers because that gave photography a scientific purpose. But he made it clear that he did not think it appropriate for her to, as he said, roam the streets looking for subjects. Perhaps that was why she had persisted, although she had stopped showing him her work.

Mr Welch's photographic journal had been such a find. She had subscribed to it for a couple of years, always making sure she lifted it from the pile of mail on the hall table before her father came home. It had been her most significant act of courage to write to Mr Welch to ask if he would agree to see her work.

'But this is something quite new,' Welch said, reaching for his magnifying glass. 'There is nothing here that is formally arranged or attractive to the eye. Here, the men are actively at their work.' He was more nonplussed than critical.

'They would not have allowed me to assemble them.' She stepped closer to him and looked at the photograph in his hand. She was disappointed that she had not caught the slick of sweat on the man's face, the anger in his eye.

'There is this area, here, that is a little out of focus. Otherwise it is good; unconventionally clever.'

He laid the photograph aside and picked up the next one. On first sight it looked more typical of amateur photography: a fountain set in a formal garden. She had caught the sunlight in the showering droplets so that the fountain appeared to be bathed in a silver aura.

'Ah.' He picked up his magnifying glass again and examined the photograph. 'Any other photographer would have removed it.'

'I put it there.' They were referring to a small bird—an Eastern Spinebill—which she had found lying at the foot of the fountain, its broken wing spread across the grass. When she had picked it up it was still slightly warm with the last of its life. In the photograph, the wing hung over the lip of the fountain bowl, its head slightly twisted back to reveal its vulnerable white throat.

May fidgeted with the button on her glove as Welch walked across to the window to scrutinise the photograph in better light, as if searching for other signs of death. 'It's a native bird,' she told him. The glove button came off in her hand.

He appeared not to have heard her as he walked back to the table. 'I will buy this one.' He laid it down carefully and turned to scrutinise her. 'Where others are using the new plates with the old methods, you have mastered just the right exposure. See here,' he turned back to the photograph and pointed to the bird's open beak. 'You can tell from the detail.' The bird looked as if it were taking its last breath. It was the part of the photograph that May was most proud of, even though it could easily be overlooked.

ꟼ

When she re-emerged onto Swanston Street, the sky had grown livid with thunderclouds, the wind had dropped and the air was so moistly thick that walking was like wading through soup.

But the weather could not dampen her joy. Her first sale. Her first published photograph—for her own artistry, not merely an image to explicate her father's writing. This made her—she took a deep breath and straightened her back—a professional photographer. She imagined that she could feel the weight of the gold half-sovereign in her purse, lying there glinting against the pink satin lining. Mr Welch had said it was all he could afford to pay; she wouldn't have cared if it were thruppence.

A cable tram came rattling along in its own cloud of dust and she climbed aboard, selecting a seat at the open rear end where she might catch a little cool air. From her purse, she took Esmay's letter, pausing to touch the raised pattern of St George and the Dragon on her gold coin. Esmay had proven to be a good correspondent, writing in the perfect copperplate May's mother had taught her.

It surprised May how easily the native woman had taken to mission life. She and her mother had visited the Lake Tyers Mission to see Esmay and the other Eastwood blacks soon after they had been moved from the farm. It had been a scorching day then, too, and they had stood with Reverend Bulmer in front of the church, behind a table laden with foodstuffs. Children's voices reached them from their small timber schoolhouse, singing 'The Skye Boat Song'. The tune had transported May back to her own childhood of hot afternoons in stifling classrooms, which smelt of wooden desks, Indian ink and sour milk. She and her fellow pupils had been expected to connect—as these little black children were—with a wet, cold country of bedraggled sheep, a prince on the run, and highland clans in tartan skirts with bagpipes under their arms.

The Reverend had rung a bell, the brassy notes ringing out over the scorched paddocks and across the lake, and the natives had straggled up to the table from the row of cottages set below the church, holding their calico bags. May tried to catch the eye of the men and women she knew as they shuffled into line. The women nodded, but the men kept their heads down. They all passively waited their turn for the Reverend to place their weekly rations into their bags: tea, flour, sugar, potatoes, jam, a bit of bully beef. Only Esmay smiled shyly at May and Liney as she received her rations.

They were no longer the blacks May had known at Eastwood, with their quick pride and erect posture; their nimble fingers picking hops; their theatrics and mimicries and their readiness to tell a story. The men especially looked lost and beaten; the women were fortified, it seemed to May, by the continuing responsibility of motherhood and domesticity.

And now here was Esmay writing about Jesus and Sunday-School picnics. She wrote about the baskets she was weaving for tourists—another thing May hated. Reverend Bulmer had found a way to supplement the Lake Tyers Mission's meagre funds by opening up the Mission to tourists. They came in hordes, having paid their shilling to the proprietor of Durham's Hotel in Lakes Entrance for the half-day package tour that included tea. Papa had returned from a visit to his friend Reverend Bulmer, dismayed by what he'd witnessed. The tourists, he had told her, stood in packs staring at the natives as if they were wild creatures, the mission a zoo. Watching an Aborigine throw a boomerang caused a frisson of excitement to ripple through the crowd. The tourists, acting as if they were Lords and Ladies from the Old Country, threw farthings and halfpennies to the black children, and left with woven baskets and carved spear-throwers.

Since coming to Melbourne, May had rarely seen a black face. Even out in Malvern, which was more country than city, there were no natives. As a girl, she had loved Esmay. The way her dark eyes danced; the way her skirt swayed when she walked; the way her broad feet belonged to the earth; the way, especially, she shared May's passion for the natural world and was full of colourful stories that fired May's imagination. They would sit together on the banks of the Backwater, or walk through the long yellow grass between the house and the blacks' camp, and Esmay would tell her how the world was made. Once she had pointed overhead to a flock of pelicans, her ancestors, wheeling their way towards the lakes. Borun the pelican had walked the long distance from the northwest mountains with his canoe on his head, puzzled by the constant tapping sound that accompanied him. He came to a deep inlet and put down his canoe, only to discover, much to his surprise, there was a woman in it. She was Tuk the musk duck. She became his wife and the mother of the Kurnai people.

The cable tram trundled past the State Library. May doubted there was one volume of Aboriginal lore in the whole of the grand building, yet she would not understand this place—her country—if she didn't have their stories to lay over the land and give it meaning. The natives' spiritual connection to the country and all living creatures explained the world inclusively, so unlike Reverend Anderson's Bible stories, that set humans apart and above everything else except God.

As a young teenager, during school holidays, she would go to the blacks' camp at Eastwood and sit quietly with the old women around a campfire, listening as they wove never-ending stories, passing the tale on from one to another. Esmay, at her side, would translate, but gradually May had come to understand enough of the language to follow the warp and weft of the women's tales. It was then that she had come to recognise the harmony and beauty, to see how they contained patterns like the contours on her father's maps; that offered understanding of place and existence.

Later, when her brothers and sisters had left home, May tried to find purpose for her life in recording the natives' stories. She took photographs of the black women but shared them with no-one; only the photographs of natives she took at her father's direction made their way into his work. From time to time, she submitted stories she'd gathered from Esmay and the other Eastwood women to the *Folklore* journal but they were always returned to her, sometimes with the cursory comment of 'unsuitable', occasionally with a suggestion to publish them as children's fairytales. The editors were looking for work like her father's, but she didn't like how her father changed the stories, removing their ethereal quality and arranging what was left systematically into straight lines and divisions. The stories weren't like that at all.

'Subjectivity is the curse of anthropology,' he would warn her. 'In the act of coming to know, we have to guard against inserting ourselves, distorting the original by viewing it through our personal prism.' She had read *Notes and Queries on Anthropology*, with its organising categories and insistence on objectivity, but she also saw the lines of bias that ran through her father's work, and that of Reverend Fison's. For one, they left out the women: wasn't that a bias? Authoritative knowledge, Papa called it, but what May saw was the way he always placed the Aborigines outside his own world, and then applied the rules of his world to his understanding of them.

Nevertheless, he praised her work, and borrowed liberally from it. When she was transcribing his scribbling, which had become her job, she was often arrested by a phrase or a paragraph, a whole tale that had been her own discovery. But the story wouldn't be quite the same. Her father's dispassion was a scalpel that he used to cut away the deep tangles of mystery, to make it clean and unambiguous. He dissected the legends as if he was looking for the cause of death in a cadaver, and missed the living, breathing *wonder* of it.

The worst of it was that the extracts he, and even Dr Frazer, borrowed were often taken out of context. In some cases, these men of science made claims that she knew to be wrong: they misunderstood the legends, or misinterpreted them, at least from what she believed was meant.

The tram rocked along its tracks. May could feel the gritty wind on her face and the rumble of motion through her feet. Esmay's letter had become creased in her clenched fist. She smoothed the sheets out on her lap, carefully folded them back into their envelope and into her purse. Others would think Esmay's life had changed for the better, but May felt a terrible loss.

When the cable tram came to a stop on the corner of Grattan Street, she alighted and walked along the bitumen pavement that had become as sticky as molasses with the heat. She came to a set of high gates mounted on bluestone pillars. For a moment she hesitated, a gloved finger tracing the university's insignia on the gate, then she took a deep breath and entered what could have been a forbidding world.

There were tree-lined avenues, broad sandstone galleries, buildings that carried an aura of sacredness. Was this how one walked? She checked her stride, trying to make it purposeful and dignified. She wanted to appear as if she belonged, distracted by lofty thoughts, when in fact she was fearful that at any moment she would be asked to leave.

Stepping out from one of the cool galleries, the humid air fell around her like a heavy veil. She walked towards a square of manicured lawn, its greenness stunning in the storm-brewing light, and sat down on a bench under an elm tree. She had no right to be there. She just wanted to know what it might feel like. Three young men crossed the green in front of her, their arms full of books, talking ardently. They paid her no notice. Dozens of butterflies came winging across the lawn, bunched together like a grey air-borne phantom. One landed on May's grass-green skirt. She could name it: a Moonlight Jewel, dove-grey wings studded with orange gems. If I could have your wings, she mused, and hover above, looking down, what would I see? A reasonably pleasant-looking woman, well-presented, old enough to be called a spinster, a bitter line to her mouth, slumped in her own self pity. When she shook the self-image from her mind she could feel the pull of the tightly bound bun at the nape of her neck. Did she deliberately try to look old-fashioned and humdrum? The butterfly lifted weightlessly from her lap and was tossed away on a current of air.

She'd been clever at school, all the teachers praised her work and she won prizes for her compositions and arithmetic: books and medals, and a creamy scroll that bore curly lettering and a red wax seal. But then her father had planted opium poppies. The immaculate green lawn in front of her was transformed into an image of a land burnt brown with drought, bare stalks clicking and rattling in the wind.

ᔓ

The storm broke as she dashed from the train station to her

home, and she arrived drenched and shivering. As she closed the front door, she could hear her mother's voice coming from the back of the house. Lying on the silver salver on the hall table was the day's mail: letters, a parcel that looked like a book, a few catalogues. Quickly, she sifted through the letters. There it was, finally: a brown envelope bearing multiple stamps, and Dr Frazer's distinctive handwriting. May slipped the letter back into the middle of the pile and went to her bedroom to change out of her wet clothing. She took the gold half-sovereign from her purse and felt its weight in her hand. It was something to cling to: a good luck charm that might put the magic words into Dr Frazer's letter. She placed the coin in her jewellery box.

In the kitchen, she found her mother rolling out pastry. The room was like a furnace, with the big Aga stove burning and pots bubbling. The deal table in the middle of the room was crowded with bowls of stewed apple, podded peas, potatoes and pumpkins cut into neat squares, and freshly picked blackberries. A strand of Liney's hair had come loose from its bun and her cheek was smeared with flour, where she had tried to tuck the hair behind her ear.

'You don't have to do that Mama,' May said, exasperated by the way her mother could not give up these tasks, even though she employed other women to do them.

'I've just sent Rose to the shops for more flour. I thought you might have come home earlier, to help.'

May looked at the dishes and bowls lined up on the table: all that fuss. But then she'd come to understand that this was how her mother measured her worth. May filled the kettle and set it on the stove.

'Where have you been? You've been gone nearly all day.' Liney expertly rolled the pastry from the rolling pin into the greased pie dish.

'The city,' May shrugged, spooning tealeaves into a pot.

Her mother sighed. 'Well, make the tea, at least.'

'I am,' May answered more crossly than she meant. 'Is there anything I can do to help?' she asked in a more reconciliatory tone, although both she and her mother knew her domestic skills were not strong.

'It's too late now,' Liney answered crossly as she filled the pie case with stewed apple.

May carried her cup back to her bedroom. For the first time she looked at the room critically and saw it as it really was: the narrow bed; the uncluttered dressing-table; the girlish pictures on the wall; her desk and its straight-backed chair against the opposite wall. She sat down in a dainty chair and tried to read, but her mind kept wandering back to the brown envelope waiting in the hall.

Promptly at six, she heard her father open the front door. He will be hanging his hat on the hallstand; now he will be picking up the mail, shuffling through the pile on his way to his study. Now he will be at his desk, picking up his silver letter knife. Then she heard him call her.

She stood at the open doorway to his study, one hand on the doorjamb, until he looked up and beckoned her to enter. He had removed his jacket and hung it on the back of his chair, and loosened his tie, making his stiff, high white collar stand agape. In his shirtsleeves he could still be the farmer of Eastwood rather than the Secretary for Mines and Water Supply. Across his broad desk he handed her a letter. 'Here. This concerns you, though I'm afraid the news won't be to your liking.' His voice was kind.

She hardly dared reach for the pale, flimsy sheet. Sitting down on the edge of a chair, she scanned the early parts of the letter—news of London's scientific circles, mutual friends—until she found her own name buried in cramped script at the bottom of the page, almost as an afterthought. She placed the letter down on her father's desk with deliberate care and left the room.

'May,' he called, but she could not talk to him now. She returned to her own room and looked down at her most recent writing lying on her desk: her meticulous recordings of legends of the Kurnai women. The stories recalled a time in her life when she had first started to feel the stirrings of what she liked to call her scholarship. After she had been taken out of school, her father had tried hard to satisfy her thirst for learning. He taught her how to classify his rock collection, and instructed her in sketching for his botanical articles. But what she had loved most were the times they went riding together through Gippsland, when her father went to visit the ever-fewer blacks' camps. While he interviewed the men, she learnt to watch, listen, ask questions, and build trust with the native women. At day's end, she and her father would camp together, often on the banks of a river, and while he fished for their dinner, he would tell her what he had gleaned from the men. She would listen closely to his words as she watched the dusk descend: dusty yellow beams of light streaming through the branches and setting the scrub aglow. The horses would become black silhouettes against a sky turning navy blue, and the air would throb with the sound of insects. As night settled, Howitt and May would draw closer to the fire and blow on steaming cups of tea.

In the letter, Dr Frazer had described her work as quaint, a hobby. He said that it was unsuitable for publication, but at the same time—in the very same paragraph—asked her father's permission to use some of her findings.

With one brisk movement she swept the papers from her desk. They flew up briefly before settling on the carpet around her feet. Her eyes fell on the scissors lying next to her pens. She snatched them up and sat down on the stool in front of her dressing-table mirror. In a swift, practised movement she pulled the pins from her frumpy bun and shook her head so that her hair dropped heavily down her back. She grasped it in one hand, pulling it over her shoulder, and began to hack at it with the scissors. The hair fell in dark, curling tresses into her lap.

ഗ

An hour later, May heard her father welcoming their guest. She opened her wardrobe and selected the first gown that came to hand, glamorous by Bairnsdale standards only. She splashed her eyes with cold water and checked her reflection in the mirror, smiling grimly and shaking her head to feel the new lightness.

Her father and Mr Deakin were talking as they passed down the passage on their way to the sitting room. When Mr Deakin had been appointed Minister of Mines, her father had become more cheerful. Finally, he had told her, there was someone to talk to who was intelligent and liberal in his views.

When May entered the sitting room, her mother was welcoming their guest to her humble home. May looked around at the Turkey rugs and jardinières, the ostrich feathers, crystal vases and brocade cloths, and thought of the men she'd seen that morning on the train and in the street. Mr Deakin turned towards her and, before he checked himself, she saw his eyes sweep up and down her body. Rather than shake his hand, she nodded politely and took the upright Queen Anne chair by the window that faced the garden. Her mother was staring at her in horror, but her father didn't appear to notice any change.

Mr Deakin was fashionably dressed and groomed. His short hair, trimmed beard and drooping moustache were grizzled, as if to confirm gravitas and wisdom. Alfred ushered him into a comfortable armchair and sat down opposite. As he sat, Deakin pulled at his shirt cuffs so that they showed just beyond his jacket sleeves—sufficient to reveal the gem-encrusted cufflinks. Liney handed around a tray bearing small glasses of sherry.

The men sipped their drinks while they discussed mining business: of the new method of diamond drilling that would reverse the decline in coal mining, and the prospects for deep lead mining. Liney, still standing, continued to glare at May, clutching her sherry glass as if she was ready to toss it.

Finally, Liney sat down on a chair by a small mahogany table, at a distance from the men, in a pool of light from one of the wall-mounted gaslights. The lamps had been lit early, as the storm clouds had made the house dark. Outside, a squally shower of rain beat on the tiled roof. May watched raindrops chase each other down the windowpane, then turned to Mr Deakin.

'Will there be jobs?' She leaned forward in her chair and felt her short locks fall onto her face. She tucked one side behind her ear. Her father gave her a small indulgent smile, but Mr Deakin's face clouded, his dark eyes going strangely dull.

'It's just that today, in Melbourne, I saw so many men who are out of work. It seems a tragedy that this country can't offer them employment.'

'It's the drought. It will pass, and there will be times of full employment again,' the Minister waved a dismissive hand in her direction.

'But how are they to live now? How are they to feed their families tonight?' Her voice rose in passion, and she felt her mother's eyes boring into her. In the silence that followed her words, the grandfather clock in the hall chimed the half hour.

'May, could you please go and ask cook if dinner is ready to be served.' Liney's voice was strained.

So, thought May, walking stiffly from the room, I am to be dismissed because I air an uncomfortable truth before a man who is responsible for a satisfactory answer. She dutifully went to the kitchen, then rejoined her parents in the dining room.

French-polished furniture usually filled the dining room to capacity: a massive sideboard, a long table and ten chairs. For tonight's small party, the central leaf had been removed from the table, and six chairs had been pushed back against the dark green walls. The walls were hung with even darker paintings of hunting scenes, which had nothing to do with anything May had known in her life. The candles on the table cast wavering shadows and made the glassware glint. Alfred sat down opposite Liney, and May was, she saw, to sit opposite Mr Deakin.

Over dinner, the men talked politics to each other. Every now and then, their guest would break off and mention some triviality to the women, explaining some overly obvious point, to keep them just on the boundaries of the conversation. May held her tongue. Then the talk turned to race.

'It is vital that Australia be kept racially pure,' Deakin said with all the certainty of his parliamentary position. He lifted a napkin to his lips and wiped his mouth and moustache.

'But think of the multitude of races that have arrived in the country in the past fifty years. They have all contributed in their own ways.' Alfred spoke carefully, but May knew it was a matter about which he felt strongly.

'We need to keep our sights firmly on the future, not the past. As the colonies move towards Federation, we must build on the foundations of our British heritage.' The Minister used his thumb and finger to part and smooth his moustache, a mannerism that looked, May thought, like an attempt to open heavy stage curtains. Her mother, May observed, was intent on cutting her roast lamb into very small pieces.

'There is, I grant you, an economic reason,' her father responded. 'As May said earlier, jobs are short. Perhaps there is an argument for ensuring what is available goes to those already here.' Alfred was being at his most diplomatic, but May could see his temple vein pulsing and noted the way he kept his eyes down and mopped up gravy with a piece of potato. She felt a surge of exhilaration at the prospect of her father losing his temper with this man.

'Yes, that's it,' Deakin answered excitedly, putting down his knife and fork. 'It is not the bad qualities, but the good qualities of these alien races that make them so dangerous to us. It is their inexhaustible energy, their power of applying themselves to new tasks, their endurance and low standard of living that make them such competitors.'

Rose came into the dining room bearing a tray of desserts that she placed on the sideboard. The room remained silent while the servant cleared the dinner plates and served dessert to each person. She placed large jugs of cream and custard on the table before leaving the room.

May watched her father, waiting for his reaction. Speak truth to power: they were the words he had passed on to her from his own father. He always said that if you grew up in a Quaker household, the tenets were stamped on you forever—truth, equality, humanitarianism—although he also conceded to what he called the realities of life. She was expecting his words of truth now, but instead he poured cream over his pudding and began to eat. May looked into her own bowl, then up at Mr Deakin.

'And where does racial purity leave the blacks?' Her question was like a whip across the table. She straightened her back against the shocked faces regarding her. There was a fault line running through his argument, wide as a chasm: that Australia was a politically progressive country, but that such progressiveness required the petty conservativeness of a whites-only policy. To her mind, Mr Deakin's ideas were more regressive than forward thinking, moving back to the dark days of the slavers' claim of white superiority. Again she turned to her father. Hadn't abolitionism been another foundational belief of the Quakers?

'Perhaps that's not appropriate in this context, May dear,' Alfred cautioned her as their guest wiped away the custard that had caught in his moustache.

May felt stifled by the table's impeccable setting: the starched white cloth, the silver cutlery in its military-correct order, the glinting wine glasses, the floral china terrines—the whole, awful, ordered perfection of it. She stood, made a small bow to the table and left the room. Just before she closed the dining room door she heard her mother ask if either Mr Deakin or Alfred would care for more pudding.

ၹ

The rain had stopped and a moon set in a hazy halo was just visible through the clouds. To the west, it was possible to make out the faint loom of the gaslights that lined Glenferrie Road. May hurried along the unmade street, stepping through puddles that seeped into her shoes and soaked the hem of her gown. She carried on the argument from the dining room in her head. Her shawl caught on a barbed wire fence and as she pulled it free she heard the fabric rip. 'Blast, blast, blast,' she said aloud. She kept walking, trying to walk away her anger. What did he know, sitting in his cushy little office, about what had happened to the blacks? Or the Chinese? Or even those men on the train this morning? Not a representative of the people, only those he deemed suitable; the few that fitted within the scope of his narrow little mind. Which didn't include women, obviously. She shuddered to think of his bushy moustache that made him look like a walrus. Beard stiff as a bristle brush, and the way his red lips peeped wetly through all that facial hair. His eyes had kept their cold, hard detachment even when he was angry, and settled on her breasts instead of her face. She shook her head to clear the image and was surprised again by the loose lightness of her hair. The wonderful daring of it.

She slowed her pace, thinking about Esmay and her people, and slavery and missions. Under her father's guidance, she had read Lyell's *Principles*. Humans were the latecomers on earth: that put us in our place to begin with. We are one species, one family, Lyell said. How would Mr Deakin like that? Your brother the Chinaman, Mr Deakin? Your black sister? The ridiculous Samuel George Morton thought he'd proven otherwise with his brain measurements: 87 cubic inches in white men, 78 in Ethiopians, so he claimed. You'd like that bit of arithmetic, wouldn't you, Mr Deakin? She broke off a branch from the she-oak she was passing and slashed the ground with it. The so-called civilised races were not necessarily the most moral.

To Lyell, the human varieties of colour and form were just that: varieties, none better or worse, superior or inferior to another. The great geologist didn't believe in Adam and Eve, but he did believe that we all originated from one pair. She should have said that, offered the rational argument of a highly respected scientist. A man's argument. She tossed the branch away in disgust.

The air was fresh against her hot skin, until she walked straight into a spider's web strung across the path between trees. Its sticky fibres coated her face and clung to her fingers as she picked them from her skin. She could feel a creeping inside her bodice, on the back of her neck, down her arms. Then her father's voice spoke inside her head and she stopped walking to listen. He was telling her about spider's webs. It must have been from twenty years ago. They'd awoken to a breathless winter morning to find the farm fences festooned in spider's webs. Glistening dewdrops ran along the threads marking out the intricate beauty of their architecture. She'd said that the fences looked like brides dressed in white lace. He'd told her how the spider sent out its initial long thread to float on the breeze until it connected with a distant point. How the spider walked along this fine tightrope, spinning more threads to make a firm platform from which to build its web. There was wonder in nature, he'd told her, even those things you might think are the most horrid. It all depended on how you looked at the world.

Mopokes hooted one to another, their calls round as vowels. Otherwise, there was complete silence. The mopokes called again. A yellow light, the size of a firefly, appeared in the distance and gradually grew larger. She heard her father calling her name.

# Chapter 9

The party of four Commissioners started their inspections at the height of summer. They left Bairnsdale, where Howitt had joined them, on a particularly sultry Sunday. Travelling by coach with four in hand, it should have been comfortable, but the further they journeyed inland, the more the roads became bone-rattling corrugations. The horses' hooves sent up plumes of white dust so that the men's dark suits and hats turned a ghostly grey and they were forever slapping at sleeves and hat rims, and coughing into their hands. The Monaro Tableland had been cleared of trees for grazing, and every time there was a strong wind the thin skin of topsoil took flight, leaving the earth barren and fissured. Dirty, scrawny sheep bunched together in the scraps of shade cast by dusty gums. The dams were at best muddy puddles; their orange clay sides fracturing like crazed china.

It could have been the desert, all over again, reflected Howitt as he watched the landscape slide past. There was the heat and aridness, certainly, but there was also the excitement that coiled tightly inside him like forbidden love. He was in the fray again, amidst the freedom of vast landscapes, in the company of like-minded men.

He'd left home under the cloud of Liney's disapprobation, which he relived with alternating waves of annoyance and guilt. She had pressed him to apply for the commission, then baulked when he was appointed. What had cut him deeply was her cynicism: she'd encouraged him, she claimed, only because she thought him too old to be considered. Too old, indeed. He watched the passing countryside, straightened his spine against the jarring ride, and gradually his spirits rekindled.

In the distance to the west he could see the evidence of bushfires tearing through uncleared country. He supposed it was a fire lit by lightening, unchecked and destructive, unlike the fires the Aborigines had once used to husband the land. They would not have burnt country in weather like this, and perhaps the land would not be burning so if they were still managing it. He didn't know.

The air was saturated with the colour of the fire, the sky turned to shades of amber. The sun appeared as an angry red eye peering through the smoke. Borne on the westerly wind, ash competed with dust to fill their mouths and sting their eyes. Even this was bearable, Howitt thought, as he and his fellow Commissioners helped the coach driver clear the road of the maggoty carcass of a cow: it all added to the adventure.

He tried to recall the lithe young man he'd been, travelling through desert storms as easily as walking down Collins Street. He'd been caught in a fearful dust storm once, his men and horses already desperately thirsty. It had been his baptism of fire and he was still proud to recall his cool management in a situation that could have been fatal.

Liney didn't understand. He might be in his seventies, but he had all that experience, as fresh as if it had happened last year. Why should it be wasted? Retirement in Metung had its charms, and gave him time to write and potter in his shed with his woodworking projects, but it was nothing compared to this: the opportunity to contribute to the selection of the most suitable site for the new nation's seat of power. From the moment he'd opened the official letter inviting him to join the Royal Commission, he'd felt the pull of the open country: Tom Groggin and Bombala, Albury and the Murray River, Bega, and up to Armidale and Orange. John Kirkpatrick, a man he respected, was leading the inquiry, and old acquaintances Henry Stanley and Graham Stewart were the other two Commissioners.

He had fallen back on the relief mission's success in his application because it still carried weight in the right circles. Burke was now thoroughly entrenched as an Australian hero in a land with few contenders. The dead explorer's fame both helped Howitt's cause and reignited his resentment. He shook his head at the trajectory the myth had taken: nothing aligned with what he knew, what he'd found. All of Burke's faults had been blown away like so many grains of sand; the bones that Howitt had brought back were revered like religious relics. Somewhere in his study he had a tobacco tin containing a lock of Burke's hair. He should hunt it out when he returned home; it would be worth a fortune.

ᔕ

As the weeks passed, the Commissioners established a disillusionment about their mission along with their pattern for assessing the towns they passed through. They inspected land during the day, held public meetings in the evenings, wrote up their findings late into each night, and set out early the following morning for the next town. They slept in rough hotels where the beds smelt of unwashed bodies, and ate stringy roast mutton night after stifling night. Yet the arduous travelling became only part of the hardship. In each of the towns they were met by hordes of petitioners desperate to have the government buy up their famished farms for the new capital city.

'Hot as hell,' Stewart complained, leaning into a furnace-like wind, removing his hat to wipe his brow. They were waiting in front of another run-down weatherboard hotel for their coach and horses to be brought around. The smell of warm beer, embedded in the timbers, reminded Howitt of hop harvests. The buildings along the mean stretch of street were dilapidated: planks warped and lifting, broken windows boarded up with tin or cardboard, once-proud business names faded to illegibility. It was as if the town had been settled centuries ago, rather than decades.

'Then you think this might be the place?' Howitt joked. He absent-mindedly ran his hand along a hitching rail and then suddenly pulled it away to inspect a splinter that had lodged in his palm. His skin had softened, like a gentleman's. Not like an explorer's at all, he thought with annoyance.

'The politicians will only add to the heat,' Stanley chimed in, hitting his dusty trouser cuffs with his hat. The three men laughed. They each had long experience of working with politicians.

'It won't much matter what we recommend. Our job will be to make whatever they decide look researched, fair and rational.' As Howitt spoke he pulled out the shard of wood between his finger and thumb, and then sucked on the beading blood. From the outset he had been aware of the speciousness of their quest, knowledge he had not dared to share with Liney.

Stanley blew out his breath through pursed lips. 'The brawls have already started between Members anxious to claim the prize for their electorate.'

'Then I suggest we don't make a firm recommendation.' Howitt spoke seriously, inspecting his palm. 'Just give them our scores for each place and let their creative accounting do the rest. We'll only look foolish, otherwise.'

'My guess is that it will be Yass. Yass or Canberra, even though our findings so far point to Tumut,' Kirkpatrick said, joining them, his arms full of documents.

Stewart looked at him in surprise. 'Canberra? That's in the middle of nowhere.'

'Everywhere on our list is in the middle of nowhere,' Stewart responded, walking to the corner of the hotel to see if the horses were coming. 'The middle between Sydney and Melbourne is what they'll want. That will be the only way to settle the rivalry.'

Two women walked past along the otherwise deserted street, their heads bent and skirts whipped behind them. The men doffed their hats. Watching the white women, it occurred to Howitt, quite suddenly, that he had seen no blacks during their travels so far. He supposed that none now lived on their traditional land; that they had been moved to missions. Just as well, he reflected. How would they have survived such a drought as this? But it seemed to him, vaguely and uncertainly, that their absence might somehow be connected to this present aridness. He wandered off a short distance, but not so far that he could not hear the others talking. He turned over stones with the toe of his boot, then picked up a stick to scratch around in the earth.

Looking cross at the delay of their coach, Stewart rejoined

the other two men. In their heavy jackets and ties, their faces were becoming increasingly red. 'They don't need us then, just a ruler and a pencil. We're wasting our time,' Stewart complained.

'Not our honourable friend, Mr Howitt. Look at him.' Kirkpatrick indicated with his chin to where Howitt was inspecting something in his hand. It was worthless and he tossed it away. He ran a finger between his collar and his sweating neck, feeling increasingly frustrated at his lack of worthwhile finds. As the weeks rolled on, he had come to think that a decent fossil might be the only thing that would make the mission worthwhile.

'Come on, Sir,' Kirkpatrick called to Howitt as their coach and horses finally appeared. 'Time to move on to the next inferno.'

In the coach, Howitt's mind turned back to Liney. Her stormy silence and ungracious help had marred the days of his preparation for the Commission. She had stood by the coach as his portmanteau was hoisted onto the roof, and turned her cheek to him when he kissed her goodbye. When he'd settled into his seat and looked out of the coach window, she had gone.

From Omeo, he'd written her a long letter, to remind her of those first years of their marriage. Did she remember her mare, Cloud? The nights they spent outside under a rug, exploring the night sky? He wrote of how good the years together had been, how much he still loved her, how he was anxious to fulfill this one last assignment then return home to her. She was to think of places she wanted to see, perhaps writing away for pamphlets so they could plan a holiday together on his return. They could even think about having the house wired for electric lighting, just like she wanted.

The other men slept through the heat of the afternoon, despite the rough road. Stanley was snoring like a trooper, and Stewart's head kept dropping sharply forward, waking him momentarily before he fell back into a doze. Kirkpatrick gave the impression of reading, but he hadn't turned a page for a good while. Howitt looked out of the coach window at the dismal landscape littered with carcasses of cattle and sheep. Black crows perched on the rumps of those animals that still retained some meat, or glided, wings spread wide, on the hot-air currents, issuing their long cawing cries. *Ngarugal*: that was what the Kurnai Aborigines called the crow. The natives revered the bird and would not allow it to be harmed. The thought made him homesick.

ও

The autumn rains failed to materialise and now the bitterly cold winter had arrived on the Snowy Mountains. A gale-force wind, edged with snow from the peaks, propelled the Commissioners through the front door of the Mechanics Hall in Adaminaby. The wind followed them into the hall and rattled the windows, and the Country Women's Association women held down the edges of tablecloths on tables set with supper. Townspeople and farmers filed in and sat on the chairs in rows in front of the small stage. Most did not speak, but gazed at the portrait of the King, at the blackness beyond the windows, at the rows of books in the bookcases that lined one wall: anywhere so long as they did not have to meet their neighbour's gaze. The Commissioners took their place at the table on the stage. As they had done dozens of times before, they outlined their mission and their criteria for selection. The crowd remained silent until Kirkpatrick had finished. Then a tall, gaunt landholder rose to his feet and spoke on behalf of his community. He broke down trying to convince the Commissioners to buy their farms.

'They shouldn't be strung along like this. We should be telling them it's an empty exercise.' It was Stewart who spoke, after the meeting was over and the farmers and their wives had drunk their tea and eaten the scones, and returned home to their children with nothing promised. Howitt was shoveling papers into his briefcase, worn down by the repeated exposure to landowners' desperation. What Stewart suggested was fair, but impossible.

It was, in the end, nothing like the adventure he had

dreamed of. He was desperately tired and cold, and felt all of his seventy-three years in every muscle and bone. But it was more than that. In the course of his travels, something had shifted in his understanding of the land and come to rest, heavy as a stone, below his heart. In the fifty-odd years since he first came to Australia, he'd seen the land change. The ruin, everywhere apparent on this journey, spoke to him of pillage; of taking more than the land could give. He recalled Mungallee, all those years ago, standing at ease on his broad bare feet, tossing his boomerang into the sky above the Cooper. Such a beguilingly simple but direct act: it disrupted nothing else in the landscape in its purpose of securing a feed of birds. It was a different way of existing: not on the land, but as part of it. He was as guilty as the next settler. He'd farmed his land using the methods that had come from another hemisphere. Even his geological eye looked at a speck of rock close up, and vast formations over eons, but missed the essential nature of the land, here and now.

> Let Mammon's sons with visage lean,
> Restless and vigilant and keen,
> Whose thought is but to buy and sell . . .

His mother's words. Neither he nor the farmers he'd met were Mammon's sons; after all, men had to make a living and feed their families. But he could see how this country was being forced into a form and pattern it was never designed for, like trying to compress water within a container. It helped to explain and made more tragic the suffering he had witnessed over the past six months: the farmer suicides he'd heard about; the woman who died from a botched attempt at aborting her child because she could not feed another mouth; the children in rags without shoes, taken out of school for want of a few pennies.

He was desperate to be home. Liney's recent letters had become tender; she too was anxious for his return.

The four Commissioners walked across the street from the Mechanics Hall to their night's accommodation. As they entered the hotel, the publican handed Kirkpatrick a telegram that had just been delivered. Kirkpatrick read the red-bordered slip of paper, then looked up at the others, his eyes red-rimmed with tiredness, his mouth grim. 'Despite our long six months on the road, we have yet another week's work, I'm afraid.' He waved the telegram at them. 'Dalgety is a late contender. We'll have to go there before we finish in Sydney.'

Howitt received Charlton's telephone call before breakfast. He had finished dressing and was standing at his hotel window, watching the Sydney street below him as it stirred into early-morning life. A mostly-empty cable tram rattled past the hotel, followed by a Clydesdale pulling a cart laden with hessian sacks, the horse's breath steaming in the cold. Beyond the street, he could see the harbour. A large liner was docking on the left, and a ferry blew its horn as it pulled away from Circular Quay.

His diary was lying open on the desk. He walked over to it and was adding some thoughts about Dalgety that had come to him during the night when there was a discreet knock at his door. 'There is a telephone call for you, Mr Howitt, down in the lobby. The party's waiting on the line for you, sir.'

At first he walked down the stairs, then felt a strangely ominous premonition. As a picture of a *Gule-wil* rose unbidden in his mind, he hastened his step. At the reception desk, he grasped the hearing piece of the telephone, clutching its neck tightly as if he might strangle the words before they could reach his ear, but they lumbered along the line, ghostly and scratchy, made almost unintelligible by his son's breaking voice. Alfred knew what he was being told. He passed the receiver back to the clerk, did not hear what the man said to him, and walked heavily back up the stairs to his room.

It had been something as inconsequential as a rose thorn. She had tugged at a weed beneath a rose bush and as it came away a thorn had pierced deeply and torn a gash along the length of her thumb. She'd bathed the wound, and bound it, but within hours her body was swinging between profuse sweating and devastating chills. Just one day in bed, she'd told May, and then she'd be fine. She became comatose during the night; the following morning she was dead.

He stood in front of the door to his room, unsure for a moment what he was doing there. Entering the room he looked around at its ordinariness: the bed with its rumpled sheets and blankets; the washstand by the window and his shaving brush with its still-foamy bristles; a desk, chair and wardrobe all in matching walnut; his portmanteau on the floral-carpet floor. He drew the curtains against the daylight.

His diary was still open on the desk. Alfred picked up the pen, removed its cap and shook out a few drops of ink onto the blotting paper. He drew a thick line under the last diary entry, dragging the nib so forcefully across the page that it tore a line of small ragged holes. Beneath the line he recorded Liney's initials and the date. He knocked the cap of his pen onto the floor, and it rolled away under the bed. He got down on his hands and knees to retrieve it but could not find the strength to stand up again. He stayed on the floor, on his hands and knees, forehead on the bedside rug, shaking and sobbing.

∽

The train rattled through the night, the timber carriage swaying and knocking. Alfred, in his private compartment, vacantly watched his reflection in the carriage window flying over the dark landscape, until the constantly moving shapes made him nauseous and he had to pull down the blind. In the middle of the night, he stumbled along the corridor to the toilet, and asked the conductor if he would bring him a cup of tea. The conductor knocked tentatively and brought the tea with a sweet biscuit, placing it carefully on the small pull-down table. The tea cooled as Alfred tied knots in his handkerchief, then untied them, then tied them again.

He changed trains at Albury in the early hours of dawn. He'd been in the town just a month ago, assessing its suitability to house the nation's politicians, discussing land values with farmers, returning the awkwardly wrapped gifts that he found in his hotel room. While the other train passengers enjoyed an early breakfast in the steamy-windowed buffet, he stood on the platform in the freezing cold and watched luggage being transferred from one freight van to another. When he boarded the Victorian train, his compartment was close and stuffy. He threw up the window for air and his face was hit by biting wind and black soot smuts from the steam engine. He closed the window again and wondered for a moment whose haggard face was reflected in the glass.

He must have slept because he dreamed of Liney. She was balancing on the top rung of a ladder while he stood below, grasping the rails and urging her to take care because he could see that the hem of her skirt was caught under her heel. She paid him no heed as she lent far, far over to prune the wild sports from a climbing rose. He called out that a branch had caught in her hair, a thick tendril that pulled her bun apart so that her hair fell down her back. Not grey hair, but the rich autumn tresses that she'd had when they'd married. He knew, utterly, that she would fall. He held his arms out ready to catch her.

When he awoke, his mouth was like sandpaper. A different conductor brought him tea and doffed his cap before quietly closing the compartment door. This time Alfred tried to drink but he could not swallow, and the cup rattled so badly in the saucer that the tea sloshed over the rim and onto his trousers. As the tea went cold and the milk congealed on the surface, he watched the sunrise gold-tip the frayed edges of cloud and wash over the countryside. Everywhere was grievously parched. The train passed rundown cottages, and brown seas of cattle being herded to the Melbourne market. It was apparent even from the enclosed world of his compartment that the stock's skin hung loosely over sharp bones. He squeezed his eyes shut against the crowding images of death.

Henry Anderson would read the service. Alfred dreaded seeing his old friend, dreaded his kindness and sympathy, the clichés of a spirit at peace, of joining God in heaven, of everlasting life. It was all such nonsense, but thinking that now made him feel desperately disloyal to Liney. He would ask Henry about his god, the loving father. Why did that god let Liney die? Why a rose thorn? Henry would answer that the ways of God are unknowable, that we cannot comprehend the Divine will. Which was no answer, Alfred thought bitterly. If only there was a god: someone to whom he could direct his rage, someone other than himself to blame.

ɕɔ

Charlton was waiting for him on the station at Bairnsdale, his head bent into the gale, his coat flapping about his legs. The station was bustling with passengers and those who had come to meet them. The rain that had travelled east, following the train from Melbourne, had eased, but the late afternoon was almost as dark as night. Seeing Charlton waiting, Howitt hesitated at the door of the train carriage. He would give anything, offer himself up to a non-existent deity if necessary, to delay the moment of speaking to his eldest son.

'Father.' Charlton came towards him, angular and darkly handsome, his hand already out to help Alfred down the step from the carriage. They embraced awkwardly; Charlton had grown up to be much taller than his father. 'I'll fetch your luggage,' he muttered, and strode away before anything further could be said. Howitt straightened his shoulders and took a deep breath. He would not let anyone see what he felt: his weakness, his guilt.

The train engine was sending up billows of steam that rolled along the platform and partly obscured the crowd. While he waited for his son, a man bumped into him and apologised, but Alfred hardly noticed. Then Charlton was back at his side, taking his arm and guiding him towards the buggy.

The region had been spared the drought that was still devastating the land to the north and east. It all looked so familiar: the well-maintained gardens, the fully-stocked shops, the bustle of Main Street; and as they made their way out of town, the lush crops and the fat, woolly sheep. Worse, it looked unchanged, which hardly seemed possible. An ethereal post-storm light made the green of the grass and foliage so luminous it almost hurt Alfred's eyes. He'd lived in this oasis for half his life. No wonder he had forgotten Mungallee's lesson: the land seemed to promise such abundance. But even here, in his own time, he'd seen hillsides erode, creeks silt up, and yields diminish.

'You're going the wrong way,' Alfred told his son who was turning the horse from the main road. Charlton had taken them over the Mitchell River Bridge and was turning left.

'Mother is at Eastwood, Papa, not Metung. We thought it best. To be near Reverend Anderson's church, and closer to the cemetery.'

'Ah,' Alfred muttered. 'Practical thinking.' But he wanted to remind Charlton of how dear Metung was to Liney: it was *her* home, and the home of their retirement. He held his breath to stifle a cry.

Tulaba had died at Eastwood, he remembered unnecessarily. He couldn't recall where the native had been buried, but he did remember that Liney had made a special afternoon tea for the blacks. She could always remember their names; that's why she'd been so good at managing the farm labour. He took a deep breath that turned into a sob, but Charlton pretended not to hear.

All the family was at the farm, Charlton told him: Charlton's wife Agnes and their two children, Gilbert and May; Maude and her husband; and Annie, her husband and their two children. It was Gilbert's farm now, but they all still referred to Eastwood as home. Alfred could picture them, sitting with their heads together around the dining room table, discussing his feelings and his future. No, he remonstrated with himself; that was unfair.

Some of his happiest memories were of his family gathered together, such as when he returned from his trips away, and they'd sit around the kitchen table to listen to his stories. Or when he had taught them The Universe game, that they played so rowdily together. It was a game he'd learnt at school in Nottingham, all those many years ago. In the games with his family, he had always taken the role of the sun, but now in his mind's eye he saw himself as a planet. He was spinning around, lost in his own orbit, while Liney and the children spun past him in their separate revolutions. And then there were the stray meteors: Welch and McMillan, that odd fellow Cameron, and Alex Aitkin. They flew towards him, made contact, then glanced off onto unknown trajectories. Had he always moved too fast, failing to look back to see the traces he left, or to wonder at the direction others were taking?

The horse had grown hot from Charlton's urging, and its furry smell reached Alfred. The wind blew across the flat paddocks, bending the long grass to and fro so that it changed from pale straw to grey-green, like a hand passing to and fro across velvet. He thought of the desert. The jingling harness could have been dry bones rattling in a box; the grate of the turning wheels could have been King's rusty, reluctant voice. Under his breath, he intoned the words from St John's that he had read over Burke's grave, keeping rhythm with the trotting horse: 'I am the resurrection and the life; he that believeth in me, though he were dead, yet shall he live.' He hadn't failed Burke, but there were others who had considerable claim on his conscience, not least Liney. He felt very old and hollow.

# Chapter 10

May was in her study, sorting through papers and journals in preparation for her day's work, when he started ringing his infernal bell. He'd bought it in England and told her it would make it easier for her to know when he needed her; she only had to follow the sound of the bell to know where to find him.

She found him on the verandah at the front of the house, sitting at the square marble table he called his outside office. The bell sat at his elbow, along with his pipe, tobacco tin and ashtray. His papers were held down by coloured-glass paperweights. He had a tartan rug around his knees, and his body, once so straight, slumped a little over his work.

The day was glorious. The deciduous trees in the garden were turning yellow, leaves dancing in the soft breeze against the blue of the sky and the bay. May stood by her father for a moment, who had returned to his writing, then walked onto the lawn to stand in the sunshine and admire the view. They had seen wonderful sights during their travels through Britain and Europe, but nothing to rival Metung. It wasn't just that she measured what was picturesque by familiarity; this place, in all its enchantment, made her feel anchored and confident.

Borun came into sight, chasing cabbage moths across the lawn. Her younger brother Gilbert had given May the dog when she and her father returned from abroad. It was a tan-coloured kelpie with a touch of dingo, a long snout, pricked ears and amber eyes. 'An Australian dog,' he'd told her proudly; the breed he used to round up the sheep at Eastwood. She called the dog Borun. Esmay had told her the natives' legend about Borun the pelican, the bird that founded this corner of Australia, along with his wife Tuk the musk duck. That touch of dingo made the dog native, and Borun became her shadow.

She walked across the lawn and picked up a ball. The dog raced towards her and bounded away after the tossed ball, leaping into the air to catch it on the bounce.

'You spoil that animal,' her father called out when the dog returned and dropped the ball at her feet. 'I thought you came out to see me.' His voice was slightly petulant. She tossed the ball again and turned to her father.

'Can you type this letter for me, May?' He held out a fistful of papers towards her.

May sighed and returned to the shade of the verandah. 'Papa, today I am working on my own research. I told you that at breakfast.'

'But this is important. I must respond to Professor Gregory today. His work is flawed, and it contradicts my own findings. I thought this nonsense of Lidgey's had been put to bed. I've already rejected his findings.'

Borun returned again with the ball. She put her hand on his head to quieten him, and he dropped, panting, at her feet. There had been such a hoo-ha over Ernest Lidgey's investigations. He had published his description of Cambrian rocks in central Victoria in a paper that refuted her father's own findings. Howitt, as Acting Secretary of Mines, had discredited Lidgey's claims in a special report published by the Department. Lidgey had subsequently retracted his findings, but there were many who thought her father to be in the wrong.

May took the handwritten pages from him and walked wearily back to her study. She had returned from their travels determined to have space and time of her own. She had taken the smallest room in the house for her study, but it had a large north-facing window that filled the room with light and warmth. She had placed her desk under the window and an upright chair before it. In the corner was an old armchair that she had covered with a bright quilt, and there was a row of potted cyclamens in bloom along the top shelf of her crammed bookcase. Next to the armchair was a small table, its entire surface taken up by an Olivetti typewriter, an extraordinary contraption that her father had bought for her in London.

On her desk were the *Folklore* journals she had planned to spend the morning reading. They contained articles that might contribute to her own writing about native customs, although rarely did she find anything that directly considered the women's traditions. Her book, when—if—it was published, would break new ground. She moved the journals to one side, put her father's papers in their place and lifted the typewriter onto the desk.

Outside her window there was a monkey puzzle tree that her mother had planted when they first moved to Metung, a mere five years ago, and already the tree was like a huge green boulder that stopped the view to the paddocks beyond their home. May had often pondered the similarity between the tree and her attempts to unravel the natives' stories: the way the branches divided and divided again, endlessly, so that from a distance it looked confused and chaotic, but up close an intricate pattern revealed itself. Today the dark green foliage looked menacing and demanding, despite the cloudless sky above it.

She took three sheets of plain paper and placed carbon paper between them. Then she fed the pages into the typewriter and started using two fingers to convert her father's scrawl into legible print. His handwriting had never been easy to read, but these notes were full of spider crawls and crossings-out, and it took her most of the day to produce two typed pages.

With the finished copies in her hand, May found her father in the living room. He had fallen asleep in the wing-backed chair by the empty fireplace. In his lap, his hands loosely held a silver-framed photograph of her mother, the one that usually sat on the table beside his chair. She lifted it gently from his hands and looked at her mother's enigmatic smile, the face so like her own. In the photograph, Liney was wearing a silk dress with an enormous skirt that showed off her small waist; one hand was partially lost in the skirt's voluminous folds. Her long dark hair was smoothly collected at the back of her head, and around her neck she wore a cameo on a velvet choker. The photo had been taken in 1864, just before May's parents had married. It was her mother as May had never known her: young and carefree before all the demands of life etched into her face. May set the photograph on the table, and then placed a hand on her father's arm to wake him.

For a moment he looked startled and lost, his eyes rheumy and unfocused. He put his hands on the arms of the chair and hauled himself to sit upright. May handed him the pages she had typed and pulled up a low stool to sit in front of him.

His eyes followed the lines of type. He was still alert when it came to his writing. When he'd finished reading, he patted her hands affectionately. 'I'm sorry, May. I have kept you from your work. These are very beautiful pages, more clearly presented than the arguments they contain.'

She nodded and, taking the pages from him, rose to her feet. 'The Kings have invited us for supper tonight. You haven't forgotten have you?'

He grimaced. 'The dreadful Mrs Montgomery will be there, no doubt. She can't understand that I am not a doctor of medicine. She shuffles me into corners to tell me about her ailments. It's all very embarrassing, what the woman is prepared to reveal.'

May laughed at his horror.

'I have a pain—here in my side.' He mimicked her voice, coy and demanding at the same time. 'Whatever could be the cause, doctor?' Then he stopped abruptly and looked at her sharply. 'There was a time when I thought you might have been a doctor. You could have read medicine at Melbourne University.'

'There was no money, remember?' May answered flatly, turning to leave. 'Anyway, it's supper and cards at eight, so we had better get cracking.'

❧

The Gregory letter was barely posted when Alfred stormed into May's study waving a journal at her. He placed it, open, on top of her work and stabbed repeatedly at an article. 'Look at this. That upstart Lang. How dare he?' She could feel his body trembling beside her, his face was a mottled red and the vein in his temple throbbed.

'Calm yourself, Papa. Let me see, let me read it.' She pushed his accusing finger to one side so that she could read the article.

As she read, he paced the narrow confines of her study, hands deep in his pockets, muttering to himself. He took his pipe from his pocket and tried to light it, but gave up.

The article was a review of her father's recently published tome, *The Native Tribes of South-East Australia*, the book she had spent so much time helping him with, both at home and in England. For her, the book still represented his thoughtlessness, if not his injustice.

Andrew Lang had long been one of her father's adversaries, but despite the condescending tone, the first couple of paragraphs appeared more positive than might have been expected. May read on and came to a section where Lang claimed that Howitt was wrong in crediting the Aborigines with deliberately devising their exogamy rules. Not believing the natives capable of creating a marriage system at once so complex and so regular, Lang argued that the rules would have come about by a series of accidents and, in particular, male jealousy. May snorted with disgust.

'How would he know?' her father fumed, grabbing the journal back from May and slapping at the article with his hand. 'It's nothing more than conjecture from the other side of the world.'

Still seated, May looked up at him, at his wild white hair and his eyes that were glistening too brightly. 'Nor can he credit the Aborigines with . . .' she started, but her father waved her words away.

'Nothing, that man knows nothing,' he fumed. He staggered and reached for the edge of her desk to stop himself from falling. May stood quickly and eased him into her chair. His hands were clammy, and his face was no longer red but putty coloured. She left the room and ran to the kitchen, returning with a glass of water. She took the journal that was clenched in his hand and handed him the glass.

'We are going to put this to one side, Papa. There have been many good reviews to outweigh this one.' She helped him up out of the chair and guided him to his wing-backed chair in the living room. She placed a rug over his knees, but he pushed it to one side, telling her not to fuss.

'Perhaps I should go and fetch Dr Hughes,' May suggested.

'No. There is nothing wrong with me.' But his voice was thin and he put his fingers to his temple, feeling along the length of the vein that was the colour of a storm cloud against his pale, clammy skin.

'Then rest for the afternoon,' May conceded. 'I'll wake you at tea-time.' He nodded, almost timidly. His acquiescence frightened her.

ꕥ

It rained heavily for the next three days, turning Metung into an island. May, standing on the front verandah, looked out at the veiled, flat bay and felt imprisoned by the water and dim grey light. Borun came and dropped his ball at her feet. 'Not in this weather,' she told him and the dog's tail drooped. She pointed to his bed on the verandah, and he slunk away. If it was up to her, he would be inside, but her father would not abide an animal in the house—although she was sure she could recall his old dog Turk in the house at Eastwood.

She went inside and lit the fire, more for its cheeriness than warmth. She had begged her father to rest. Instead, for three days he had wandered around the house, getting on her nerves with his absentmindedness and mumblings. He would seek her out in her study to ask some trivial question, or he would sit over a meal she had prepared, gazing vacantly at the kitchen window and letting his food go cold. Finally, after a drizzly morning, the day ripened into clear blue skies and a sea breeze as soft and fresh as just-washed sheets.

May, drying the lunch dishes, spoke over her shoulder to her father sitting at the kitchen table. 'We could take *Prelude* to the ocean beach to collect cuttlefish bone for your French polishing.' She offered her suggestion with forced gaiety.

The bay, which lay like the forecourt of their home, was bordered to the south by a line of sand dunes that divided the inland waters from the ocean. They could moor the boat and walk over the dunes to the ocean beach, which, after the stormy weather, would be littered with cuttlebones. The chalky fishbone was the finest of sandpapers, giving a silky lustre to a wood surface.

'I've given up French polishing,' he said grumpily.

May placed a cup of tea before him, but he did not raise his eyes from the journal on the table, open at Lang's article. 'No you haven't. There's still that table to finish for Mrs Thompson.' She put the dishes away and wiped the sink and table.

On his retirement, Alfred had taken up furniture-making, entranced by the colours, textures and grains of the native timbers. He'd made some nice pieces for the house, in blackwood and mountain ash, and blue gum, including an ingenious stool that doubled as a ladder for the high shelves of the bookcases that lined his study, and a small table that was made from fiddleback redgum. The striking figure in the timber looked like ripples passing endlessly over a red sea. On seeing the table, their friend Mrs Thompson had insisted he make her a replica.

May tipped his untouched tea down the sink and went to fetch their coats and hats. When she returned he was still at the kitchen table, looking at Lang's article. She picked up the journal and placed it on the kitchen bench.

Alfred made a fuss about putting on his coat, getting tangled in the sleeves and sighing theatrically. She held the door open for him and glared until he followed her out of the house. Borun rushed up to them with his ball in his mouth and dropped it at Alfred's feet, his tail wagging madly.

'Not the dog. He'll get wet and shake all over us.'

May picked up the ball and put it in her coat pocket. Borun preceded them down to the garden gate and onto the track that led to their boat *Prelude*, moored at a small jetty. The grass of the track was still wet from the rain, and the ground was spongy, but everything looked washed clean and bright and the gums had released their sharp eucalypt scent. Wattlebirds in the banksias clattered tunelessly, and a countless flock of little terns wheeled in the sky over the bay. The track crossed a dirt road that was Metung's main thoroughfare. On the far side of the road, a row of fishermen's cottages lined the foreshore, paint peeling from tin roofs and nets lying in stiff heaps redolent of old fish and seaweed. Chooks poked about in weed-clogged gardens and, at one cottage, a cockatoo in a cage hung under the verandah screeched as they walked past.

The dog bounded onto the boat and sat expectantly on the seat by the tiller. May stepped down from the jetty, and held up her hands to steady her father. He brushed her away, but after almost falling, reluctantly accepted her help. He sat on the forward thwart, on the starboard side, while May half raised the gaffer sail. Single-handedly, she cast off the mooring lines, pushed off from the jetty, and as the boat turned, raised the sail fully and took the helm.

The sunlight caught the small peaks of waves and turned them into millions of twinkling stars. From time to time May glanced at her father's back: he was hunkered down in his coat, his shoulders up near his ears so that they touched his hat brim.

It felt good to be steering the boat. When they were growing up at Eastwood, the family often holidayed in a shack on the beach at Cunninghame, further along the coast to the east. *Prelude* had been built for those holidays, and her father, with infinite patience, had taught all the children to sail. There was May and her brothers and sisters, and all the other children who holidayed in the neighbouring shacks.

'I was just thinking about those holidays we used to have at the beach,' she called out to her father above the chattering sound of water along the hull. She laughed. 'Do you remember how the McLeods always brought a cow with them, because Mrs McLeod wouldn't trust any other milk?'

Her father remained unresponsive.

May tacked the boat into a channel that wound past low scrubby islands and around sandbars, heading for the Short-Longway.

An egret took flight from the nearby shore, its neck an elegant 's' and its feet trailing behind like a weathervane. May raised the centerboard, dropped the sail and *Prelude* slipped up onto the shore. Stepping into the shallow water, getting her boots wet, she took the anchor and dug it into the sand. Her father sat watching the play of wind across the water so that May had to call to him, then bustle him out of the boat.

'Now look,' he complained, pointing to his wet boots. She took his arm and led him along the bush track through the dunes towards the ocean beach. Borun bounded ahead and looped back and around them as if they were sheep to be rounded up. The track was hedged in on both sides by the twisted trunks and branches of tea-tree. It was a haunted forest, made more eerie by the silence of their footfalls on the leaf-littered black sand. The breeze stirred the canopy but did not penetrate below.

Suddenly, they stepped out of the gloom into the dazzling light of sky and sand and ocean. She looked at her father expectantly but his face still bore a scowl. There'd been a time when this sight would have made him shout with joy. May shook her head. She left him gazing out to sea and walked briskly along the beach, tossing the ball for Borun and filling her bag with cuttlebone

If she kept walking for a mile or two, she would reach Cunninghame. One year, the Tatungooloong tribe had camped at the top of Cunninghame Arm—they called the place Ngrungit. The other farming families had been scathing of the blacks' presence, but her father was pleased to find them there, and had taken her with him when he went to talk to them.

The natives had an upright piano, of all things, salvaged from the ocean. They called it a *yay gri*, a sorrow canoe. A pedal and the lid were missing, and the brown varnished panels had swollen and buckled, and split down the sides like over-ripe fruit. Her father had rolled up his sleeves and played the thudding keys as he sang 'The Wild Colonial Boy'. The natives had clapped and laughed.

She had listened carefully to the respectful way he talked to them, watched the trust they put in him as they answered his never-ending questions, happy to wait patiently while he wrote their words into his notebook. Then the women had taken May into their own circle, amongst the black children and babies, and had given her food. She smiled to recall: a small roasted bird, perhaps a little tern, on a piece of bark. She had eaten it, to be polite, following her father's example.

She might have been ten at the time. The Eastwood natives were so familiar to her to be not particularly interesting. Around the farm and the house, they did much the same chores as her mother and father. Even when she went to their camp, further along the Backwater, Esmay and the others she knew well made the camp seem commonplace. But on the beach that year she had registered how utterly, unfathomably different a way of life could be.

They were gone now, of course, the Tatungooloong people and all the other wild-living natives. She thought of Esmay, how she had adopted Christianity. Esmay, who willingly lived at Lake Tyers Mission and spent her days washing and ironing for Reverend Bulmer. Like her father, she was sorrowed by so much loss, and wanted, in her own way, to preserve some remnant of what had been.

The sun tipped the top of the dunes, making the marram grass glitter, and Borun ran in and out of the waves and pushed his nose through the spume along the tideline. Gannets dived into the waves, lifting out effortlessly with full beaks, and ahead, a couple of oystercatchers scuttled along on their red-twig legs, always keeping a few yards away.

Her book was still a dream, but it was becoming more possible. Despite the training her father had instilled in her, she had given up on objectivity, allowing herself to sink into something more heartfelt. Capturing the soul of the women's stories—that was the goal she'd set herself, even though, at times, it felt like stealing. They weren't her stories, but at least the book would be her own achievement, and her gift.

A chill wind off the ocean was blowing up and May retraced her footsteps, most of which were now only ghostly outlines in the wet sand. She pulled her coat more tightly around her and quickened her pace. As she drew closer to her father she watched him stand up and walk down to the shoreline. He took his compass from his pocket, flipped off the lid and turned slowly in a half circle. His shadow fell long and stick-like on the sand, and the wind blew his trousers against his legs so that she could see the sand and surf between his shins. When she came up to him he smiled shyly.

'Just checking on home,' he said, holding up the compass to her.

May had known that compass all her life. Riding with him in the mountain ash country up past Errinundra, or through the dense Tarra Valley, he'd taught her to use it. He'd unfold a map and point to their destination, then pass her the compass and ask her to set their course. The time they went in search of the legendary Lake Tarli Kargn, she'd led the way: from the high country, down along the Moroka River to Moroka Gap—what the natives called the Valley in the Sky. Then they had ventured on into the narrow, echoing gorge of Nigothoruk, known as the Valley of Destruction, to the Barrier Creek and finally to Lake Tarli Kargn. Hills rose sharply around the lakeshore and the trees were reflected so perfectly she might have counted the leaves. The place was eerie with silence—not a bird call or rustle of creature in the undergrowth. It was as if the still water drew all sound down into its dark depths. Her father had claimed they were the first white people to ever see the lake. She had been the one to guide them there.

'The great poet Wordsworth gave it to me. He was a friend of my parents.' He weighed the compass in his hand. May smiled indulgently; she had heard the stories many times. 'They all were, you know. Dickens and Tennyson, Mr and Mrs Browning, and Mrs Gaskell. They were all regular visitors when I was a boy.' He laughed to himself, raking his fingers through his long white beard. 'And, of course your mother's father, Grandfather Boothby, he was often at our house in Nottingham. Always cantankerous. Didn't approve of me proposing to your mother. Said he thought I'd never settle down and be responsible. Or was it respectable?

'Me!' he pointed to his breast with mocked injured pride. 'Me, an Honorary Doctor of Cambridge and Melbourne

Universities, a Fellow of the Geological Society of London and of the Royal Anthropological Institute. A Companion of St Michael and St George. He never achieved half so much.'

May patted his arm, and Alfred returned the compass to his pocket. As they walked back through the bush towards the boat, her father ahead, Borun at her heels, she thought about all those awards and honours that he had received over the years; all the things he had achieved.

The Burke and Wills monument had been moved from the busy intersection in the middle of Melbourne to a reserve up near Parliament House, but the explorers' fame had not waned. She thought of her father depicted in the bas-relief below Burke's bronze feet, yet it had been up to Papa—finally—to tell the true story of that ill-fated mission. The Australasian Association of the Advancement of Science had invited him to Adelaide earlier in the year to give an account of Burke's expedition and his own role in the relief mission.

In preparation for that talk, he had unearthed his journals from forty-odd years ago, placing the pile on her desk with a small thump that sent up motes of dust. He'd held a journal to her nose, asking if she could smell the sand and camels. As she prepared his notes, the journals fell apart in her hands; the ink had faded to the palest desert-sky blue.

It was January when they caught the train to Adelaide, travelling west into increasingly hot weather. At their hotel, she helped her father prepare for his evening address. As she buttoned the cuffs of his shirt, he lamented that he had chosen not to wear either his Cambridge or Melbourne University gown, fearful that some in the audience might think him arrogant. Such a shame—he did love his gowns. He also loved his medals and decorations, but if he wore all his honours he'd jangle like a streetcar. He could not, however, go without the Mueller Medal. He lifted the bronze insignia that was pinned by its ribbon to his lapel and studied the upside-down profile of his old friend, plant in one hand, pen in the other.

'A good man,' he had told May, tapping his finger on Ferdinand von Mueller's nose, then he had bent his head for

May to place around his neck the ribbon bearing the seven-pointed star of the Companion of St Michael and St George. No-one, he assured her unnecessarily, would begrudge him wearing that.

'*Auspicium Melioris Aevi*,' he read aloud from the medal. 'How apposite: augury of a better time.' Those youthful years had been, he mused while May straightened his tie and buttoned his jacket, a time of spirit and certainty; a time when he had believed he could conquer anything without consequence.

May passed him his walking stick and his notes. 'Come on Papa. We mustn't keep your fans waiting.'

The hall was close and crowded, smelling of dust and wooden seats that had borne human bodies over many years. Her father had climbed onto the podium and gradually warmed to his theme of Burke's incompetence and the Victorian Exploring Expedition's failure. From his pocket he had taken his compass and laid it on the lectern beside his notes. With even more certainty, he moved on to his own role, and to the day that King was found.

But he had paused and swallowed, and peered into the audience. Then, out of the blue, he announced that it had been Mr Welch who had found John King. May had jerked upright in her front-row seat. That wasn't right. He was not following the notes she had prepared for him, and now his memory had lapsed in the most alarming manner. Fortunately, no-one else in the audience appeared to have register his blunder.

He touched her sleeve, waking her from her reverie. 'We'd better walk more quickly, May dear. We don't want to be caught out in the dark.'

They emerged from the gloomy bush onto the lake beach. *Prelude* sat nudged up on the sand, and Borun ran off barking after seagulls. May dragged her eyes away from the water and helped her father into the boat, more gently than when they had arrived. The sun had disappeared behind the dunes and the light was soft and subdued. May whistled to the dog, pushed the boat off the beach into deeper water, and climbed aboard to take her father home.

Printed in Australia
AUOC02n2201090415
266882AU00002B/2/P

9 781925 003765